The Devine Case

LORILYN WHITE

WORTHYWHITE PRESS

Published by: WORTHYWHITE PRESS

This is a work of fiction. Names, characters, places, and incidents are either used fictitiously or are the product of the author's imagination. Any resemblance to actual persons, living or dead, business establishments, events, or locales is entirely coincidental.

This novel contains mature themes. Reader discretion is advised.

ISBN Paperback: 979-8-9893691-4-0

ISBN Kindle: 979-8-9893691-5-7

Printed in the United States of America

DEDICATION

In loving memory of Jon Erick White

Chapter 1

The judge slammed down his gavel. "Court is adjourned." He stood up and stepped down from his perch, flipping his robe behind him.

Alicia wasted no time swiftly gathering her briefs into her tote as the bailiff commanded, "All rise!" Glancing at her watch, she noted the time with a sense of urgency. It was already two-forty, and she needed to be in Mamaroneck by three. This hearing had been a fruitless endeavor. Her client's absence spoke volumes, despite her preparedness with the power of attorney documents. Still, Mrs. Barton insisted on her day in court, oblivious to the judge's disinterest in her grievances.

Exiting the courtroom in a rush, Alicia quickly nodded to the opposing counsel. She hurried down the hall and boldly stuck her arm between the closing doors of a crowded elevator. Annoyed faces glared at her, and they released sighs as she wiggled in and the doors closed. When the elevator stopped at her floor in the parking lot, she sprinted toward her car. No simple feat considering her three-inch stilettos and tight skirt. This wasn't her typical dressing style, but her best friend, Diana Foster, convinced her it was time to upgrade her wardrobe now that she was single again. "Show some leg, give 'em some cleavage," had been Diana's advice. *Diana better appreciate all my efforts to help her cousin's baby daddy beat a speeding ticket.* Normally, Alicia would never waste her time with such a petty case, but Diana had begged her to go, so the brotha wouldn't lose his license. One more check of her watch confirmed she'd only lost five minutes between the courtroom and her car. Except she couldn't figure out why her car was leaning. On closer inspection, her Jeep Grand Cherokee had a flat tire.

"Oh, hell!" Bending over, she glared at the deflated tire. "I'll never make it to traffic court on time now." She wasn't speaking to anyone in particular. The parking lot was empty. Taking out her phone to call Diana, she continued to look around, hoping to see some sign of life, someone who could rescue her. "Where are you?" Diana's voicemail was politely instructing the caller to leave a message. "I don't even know how to get in touch with this Negro!"

When she heard the beep, she frantically shouted, "Di, it's me, and I'm stuck with a flat tire at the courthouse. If you want me to help your homey, you need to help me. Call me back right away!" She tapped her foot for a moment and hoped for a quick response. When she didn't get one, she called again. "Ok, well, when you get this message, you'll know why I didn't show." Alicia tossed the phone back into her tote. As she scanned the lot again, she chastised herself for not adding roadside assistance to her car insurance policy. *I could change the flat myself, but I just bought this suit. Dior does not do flat tires.*

Her ears perked up like a puppy dog as a car approached from the far end of the parking lot. Determined to strike her best pose, she moved into the traffic lane, stuck her leg out, and daintily waved her hand in the air. The elderly white man driving the red Volkswagen Bug glanced over and sped up to avoid further eye contact. Alicia mumbled "old coot" under her breath and turned back to the backside of her Jeep. *I'll rip my skirt if I have to reach under there to get the spare. Never mind the damage jacking up this behemoth will do.* Suddenly, another car headed her way. She stepped back into position, this time a bit further in the line of traffic. As the big daddy Benz swerved past her, the tinted windows concealed the driver's identity. A few feet away, the car slowed and came to a stop.

Hallelujah. A tall man with broad shoulders and a bald head emerged and walked straight toward her. She shook her head in disbelief. *This cannot be!* Her eyes widened as her hand went to her throat. "Kevin?" she whispered.

"Hey, are you crazy or something?" the man yelled. "I almost hit you."

Am I seeing a ghost? Then the voice. It was all wrong, and once the man was close enough, it was clear he was not Kevin. Yet, she was experiencing a weird Déjà vu kind of feeling.

It took a moment for Alicia to regain her composure. She gently gave her belly a quick rub to soothe away the flutters flowing through it. The eyes were smaller, the nose thinner, and the shoulders not quite broad enough. *Nope, it's not Kevin, but this brother is definitely as fine. Is that why this flutter in my stomach won't fade?*

The man leaned forward, putting his face closer to hers as his hand lighted on her shoulder. "Hey," he said in a gentler tone, "are you all right?"

The touch of his hand on her shoulder brought her back into the moment, and Alicia focused on his face. She gently pushed his hand away and stumbled to the car's other side. "No. I mean, yes, I'm all right, and no, I'm not crazy. But I could use your help. I've got a flat." She pouted, pointing at the tire.

The man approached her side to get a good look at it. "Yup, you sure do. Do you have a spare?"

"Uh, yeah, I think so. Isn't it under the truck, there?" She pointed again.

He leaned down to take a look. "Yea, it's there. That's what I hate about these big SUVs. They put the spare tires in the most ridiculous places. There must be a jack under there, too." He stood up, and Alicia felt him give her the once over. "I guess I can help you out." He took his suit jacket off.

"Oh, thank you, thank you so much. I have a blanket in the back of the Jeep. We can put it on the floor so you won't get too dirty." She opened the door and took out a wrinkled, grass-stained baby blue thang.

The man shook his head as she tried to hand it to him. "I think I have something better in my trunk." He went to his car and returned with his folded black felt throw over one arm, and extended his other hand to Alicia. "I'm David."

Grabbing his hand, she gently shook it. *His hand feels strong yet soft all at the same time.* "Alicia." Their eyes connected, and Alicia suddenly felt warm and safe, like she was with Kevin. Heat radiated from his hand through her body.

"Well, Alicia, you might want to sit in my car while I take care of this. It could take a while. I left the doors open."

"Are you sure you won't need my help? To hand you some tools or something?"

David grinned at her. "Yes, I'm sure; I won't need your help." He opened his throw, placed it on the floor, and crept under the SUV. Strangely, Alicia didn't want to leave. She wanted to watch him work, see how he moved. But he had dismissed her, and she didn't want to irritate him by standing there. After tossing her blanket back into the Jeep's backseat, she slowly sauntered to the Mercedes Benz to sit and wait.

As she sank into the car's plush leather seating, she couldn't shake off how much David looked like Kevin. To soothe her nerves, she turned on the car radio. A mellow saxophone floated through the air, perfectly accompanying the musky, manly scent. She closed her eyes, and Kevin's face appeared. It had been two years since his death, and her mind was no longer filled with thoughts of him every waking moment. Nor did she dream of him every night, but this man had stirred up her memories. In her mind's eye, Kevin's big brown eyes glistened in the dim light as he dressed to go into the night and meet an informant. They had just finished making love when the phone rang. She moaned, "Don't answer it," but he always answered the phone, saying, "It could be important." His voice was booming and deep as he spoke, "Yeah, this is Kev…. oh yeah? I'm on my way." He turned back to Alicia and said, "I gotta get uptown."

She rubbed his round, bald head and kissed him on his full lips. Her hand slid down the side of his face to feel the stubble on his chestnut-colored chin, whispering, "Hurry back." Taking her hand, he kissed it. *What would I have done differently if I had known it would be the last time I would see him alive?*

David startled Alicia when he opened the door and stuck his head in. "Hi."

She sat up, adjusting her skirt. "All done?"

"Ahh, no. I had a bit of a problem. One lug on your tire froze. I can't get it off. You'll probably need to have it removed with a mechanical jack." He shook his head. "I'm sorry."

Alicia had no idea what he was talking about. "Oh."

David slid into the driver's seat and threw his blanket onto the back seat. "Is there someone we can call? Do you have a regular mechanic?"

Again, she cursed herself for not signing up for roadside assistance. "No."

"Is there somewhere I can drop you off?"

"I hate to have to leave my car here. Don't you know someone who fixes cars?"

"No, I'm sorry, I don't. I'm relatively new to the area, and fortunately, I have had no car trouble yet."

"Oh. Well, you could drop me off at my office, if you don't mind. I'm sure someone there will know whom to call. Let me get my things. I'll be right back."

David started the engine. "Great."

Alicia went to the Jeep, grabbed her leather tote, and quickly returned to the Benz. Her eyes strayed to David's hands on the steering wheel and they were ring free. After giving him her office address and watching him punch it into his Garmin GPS, she smiled. "You're new in town?"

David put the car in gear and gently glided toward the parking lot exit. "Yes. I moved up here from Brooklyn a few weeks ago."

"What do you think of White Plains? How do you like it?"

"Seems nice. I've been busy working and haven't had time to look around much. But I like what I have seen so far." He glanced over and gave Alicia a wink, and she rewarded him with her big, beautiful smile.

"What kind of work do you do?"

"I'm Westchester's newest Assistant District Attorney." Alicia didn't say anything, just frowned. "What's the matter? You got something against lawyers?"

"No, no. Some of my best friends are lawyers. But they are lawyers for the defense. Quite frankly, counselor, are you sure you're sitting on the right side of the law?"

The car slowly curved around the last parking lot ramp and turned left onto Main Street. David gave her a quizzical look. "The right side of the law?"

"Yes." Alicia's tone got sterner. "You ought to be defending brothers instead of locking them up. "You know, statistically, black men make up more than their twelve percent of the total population in jail."

"Yeah, but I...."

"I bet you used to be a cop. Turn right at the next light."

"Yes, I was, but…."

"That's what's wrong with black people these days. We're always so hard on each other, holding each other to some high moral standards, yet doing nothing to alleviate the miseducation and poverty prevalent amongst our people."

"If you'd let me get a word in," David said, "I believe we need fair representation on both sides of the bench. We need black cops and prosecutors to ensure laws are equally and properly enforced. As long as I am not participating in criminal activity, I am on the right side of the law. Besides, what side of the law are you on when the crime is a case of black-on-black crime?"

"Then I'm on the side of the Lord. Right is right, and wrong has got to be punished."

"Good. Me, too. I understand the law is imperfect, but it's all we have. I believe genuine change can be initiated from the inside out."

"Pull over here. This is my building." The car slowed and pulled up to the curb. Alicia gathered her tote and prepared to exit the vehicle. "Thanks for the ride. And for trying to change the tire. I don't know what I would have done if you hadn't stopped."

David threw the car into park and turned to face her. "No problem. I only wish I could have finished the job."

"Well, if there's anything I can do to repay you…."

"As a matter of fact, there is." He grinned. "How about showing me around town and letting me take you out to dinner?" Their eyes connected, generating a charge in the air. A palpable energy that forced her to pause and catch her breath.

"I would, but I don't know when I'll have the time. My calendar is pretty full. And you, Mr. New Assistant DA, I'm certain you're a busy man."

David reached into his breast pocket and pulled out a business card. As he handed it to her, he winked. "Don't worry about my calendar. You clear yours and give me a call."

Alicia plucked the card from his hand and shoved it into her tote. "Okay, counselor. I'll give you a call." She exited the car and strolled into the office building. Adjusting her skirt while waiting for an elevator, she sighed. *I can't call him. Everyone in the firm is buzzing about the new black Assistant DA Janice DeLeo hired. What they didn't say was how sexy he is. Or how much he looks like Kevin. But I can't date an ADA. At the Law Offices of Burke and Powell, that is considered sleeping with the enemy.*

Stepping off the elevator on the seventh floor, it was eerily quiet. The sound of her heels clicking as she walked down the short corridor to the law office doors resonated in the air. As she entered, Diana rushed to her side. "Thank God you're here. Did you hear the news?"

Alicia shook her head while gazing around the office. Each secretary and paralegal stood behind their desk; attorneys were in their doorways. Everyone was speechless, staring at the two large overhead TV sets tuned to CNN. Alicia focused on the news anchor as he said, "Again, we are sharing this late-breaking news with you. Popular R&B singer, Jerri Devine, was arrested this morning for the murder of her husband, Jake Devine, whose body they found early this morning in a secluded cabin in Katonah, New York. Jake Devine, whose real name was Jason Meeks, was shot several times, and while the details being released by the police are sketchy at best, they apparently had reasonable cause to arrest his wife of twenty years. Just weeks ago, Jerri Devine gave a spectacular solo performance at the BB King Blues Club in Times Square, showcasing her new CD, *Ms. Devine Rocks!"*

The TV screens displayed a video of Jerri Devine singing, gyrating, and sweating under the glow of red light while the announcer rambled on about the evolution of The Devine Music and Jake and Jerri's tumultuous relationship history. Alicia clutched her neck as her mouth dropped open.

Suddenly, Carlton came out of his office. "Alicia, may I speak with you?" His tone told her it was urgent. She hurried through the oak door and closed it behind her.

"Hey, boss, what's up?"

"I'm sure you heard the news." Carlton gave her an intent gaze. "I just had a phone call with Jerri Devine's business manager. Jerri has requested our firm handle her defense."

Stunned, Alicia said, "Wow, that's huge. Of course, you said yes."

Carlton didn't answer right away. Instead, he reached for his pipe and lit it. He slowly took a few puffs and turned his back on her as he gazed out his window. "She said she wants to be represented by AK Stone."

Alicia slowly turned away from Carlton's back and faced the door. "Oh."

"I informed her that we have several highly qualified attorneys here at the firm who might be better suited to handle her case. But she insisted she wants you."

Turning back, she grimaced at her boss. "Did you explain to her I haven't handled a criminal case in quite some time?"

Carlton turned from the window to face her. "I couldn't. The woman was just arrested." He walked closer to gaze her in the eyes. "This is a huge case for the firm and you. You know, I believe your talents are being wasted in divorce court," Carlton said in a passionate voice. "You are a criminal defense attorney, a justice fighter! It's time to get back to what you're best at. I truly believe that is what Kevin would have wanted for you."

"I'm not ready yet."

"Yes, you are."

"No, no, I'm not, Carlton." Moving away from him, she began pacing around the office. "I know this case would be huge for the firm to win, and I don't want you to lose Jerri Devine as a client. I don't think I'm ready to defend a murder case, especially not one this huge."

Carlton waited a moment before he pressured her with one final plea. "Please, just think about it. I'll supply all the support you'll need. Will you at least think about it?"

Diana was waiting outside Carlton's door as Alicia walked out, feeling shell-shocked. "Where do you want to start?" she asked.

"What?" Alicia's head was still reeling from her conversation with the boss.

"The Devine case. Where do you want to start with the investigation? Didn't Carlton tell you I would be your lead investigator?"

"I didn't agree to take the case. I told him I would think about it."

An uncomfortable silence set in as they stood there. Abruptly, Diana said, "By the way, I got your message about cousin Pookie's baby daddy. No need to feel bad about missing his court date. That lucky Negro got off anyway. The cop who gave him the ticket never appeared in court, and the charges got dismissed. All is well. What happened to your car?"

"Thanks for reminding me. I need to arrange for a tow." As they walked down the hall to Alicia's office, she told how she met Westchester's newest Assistant District Attorney.

Chapter 2

David chuckled to himself as he navigated towards Katonah. The lush, rolling green hills filled with large, mature trees surrounding the parkway sharply contrasted with the city feel of White Plains. His paralegal, Jamal, quickly briefed him before he left the office with a glow of admiration in his eyes. "Man, you getting ready to go up into the yard of the rich and famous. I hear Richard Gere's got a big old mansion complete with horse stables and Martha Stewart has a farm up there." A city boy at heart, David was unimpressed with the remote location. *Why the heck would anyone want to live out here in the woods? I prefer people, stores, and streetlights.*

Relaxing behind the wheel, he reminisced about meeting Alicia. He had enjoyed the little sparring match with her over the right side of the law. It had been a while since he enjoyed the company of a beautiful, intelligent woman. A tingle went down his spine as he passed the petite, honey-colored beauty posing in the parking lot. Clad in a sleek royal blue suit, accentuating every curve, she effortlessly commanded his attention. Slapping his forehead, he muttered, "You idiot," when it registered he knew nothing about her but her name and the building where she worked. From her banter, he deduced she was familiar with the legal profession, but he didn't know whom she worked for, what she did, or where she lived. He wanted to see her again, but he was at her mercy. He would have to wait for her to make the first move.

This is turning out to be quite a day. First, a big case, and now a mysterious woman. His day had started at five am when he got a phone call that Janice DeLeo wanted to meet with him at once. Jake Devine, a well-known R&B music producer, had been found dead, and the police had collected damning evidence. A decision needed to be made on whether there was enough evidence to arrest Jerri Devine for murder.

At six am, he entered the big chief's office. Janice DeLeo, the Westchester County District Attorney, had been courting David for two years, making enticing offers to lure him from the Manhattan DA's office. Since he had successfully convicted a New York City slum lord, Max Glass, for murder in an extremely high-profile case, David received widespread recognition for his prosecution skills. The neighboring county district attorneys wooed him, but he finally accepted DeLeo's offer two months ago after a messy breakup with his fiancé, Elizabeth.

As David entered the office, Janice DeLeo stood and smoothed the wrinkle on the front of her dark navy-blue suit skirt. "Good morning. I hope you slept well. We've got a busy day ahead." DeLeo, a middle-aged white woman, took great care to always have her dark brown hair perfectly coifed and her porcelain face perfectly made up. Her fashion style screamed money.

Janice gestured for David to follow her into the adjoining conference room to sit at her war table. Massive bookshelves filled with law books surrounded the large mahogany table. This is where the DA held court with her assistants and other legal associates. DeLeo pushed a large folder across the table towards David. "Here's the case file with crime scene photos and police interview notes. Take a moment and read through it." David did as instructed. Once finished, he looked up at DeLeo, and she said, "I know it looks like we've got a slam dunk here, but I don't want anything slipping through the cracks. Once we decide to arrest Jerri Devine, there's no turning back."

"Jake Devine was a known philanderer and an abusive man. Jerri probably hated him and wanted revenge."

Janice nodded as she gazed at David. "But why now? She's had that motive for years. Everyone knows Jake Devine was a lousy husband. Why make a move now?"

David reached into his jacket and held up the CD, *Ms. Devine Rocks!* "I believe this is why. It looks like Jerri was already moving on." He'd brought in his copy of the CD from his car and placed it on the table. "Jake does not perform on this new CD, and they're not calling it The Devine Music because Jake didn't write it. Maybe Jake was making waves because he didn't like Jerri Devine's new direction."

"I don't think so. Jake Devine is the executive producer of that CD. He wouldn't spend his money on a project he didn't believe in," Janice said. "No, there's something else going on. What do you know about Bryan James?"

David was confused. "Who?"

"Bryan James. He's the one who wrote all the new music for that CD. He's also the guitarist in the band. My gut's telling me he's got something to do with Jerri's motive."

David opened the case folder to scan the list of witnesses. "The police detectives never talked to him. They must not think he's involved. Look, we've got the murder weapon, complete with fingerprints and a strong motive of revenge. Both Raymond Meeks and Billy Whitmore, who were also at the cabin when the body was found, have an alibi, but Jerri has none, which gives her opportunity. I say we arrest Jerri Devine for the murder. You know, in cases like these, the spouse is always the most likely suspect. I'm certain I can convince a jury with our evidence that she is guilty of first-degree murder."

"All right, let's bring her in."

David was on his way to view the crime scene when Alicia intercepted him in the parking lot. *What could be wrong with a sister to make her jump out in front of my car?* He stopped to find out. She had a strange look on her face as he approached her, but he couldn't tell if she was drunk or high on something. *Thankfully, she was of sound mind with a very beautiful face. Seeing her through the driver's side window, bathed in the low light, she looked like Sleeping Beauty awaiting a kiss. I wanted to awaken her with a kiss right on those plum-colored lips.* She took the bad news he delivered well, though, and she turned out to be quite a pistol, giving her passionate speech on justice.

Once upon a time, Elizabeth had spoken passionately about the law. A vision of her beautifully made-up chocolate brown face floated through his mind. "It's so important what Daddy is doing, dispensing justice amongst the masses." As he drove to the cabin where Jake Devine's body was found, David remembered the day he shared his dream of becoming a judge with her. "I'm thrilled you plan to follow in Daddy's footsteps. You're a brilliant attorney, and I know you'll be a great judge." She'd smiled brightly at him, tucking a lock of hair behind her ear. *But she hadn't meant it.* Gripping the steering wheel tighter, he took a deep breath while fighting off the memory. The wounds Elizabeth had left were still fresh. *She was not a diamond. Just cheap cubic zirconium. I shouldn't even be thinking about meeting a new woman now. I need to stay laser-focused on winning this case. Now is not the time for a new romance.*

The GPS directed David to make the next left. Slowly, he turned onto a gravel road marked 'Private Property.' Two officers stood guard, and David had to show identification to get past them. Continuing slowly up a slight incline under a canopy of trees for a several yards, the gravel pinged against the undercarriage of the car, until the road transitioned to smooth pavement. Emerging from the shadow of trees, David entered the circular drive and maneuvered around the multiple police vehicles to park. The impressive stone and wooden farmhouse did not resemble any cabin he'd ever built as a child with his Lincoln logs. Once inside, the dark wood and forest green décor dripped with masculinity, totally devoid of a feminine touch. Through the large glass living room windows, a sprawling green lawn extended as far as the eye could see beyond the slate patio and enormous pool deck. It was hard to believe such a hideous crime had taken place in such an idyllic setting.

A forensics team, uniformed and plainclothes officers crawled all over the house and grounds, dusting for fingerprints, taking pictures, and cataloging home contents. David approached a uniformed officer and requested them to point out the lead on the case. Amidst the chaos, the officer led him to the tall and gangly, red-haired Detective Jones.

"We found the body in the bedroom upstairs," Jones said, pointing to the wooden staircase at the back of the great room.

Staring at the bloody quilt, David conjured up an image of how the murder had occurred. Jerri Devine stood over her husband as he slept peacefully under a quilt, grasping the pink pearl handle of her 22LR Derringer and pumped four shots into his body. *No one deserves to die like that.* Struggling to understand Jerri's frame of mind, he couldn't fathom the tidal wave of anger it would take to cause her to commit the act. Afterward, in a panic, she dropped the gun before racing from the room. The gun was now in a police evidence bag, which David examined thoroughly. Shaking his head, he walked from the room and surveyed the other bedrooms on the second floor. As he gazed around the media room filled with audio and video equipment, Detective Jones came up behind him.

"I'm always amazed at how rich folks waste their time and money," Jones said with a smirk. He pointed to the racing sheets on one of the glass tables. "Judging by the living room's interior design and these sheets, it appears that our victim had a passion for the ponies. He should have been focusing on his wife. Maybe he'd still be alive."

David shrugged his shoulders in response. Satisfied with his review of the crime scene, he returned to the office to begin outlining his prosecutorial strategy.

Periodically, David checked his phone for messages throughout the day, but there was nothing from Alicia. *I shouldn't be thinking of her at all.* Attempting to distract himself, he focused on the police notes for the case. Yet, he couldn't get Alicia out of his mind. *Seeing her in the parking lot stirred something within me like never before.* The vision of her sitting in his car and his strong desire to kiss her wouldn't leave him alone, and it haunted him.

Elizabeth never had this kind of effect on me. The match made between them through her father, who was also his mentor and boss, was one of convenience. *I was wrong to think we had a great relationship based on mutual respect and admiration. Elizabeth didn't respect or admire me at all. It was all an act for her father.* Memories of Elizabeth continued to prick at his brain in spite of his determination to be okay with the breakup. Their relationship, devoid of passion, had crumbled under the weight of pretense. *I don't want to be madly in love with anyone. Running your life based on emotions will only get you in trouble. Emotions unchecked can go sideways fast and often lead to violence and sometimes murder.* He had prosecuted enough cases of domestic violence and aggravated assault between people who claimed to love one another and prided himself on his ability to remain disciplined and self-controlled. *If I act on this feeling I have for Alicia, will it lead to trouble? It already has me thinking irrationally. I should not be thinking about getting into a new relationship right now. I need to be focused on the case. Period.*

The following day, David briefly met with Jamal and Eddie, the ADA, assigned by DeLeo to help him prepare the case. Instantly drawn to Jamal's eagerness to learn and his willingness to embrace his responsibilities, David got positive vibes. Eddie, on the other hand, seemed a bit hostile. The short wisp of a man was probably wondering why David got the big case instead of himself. Eddie was a caricature of Elmer Fudd in his rumpled brown suit and dusty loafers. A modern-day version with glasses and better speech, while Jamal's preppy ensemble of khaki pants and Izod sweater displayed his sense of professionalism. Eddie grunted while Jamal smiled as David laid out their agenda for the day. He left them to their work and headed down to see the boss lady.

DeLeo sat at her desk wearing a black pantsuit with a multicolor scarf tied around the collar. Her brow furrowed as she looked up at David. "How's the case progressing? Any recent developments? Did the police speak with Bryan James yet?"

"No," David replied. "I surveyed the crime scene yesterday but didn't uncover anything new."

"Well, have the police follow up on Bryan James and question him about his relationship with Jerri and Jake." Janice picked up the CD, still lying on the table, and examined the cover picture of Jerri. "By the way, you should know Jerri has hired AK Stone to represent her."

"AK Stone?" David asked. "Is that a name I should know?"

"Yes," Janice replied, putting the CD on the table. "I keep forgetting you're new to this territory. AK Stone is a very tough defense attorney. Young but smart, and she's got a great courtroom presence. I've lost a couple of cases to her before, which I thought were slam dunks. Her only logical defense for Jerri will be to point the finger at someone else. We must be certain there are no other credible suspects for the murder besides Jerri. She's been on hiatus for a while, but I'm certain Ms. Stone will use this case to make a comeback." Janice looked sternly at David as she put her hand on his arm. "I don't want her to come back, David. I want her down on the mat for the full count. You understand?"

David put his hand over Janice's. "I got you."

Chapter 3

On a crisp autumn morning, Alicia wrapped herself in the comforting embrace of her baby blue sweatsuit, pulling up the hood to shield herself from the damp chill. With determined strides, she ventured along the trail, admiring all the beautiful foliage along the way. This was her favorite time of the day, basking in the quietness of the early hours. Soon she wouldn't be able to work out outdoors. She cherished these last days of outdoor exercise before the winter's icy grip would confine her to the gym.

Having relocated from Manhattan to Peekskill in the wake of Kevin's tragic death, Alicia had found solace in the serene embrace of the Hudson Valley city. She found the ranch-style townhouse after searching for a home in all the towns surrounding Ossining, where she once lived with her mom and sister for years but did not want to live there again. Sing Sing Prison loomed large in her mind, and Alicia didn't want to be anywhere near it. It triggered memories of her uncomfortable visits to her father as a young girl, something she wanted to forget.

On her tour with a realtor, a *'this is home'* feeling struck her as she entered the large eat-in kitchen with a bay window in the townhouse. Across from the kitchen was a living room with a fireplace and a long hallway leading to the two bedrooms and a bathroom. She immediately bought the place and infused it with her signature blend of blues and vibrant yellows to make her home warm, peaceful, and inviting.

Each morning at sunrise, Alicia embarked on her ritual journey to Depew Park, where echoes of the NY Jets football team lingered on the grassy fields. They had practiced there during their heyday in the 1960s, still a point of pride for the entire town. She'd jog four times on the gravel track surrounding the now high school football field and then walk briskly uphill back home. Once inside, she flipped Mr. Coffee on and headed for a shower. The scent of the strong Columbian brew wafted through the air when she emerged from the steamy bathroom. Wrapped in her pink terry cloth robe, with a large mug of coffee, she sipped her way to the powder blue sofa. Faithfully, Alicia picked up her devotional, *God Calling* to read the daily inspiration.

October 10

Extra Work

Our Lord and Our God. Help us through poverty to plenty. Through unrest to rest, through sorrow to Joy, through weakness to power.

I am your Helper. At the end of your present path lie all blessings. So, trust and know that I am leading you.

Step with a firm step of confidence in Me into each unknown day. Take every duty and every interruption as of My appointment.

You are my servant. Serve Me as simply, as cheerfully and readily as you expect others to serve you.

Do you blame the servant who avoids extra work, who complains about being called from one task to do one less liked? Do you feel you are ill-served by such a one? Then what of Me? Is not that how you so often serve Me? Think of this. Lay it to heart and view your day's work in this light. *

Alicia had to truly meditate on that. Yesterday, she had been called upon to take on what seemed to be a long and challenging defense. She didn't want to do it, but she didn't want to disappoint Carlton. She hadn't tried a criminal case since Kevin's death, focusing instead on matrimonial law, which somehow felt safer. Before that, she had built her reputation on winning criminal cases for the firm, using the moniker AK Stone. It threw the opposing counsel off when they heard the name. It sounded hard and was non-gender specific. Nobody knew what to expect when she walked into the courtroom. *I don't know if I'm AK Stone anymore. Can I tackle a criminal case without Kevin by my side?* He was her eyes and ears on the street, as well as her friend and lover. Someone fatally shot him in Harlem only a month after they got married.

Closing her eyes, his face floated to her mind, smiling at her with a gleam in his eye. The thought of him no longer automatically brought on tears, but sometimes brought warm memories of their love. *Yes, God has brought me through a lot. I have gone from poverty to plenty, from weakness to power. Even through the sorrow. But I'm not ready to fully claim Joy yet. I became an attorney to act as an earthly angel, ensuring justice was dispensed amongst God's people. If only my father had been able to obtain good counsel when he needed it, he might be alive today. There were so many souls I couldn't save. Dad, Mommy, Nanny Kay. Shouldn't I do my best to save those I can? I had a talent for defending the innocent against ruthless prosecutors, and I'm not using it. Have I become a lazy servant?* She picked up her bible, compelled to read several scriptures from 1 Samuel about the disobedience of King Saul. After reading, she spent time in prayer before proceeding to her bedroom to dress.

Alicia opened her closet and pushed aside the older outfits on the left. Kevin's passing caused her to lose several pounds and they no longer fit. Once again, she scolded herself for not donating them. *Someone could use those clothes. I need to pack them up and send them to the Salvation Army.* Fingering through the newer items on the right, she settled on a black and brown tweed maxi skirt paired with a golden cashmere sweater. Accenting the outfit with a black leather vest and belt, she cringed a bit when she put her black stilettos on, but once she stood and walked around a bit, her feet settled into a more comfortable position.

Despite the daunting prospect ahead, Alicia went straight to Carlton's office when she arrived at work. His secretary, Theresa, was on the phone but gave her the signal to proceed. Alicia knocked lightly on the door before opening it.

Carlton was sitting on the edge of his large cherry wood desk in his gray suit, waiting to greet her. "Good morning, Alicia. What brings you to see me so early in the morning?" He reached out to hug her briefly before sitting behind his desk.

"The Devine case, what else?" She gave him a terse look as he gave her a knowing nod. Removing her leather coat, she draped it over one of the winged chairs facing Carlton's desk as she sat in the other. Carlton Burke may have been fifty-seven years old, but he was still a suave gentleman with an excellent legal mind. She'd learned much under his tutelage, and he always encouraged her. His salt and pepper afro was always perfectly trimmed to frame his rectangular brown face, and his suits fit perfectly since they were tailor made for his large frame. She considered Carlton to be more of a father figure now. There was a time when she'd first started working for the firm when they both thought of making more of their mutual admiration. But Carlton was married, and Alicia refused to be the other woman in his life. Besides, he was too old for her, and beyond their love of the law, they had little else in common.

"Who handled the arraignment this morning?" she asked.

"I did, but I'd happily turn the case over to you." Carlton smiled like the Cheshire cat. "Shall I bring you up to speed?"

"Please."

"We pleaded not guilty today, of course," he said. "Jerri surrendered her passport, and we got her $1 million bail posted. She's resting at home. She found the body at their cabin, and her fingerprints were on the gun the police identified as the murder weapon. But Jerri insists Jake was already dead when she arrived, accompanied by Jake's brother, Ray. He'll corroborate her story about what happened when they arrived at the cabin. The police have estimated the time of death to be one or two am." Carlton paused and took out his pipe, already loaded with tobacco, to light it. "The problem is, Jerri was drinking heavily the night before and passed out. Home alone, of course."

Alicia nodded as she got up and paced around the office a bit. "She doesn't have an alibi for the murder, and her fingerprints are on the murder weapon. Why do you think she's innocent?"

"Because I talked to her, and she loved the man. She insists she didn't do it, and I believe her."

"I'll need to interview her. I want to be as certain of her innocence as you are before I agree to take the case."

"Of course. I've already arranged for a meeting this afternoon." Carlton rose from his chair. "Somehow, I convinced Jerri you were tying up loose ends on another case this morning, which was why I oversaw the arraignment." He picked up a folder from his credenza and handed it to Alicia.

"You already set up a meeting?" Her eyebrow went up, taking the folder from his hand.

"I took a chance. Glad you're taking one too."

Alicia shook her head, picked up her coat, and went to the door. "Thank you."

"For what?"

"For never losing faith in me." She smiled at him and left.

Anticipation pulsed through Alicia as she drove her Jeep to Manhattan to meet Jerri Devine. She had always been a fan of The Devine Music, and though she didn't relish the idea of meeting Jerri under these circumstances, she wanted to hear Jerri's story. To keep herself from imagining all scenarios today's interview could lead to, she focused on the change in the landscape as she sped down the parkway. As she approached the heart of New York City, the foliage became thinner and more skyscrapers filled the view until, finally, there were no trees left at all, just a concrete jungle.

Alicia didn't go into the city much anymore. Manhattan used to be her playground when she shared an apartment with Kevin for over a year on Avenue C. They were always on the go, to museums, restaurants, and shopping. The Big Apple lost its flavor after Kevin died, and she no longer had an appetite for socializing. Instead, she focused on her work.

Jerri Devine lived in a penthouse apartment on the lower West Side of Manhattan, on West 15th Street. Alicia was fortunate to find a parking spot on the street only two blocks away from the building on 8th Avenue. As she entered the pristine lobby, the doorman asked who she wanted to see. "AK Stone to see Ms. Devine."

Once he received clearance from upstairs, the doorman escorted Alicia to the elevators, pressing the P button for her in the empty car. The elevator pinged, and the doors slid open inside a small apartment foyer.

Two big, burly brothers greeted Alicia. "Sorry, Ms. Stone, but we gotta check ya," one of them said as he reached for her handbag and tote. The shorter brother gave her a light pat down as Alicia raised her arms. After they finished checking her out, they led Alicia to a door down the hall. The bigger brother knocked twice and a gorgeous, light-skinned redhead opened the door. "Jerri, this here is AK Stone."

The redhead extended her hand to Alicia. "Jerri Devine. So pleased to meet you. Please come on in." Alicia shook Jerri's hand and followed her into a sizable study. Dark brown leather sofas surrounded a big square coffee table, and dark wooden bookshelves lined two walls.

"Please have a seat," Jerri said as she strolled to the bar. "I'm having a brandy. Would you care to join me?"

Alicia sat as Jerri poured her drink. "No, thank you." Although clad simply in blue jeans and a white crochet knit top, she couldn't help being amazed at how good Jerri looked with beautiful cat-like dark eyes, a small perky nose, and full lips painted red. The pictures Alicia had seen of her before had not done her justice.

"Thank you for coming," Jerri said as she sat down across from Alicia, swirling her brandy glass. "And for taking my case."

"I haven't exactly agreed to take on your case yet."

Jerri stiffened as her cheeks flushed red. "Oh, when I spoke to Carlton, I was under the impression you were on board."

"Jerri, I'm here to talk and hear your story. After we've had a chance to go over everything, I'll know if I can properly represent you."

"Oh, you can properly represent me. A lot of folks speak real highly of you. And you're a sister and a widow." Jerri took a sip of her brandy. "Since you lost a husband, I kinda figured you could understand how I feel. How much I'm hurting inside." She took another sip and continued, "And then to be going through all this. Being called a killer. It's just too much."

It was Alicia's turn to be surprised. "How did you know about my husband?" she asked, taking out a notepad and pen. "It was not a highly publicized event."

Jerri stood up and downed the rest of her brandy before strolling to the bar for a refill. "I didn't hire you 'cause of people's word. My business manager, Ray, had you thoroughly checked out. You are quite the attorney. If anybody can properly represent me, I believe you can." Jerri raised her glass as if toasting Alicia. "What do you want to know?" she asked as she returned to her sofa seat. "Where do I begin?"

"Why don't you tell me about your relationship with Jake?"

"That's a long story. Right now, I feel like my arm's been cut off. I don't feel whole. That man's been a part of my life for so long, I can't believe he's gone."

"Did you love him?"

"Of course, I loved him." Jerri stifled a sob. "You don't stay with somebody for all those years if you don't love 'em."

"People stay together for all sorts of reasons, most of which, in my experience, have nothing to do with love. How could you love him while he abused you and had affairs with other women? Jake was notorious for extramarital affairs in the press over the years. It's no secret."

"No, it wasn't a secret." Jerri's eyes filled with water. "He could be mean, and he could be rough, but I loved Jake. He hurt me plenty, but I always forgave him. Jake was family. I've known him my entire life. We started out singing in the choir together when we were young. Later, when Jake got inspired to write The Devine Music, he said he was writing it for me, and no one else could make his songs come to life as he imagined." Jerri swirled her glass and looked down at it. "Everyone expected us to get married, so we did. But Jake never cared much for anything else besides the music. And the power that came along with success. All his gallivanting around town was just for show." Jerri drained her glass and proceeded to the bar for a refill.

Deciding to change the line of questioning, Alicia said, "Tell me what happened the day of, you know, at the cabin."

"Well, Billy called and said Jake wanted to see Ray and me. Jake used to go and stay at the cabin when he wanted to be alone to think."

"Who's Billy?"

"Billy is a part of our management team. Ray came here early and rushed me getting dressed. That's why I never picked up my purse and noticed the gun was missing. Anyway, Billy came over here, picked Ray and me up, and drove us up to the cabin. When we got there, Jake was not around. We called Jake, but he didn't answer. We spread out to look for him. I found him in the bed, but he still wasn't answering me. I pulled back the covers and started screaming when I saw all the blood. Ray came running in when he heard me screaming to pull me away from Jake's body. Then Ray saw Bella was there, on the floor."

"Bella?"

"My gun. Bella is my gun." Jerri started to cry, and Alicia rose from the sofa and walked over to the bar. She picked up a cocktail napkin and handed it to Jerri. Jerri dabbed the tears from her eyes. "I swear I didn't shoot Jake, and I don't know how Bella got there. I carry her in my purse for security, but I haven't fired my gun in months."

"What happened next?"

"I don't know. Ray said I fainted. The next thing I remember is being back here in my bed."

Alicia waited a moment before asking her next question. "Where were you the day before you went to the cabin?" She took the brandy glass from Jerri's hand and put it on the bar. Gently touching Jerri's elbow, she led her back to the sofa for a seat.

"I was here," Jerri stammered, "alone. Bryan and I had lunch together, and then he left with Billy. Something about his mother being sick."

"Who's Bryan?"

"Bryan James. He's the one who wrote all the beautiful music for my new CD. We met to go over a new song." Jerri's expression softened as she spoke about Bryan. "You know, before he showed up, The Devine Music hadn't recorded any new music in five years. He's a musical genius like Jake used to be. And he, too, says he writes his music only for me."

Alicia made a note to check out Bryan James. "Okay, you had lunch with Bryan and then?"

"Ray came by around eight to check on me, as he always does. He said he was going to meet Jake after he tucked me in. I was already pretty tipsy, and I let him put me in bed."

"What's Ray's relationship with Jake like?"

"They're brothers, and Ray loved his little brother. Thought he was a genius." Jerri shook her head and continued, "I know what you're thinking, and I'm telling you, there is no way he could have shot Jake. He spent his entire life looking out for Jake and me. And Jake, in return, took good care of him. Ray's always been a part of The Devine Music."

"Okay, it wasn't Ray. Who do you think did it? Who wanted to kill Jake?"

"I don't know. I don't know. Jake could be a ruthless bastard when it came to getting what he wanted. You don't get to be big in this game, being a wimp. I'm sure Jake made a lot of enemies along the way. I didn't get involved in the business end of things. I sing, and I perform. That's it. It could be anybody. One of the past producers, musicians, or even one of those women he messed around with." Jerri looked bewildered. "I've been racking my brain trying to think who would do this. I don't have any idea." Jumping from the sofa, she walked to the bar to retrieve her glass and fill it with brandy.

There was a light knock on the door, and a man stuck his head into the study. "Jerri, you all right?"

Jerri turned to wave him in. "Yeah, I'm okay. Come on in, Ray. I want you to meet Ms. AK Stone." Ray was a tall, well-built, dark-skinned brother sporting a low cut afro, a mustache and goatee. He wore a beige turtleneck sweater and a long, black leather coat. He had a facial resemblance to Jake. Same long face, big brown eyes, full nose, and lips,

31

but Jake was shorter with a lighter skin tone. Ray walked over to Jerri and draped his arm around her shoulder.

"Please, both of you, call me Alicia." Rising from the sofa, Alicia went to shake Ray's hand. "Pleasure to meet you, Ray. If you don't mind, I need to finish interviewing Jerri, but I'd like to talk to you later."

"Sure, sure. Whatever you need." Ray was speaking to Alicia, but his eyes never left Jerri's face. He gently squeezed her with his arm around her shoulders. "You really shouldn't drink too much, baby girl." He took the drink from Jerri's hand. "Come on, let's sit down." Ray led her back to the sofa as Alicia trailed behind them. "If you need anything, call me right away," he cooed, releasing Jerri and sitting her down. Ray turned back to Alicia. "I guess I'll get out of your way," and headed for the door. He turned, giving Jerri another long gaze before he walked out.

Alicia waited a moment before asking the next question. "When was the last time you saw your gun before Ray found it at the cabin?"

Jerri thought for a minute. "I think it was last week. Or two weeks ago. I don't know." Then her eyes widened, and she raised her hand. "No, it was last week. I took it out of my purse and threatened to shoot Ray. We were just playing, of course. Me, Bryan, Ray, and a few other fellas in the band were sitting around talking junk after a rehearsal for an upcoming show. We ordered food and were hanging out, relaxing, and Ray said something funny about how I might not fit into a certain outfit if I didn't ease up on the fried chicken. That's when I took out Bella and pointed it at him, saying, 'I'll shoot you if you try to come between me and this chicken leg,' or something like that. We all laughed, and I put Bella back in my purse. That's the last time I saw the gun."

"And you kept the gun loaded?"

"Oh yes. Always ready. Jake gave me Bella a long time ago. A cute little Derringer with a pink pearl handle. Said I needed it for protection. You know you get approached by a lot of crazy fans when you're famous. Jake taught me how to use it and told me to always keep Bella loaded and ready to fire. Thankfully, I've never had to use it on anybody."

"If everyone at the rehearsal saw you put Bella back in your purse, any of them could have taken it when you weren't looking."

"I guess."

"I'm going to need the name of everyone at the rehearsal." Alicia wrote down each name as Jerri called them out. Alicia reviewed the notes she had jotted down during their conversation. "One more question. Why would Jake call Billy to say he wanted to see you? Why wouldn't he just call you himself?"

Jerri thought momentarily and then said, "You know, that's a good question. Jake never really cared for Billy. Maybe he tried to reach Ray or me but couldn't, so he called Billy."

"All right, enough for now." Alicia stuffed her notes into her tote, preparing to leave. "Based on what I've heard today, I will take your case. Try to get some rest. I'll be in touch."

"Thank you, Alicia."

As Alicia drove back to the office, a heaviness filled her heart. Putting one of Jerri's older CDs into her car player, she swayed as Jerri crooned, "I never thought our love would ever end. How could you leave me?" Amidst the somber strains of the song, she understood how Jerri was feeling, wincing as the memory of the shocking jolt that rocked her body when the sergeant, Officer Grimes, came to her home to deliver the news about Kevin. She refused to believe him and demanded to see his body. Upon seeing it, pain flooded throughout her body, as if her heart got carved out, and it persisted for days, then months. The only way to end it had been to tuck all of her feelings away deep, deep within. Gripping the steering wheel tighter, Alicia took a deep breath. *At least Kevin's killer is behind bars. I need to get justice for Jerri.*

*Excerpt from *God Calling*, 1989 by Arthur James, LTD., Eversham, UK

Chapter 4

Now that she'd committed to Jerri's case, it was time to get to work. Alicia was already brainstorming when she arrived back at her office. *If Jerri didn't kill Jake, who did?* She needed to compile a list of potential suspects and get enough dirt on one of them to give the jury reasonable doubt. Alicia preferred to find the actual killer, but she'd settle for that shadow of doubt to vindicate Jerri.

Alicia hung her coat behind the door, sat behind her large walnut desk, removed her stilettos, and rubbed her feet. She opened the box atop her desk from the DA's office. The first folder summarized the charges against Jerri and listed the Chief Prosecutor, David King. Alicia shook her head as she read his name. *Much sooner than later.* She remembered the business card he had given her yesterday and fished it from her tote. David's handsome face floated in her mind as she tried to figure out the best way to approach him. Putting the business card down, she looked through the other folders in the box.

Alicia was flipping David's business card around in her hand when Diana walked into her office. She wore navy blue Dickies with a white thermal shirt covered by a red down vest. Her curly dark hair, cut low, complemented the glittering diamond studs in her earlobes and right nostril, especially when the sunlight hit them.

Sitting in the chair across from Alicia, she asked, "Hey girl, you ready to free Jerri?" Diana was mocking the fans gathering outside the courthouse with their signs, chanting, "FREE JERRI! FREE JERRI!"

"Yeah," Alicia chuckled. "Someone needs to tell them she's out on bail, and the trial won't start for weeks. We must review all this discovery material the DA's office sent over." She pushed the box in Diana's direction. "Guess who's the lead prosecutor on the case?"

"I don't have to guess. It's David King. Everyone's talking about it. Why are you never up on the good gossip floating around this office?"

"There's no such thing as good gossip," Alicia said. "So, I choose not to listen to it. Half of it isn't true anyway."

"But a lot of it is. Granted, exaggerated truth. How do you feel about it, going up against Mr. King?"

"I feel the same way I would about any prosecutor. I'm better than him, and I'm going to win." Alicia looked at the small, framed black-and-white photo of Charlotte E. Ray she kept on her desk. Charlotte Ray was the first black female lawyer in the U.S. Alicia revered her fellow alum, who opened the door for future generations of black women to practice law in this country. Whenever the going got tough, Alicia imagined how hard it must have been for Charlotte, yet she persevered and earned her credentials. Even though Charlotte could never garner enough business to launch a successful practice in the late 1800s, she continued to educate people on justice and the law. No matter what Alicia faced, her struggles were no match for the monumental obstacles Charlotte faced and overcame. Thoughts of Charlotte's fierceness spurred Alicia on.

Diana got up and walked over to the whiteboard on the side wall. She glanced down and saw Alicia barefoot. "Girl, what happened to your shoes?"

"I'm going to have to give them up. I know you meant well, telling me to upgrade my wardrobe, and to some extent, you were right. But the stiletto heels, they've got to go." Alicia reached down and rubbed her right foot as she looked up at Diana. "I think I'm getting a corn on my toe. I've never had a corn before."

Diana chuckled, "That's the price of beauty."

Alicia groaned. "From the looks of you, that's something you're not very concerned about."

"Hey, I've dressed appropriately for my job. I figured I'd go to the cabin today and take a look around. Could be muddy up there; definitely buggy. And I don't want to draw unnecessary attention by being too flashy while peeking around. You, on the other hand, need to present to the world. You need that glam factor, that flair that keeps the jury, hell, the whole courtroom riveted, and they can't take their eyes off you."

"Hopefully, they won't be looking at my feet because I cannot wear these shoes to court again. And this track of weave?"

Diana batted her eyes as she looked at Alicia's auburn hair framing her honey-colored face. "What about it?"

"It's got to go, too. It started itching and irritating me when I sweat during my morning walk."

"I think the extra length looks good on you, but if you're unhappy, take it out. You don't need it. You'll still be beautiful without it." Diana picked up a red marker and wrote on the whiteboard JAKE DEVINE. She drew a line across the board and wrote JERRI DEVINE. "Who else do I need to put up here?"

"First up," Alicia took out her notepad. "Raymond Meeks, Jake's older brother and business manager for The Devine Music. Although Jerri is oblivious to the fact, Ray is clearly in love with her. According to her, Ray had a meeting scheduled with Jake the night he was murdered. In the police notes, it says Ray left the meeting with Jake at the cabin around ten pm and went to a jazz place in Harlem called Pearl's Supper Club. It's one of his regular hangout spots, and several people confirmed Ray was there that night until the wee hours of the morning. I need you to go over there and talk to them. See if he could have slipped out at some point and gone back up to the cabin."

Diana wrote his name on the whiteboard, with lines connecting him to both Jerri and Jake.

"Next," Alicia continued, "is Bryan James. He's the genius behind *Ms. Devine Rocks!* Jerri seems quite taken with him. I wonder how he feels about her. She said he told her that he wrote his music only for her. Makes me think maybe he wanted to take Jake's place, not only as a writer and musical partner but also as her lover, husband even." Alicia reached down to rub her feet as she ticked off the names of the other band members who witnessed Jerri using Bella while Diana wrote them on the board. "Last but not least is Billy Whitmore. Billy received the call from Jake requesting to see Jerri at the cabin and drove her and Ray up there. Jerri wasn't sure why Jake called him and said Jake never cared for him." Alicia cocked her head as she looked up at Diana. "Why did Jake dislike Billy? According to the police notes, Billy's alibi was that he was with one of the ladies of the night at the time of the murder. You know a ho will say anything if you pay them enough money."

"That's quite a list," Diana said as she stepped back to take it all in.

"Yes, it is. And the police didn't bother to talk to most of them. They took the easy way out and arrested Jerri too quickly. It seems pretty obvious to me that someone is framing her for this murder. Why would she leave her gun on the bedroom floor if she shot Jake?"

Diana nodded in agreement. "I'm sure they were under a lot of pressure to make a quick arrest."

"We need full background checks and phone records on everyone and ask them where they were the night of the murder," Alicia continued. "I also noticed the police didn't even look at potential rabid fan suspects. There's got to be some. Ray should have some info on crazy fans since he's the business manager. And check out the neighbors around the cabin and the penthouse. Someone might have seen something interesting."

"Okay," Diana said. "This is a good jump-off point." Her eyes went to the ADA's business card on Alicia's desk. "What are you planning to do with that? Are you going to call him?"

"I don't know. I want to, but I don't know if it's the right time to reveal myself." Alicia picked up the card and rubbed her thumb over the raised print. "I wish it didn't have to be this way. He seems like a nice guy." She gave Diana a hopeless look, and Diana nodded in agreement. "Do me a favor and get a full background on David King too. I want to know whom I'm going up against."

"You got it," Diana picked up the box and prepared to leave. "I'll get my team started on this, and we'll talk later."

Alicia waited a while after Diana left before she picked up the phone to call David. "Hey, counselor, how are you? It's Alicia."

"Alicia? I'm good. I'm glad you called. I hope this means you were able to find some time for me in your busy schedule."

"As a matter of fact, I had a cancellation today. I know it's short notice, but are you free this evening? I want to repay you for yesterday's kindness in the garage."

"What did you have in mind?" David asked.

"Ribs, collard greens, cornbread. My treat, of course."

"Girl, you are speaking my language. I can definitely make time for ribs. A brotha's working hard over here on a big case, but I do have to eat. You know, keep my strength up."

"Great. I know a local spot, nothing fancy, but the food is delicious. It's called The Smoke House. Can you meet me there in an hour?"

"I'd be happy to. Text me the address."

Alicia smiled. "I'll see you soon.

The restaurant resembled a big red barn with chickens, pigs, and cows painted on the sides, and it sat in the center of a worn parking lot.

Alicia spotted David as he entered the restaurant door, and she jumped up from her booth towards the back to wave him over.

Alicia rubbed her tummy to calm the flutter rising there as David walked nearer. A smile slid across her face at the sight of him. He'd removed his tie but still wore his black suit jacket. David smiled, rubbing his mustache as he made his way toward her as if he was up to something. He wasn't Kevin, yet the Déjà vu happened again. She honestly did not want to see him with egg on his face for prosecuting the wrong person. This was his first big case under DeLeo, and Alicia didn't want to be responsible for ruining his sterling reputation by beating him in court. *Together, we can see that justice was served. Once we apprehend and bring the real killer to court, David's reputation will remain fully intact.* They sat across from one another in a red cushioned booth.

David loudly inhaled. "Mm, smells good in here. Hope the food tastes as good as it smells."

Alicia laughed, "Well, like I said, nothing fancy, but they serve up the best southern cooking around these parts."

"Good, because I'm starving." He paused, gazing into her eyes. "You're looking lovely tonight. How was your day today? I noticed you got your car back on the road."

Alicia got lost in his warm brown eyes. "Yes, thank you." She tore her eyes away from his penetrating stare and grabbed her glass of water. She took a big sip, trying to compose herself. "I got a tow, and they had to use a machine to get the frozen lug off the tire. I also signed up with AAA today for a roadside assistance plan to avoid getting stuck like that again." Looking back at David's eyes, they still waited on her. "Thank God you came by when you did."

"It was my pleasure." David leaned in, bringing his face closer to hers. "I was sorry I couldn't finish the job." The waitress came over to take their order, breaking the spell. Once she left, David focused his attention on Alicia again. "What were you doing at the courthouse yesterday?"

Alicia cleared her throat. "Divorce proceeding."

"Oh, I'm sorry. Were you married long?"

"Oh no, I'm not the one getting a divorce." She held up her right hand, wiggling her ring finger with the white gold band. "Actually, I'm a widow."

"Oh wow, I'm sorry."

"No need to apologize. I'm all right. My husband passed away a couple of years ago."

"I'm still sorry for your loss. It must be difficult losing a spouse." David paused before asking, "So, why were you in divorce court? Do you work for the court?"

Alicia took a deep breath and slowly let it out. "I was representing a client. I'm an attorney." Staring intently at David, she awaited his reaction.

David looked at her and started to laugh loudly. Alicia liked his hearty laugh and joined in. She was glad he received the news so well. Once he stopped laughing, David gave her a skeptical look. "You're not kidding."

Alicia shook her head. "Nope."

The food arrived, breaking the tension building between them. David rubbed his hands together as he looked at the platter filled with a large rack of ribs, a mound of collard greens, and a generous helping of macaroni and cheese. The waitress set a bowl of hot cornbread with butter on the table between them. Alicia's salad also appeared appetizing, since the field greens had piles of beef brisket and smoked chicken atop. David plunged into his food and began moaning.

"Mm, you were right. These ribs are delicious, so tender they're falling off the bone. And the collards, mm mm. You know, everyone can't make good collard greens."

Alicia bobbed her head as she took small bites of her salad. "Told you. Trust me, counselor, I wouldn't steer you wrong. I don't play around when it comes to my food."

It was quiet for a few moments as they each concentrated on their meal. Eventually, David took a breather. "How long have you been a divorce attorney?"

Alicia averted her eyes. "About a year." She waited until he finished drinking his water before she added, "I'm also a criminal defense lawyer."

"You are?" David set his water glass down. "Well, that explains why you were so passionate about defending brothers rather than prosecuting them."

The moment of truth had arrived. Taking the business card she had laid on the seat beside her, Alicia handed it to David.

Looking down at the card, his eyes widened as he read it. "You're AK Stone?" He burst out with another laugh, but not quite as heartily or as long as before. "Well, well, well. You are full of surprises, Ms. AK Stone."

"The K is for Katherine, after my grandma."

A serious expression filled David's face. Crossing his arms on the table, he leaned in, gazing sternly at Alicia. "Okay, Ms. Stone. Why did you invite me here tonight? What do you want? I know you're defending Jerri Devine, and you know I'm the lead prosecutor on the case. So, what is it you want?"

Alicia gave him an equally sober look. "I want you to drop the charges."

David's head jerked up. "What? Why would I do that? Don't get me wrong. You're beautiful and witty, but surely you didn't think you could talk me into dropping the charges by serving up a big helping of your charm, along with a plate of ribs."

"Jerri is innocent." Alicia raised her voice slightly. "The police rushed to make an arrest. I'm certain DeLeo was all over them to button this up quickly, but I'm telling you, Jerri is being framed."

David flagged their waitress as she walked by their booth. "Um, I will need a to-go box, please."

The waitress answered, "Right away, sir. Miss, would you like one too?"

"Sure, thanks," Alicia said, dismissing the waitress. She tried to recapture David's attention. "Think about it, David. Your evidence was awfully easy to find. Why would Jerri leave her gun at the scene, covered with her fingerprints? She's not stupid."

"Because she's an amateur. She killed Jake and staged the whole discovery scene, thinking she'd throw us off her trail. She had means, and she had a motive. I think we've got our girl."

"Many other people had a motive and could have killed Jake. The police didn't thoroughly investigate anyone else as a suspect."

David raised his eyebrows. "Many other people? Like who? Who do you think killed Jake Devine?"

Alicia sighed. "I don't know yet. We are interviewing persons of interest the police never bothered to talk to, like all the band members."

The waitress brought the to-go boxes, and David, snatching one up, began transferring his food from his plate into it. "And have you come up with anything solid to exonerate Jerri?"

"No," Alicia said. "But there's enough circumstantial evidence to cause reasonable doubt. I plan to file a motion with the judge on Monday to dismiss the charges."

David slapped the lid shut on his to-go box and gave her an incredulous expression. She continued trying to convince him. "David, you said you were interested in seeing justice served. I'm telling you, Jerri is innocent. Don't let DeLeo get you all puffed up and overly confident this case is all sewed up. DeLeo loves all the media attention a big case like these garners, but to her, you're just another one of her gladiators. She'll take all the glory if you win. But if you lose, she'll feed you to the lions."

David stood up to leave. "Well, thank you for dinner. You did say this was your treat?" Alicia nodded. "And thank you for your concern for my welfare, even if it's not needed." He picked up his food and gave her a sharp look. "I look forward to reading your motion brief. You enjoy the rest of your evening." He turned from her and left the restaurant.

Alicia pouted as she dumped the remains of her salad into the to-go box. *Guess that didn't go so well after all.*

Chapter 5

David fumed behind the wheel as he drove back to his office, his thoughts racing like a getaway car chased by sirens. *She's AK Stone? How could she be AK Stone?* The revelation slammed into him like a collision in the dark. *Had she orchestrated their meeting in the parking garage? Did she know who I was all along? Who is this woman?* The transformation from a soft, sexy siren to a ferocious tigress right before his eyes left him reeling. *Drop the charges. Is she crazy? How dare she talk to me about justice.*

Furrowing his eyebrows, David frowned as he stepped off the elevator. His young paralegal, Jamal, stopped him. "Hey man," he asked, "are you all right?"

"I just met AK Stone for a friendly dinner." David raised his to-go box as evidence.

"Ah man," Jamal swooned, "She fine, isn't she? I hear she's tough in court, but she's one fine sister. A few guys around here tried to rein her in, but no dice. I figured she'd be attracted to you, though."

David's head snapped back. "Why is that?"

"Cause you're a dead ringer for her late husband, Kevin Green." David could tell Jamal thought about what had just come out of his mouth. "Excuse my bad choice of words, man, but I swear, you could be his twin brother." He pushed the button to summon the elevator. "Anyway, man, I'm glad you're okay. I'm out of here, heading home." The elevator doors opened, and Jamal stepped in, leaving David more confused.

He sat behind his desk in his office, but David couldn't concentrate on much of anything as Alicia's words and Jamal's comments swirled through his head. *It's late, and I'm tired.* He picked up a legal pad with some notes he'd made on it and went home.

Armed with two glazed donuts and a large coffee, David headed to the office early the next day. He preferred working in the office, where he could access all his books, files and secured computer tech, rather than in his hotel room. He was staying at the Springfield Suites, which was more comparable to a studio apartment than a hotel room, since it had a small kitchen, office desk, living area, and a king-size bed. Yet, David wasn't comfortable there. He wasn't much of a cook, but the refrigerator and microwave were convenient for heating leftovers from takeout and keeping a cold drink. The desk was too small to work on, and he was never one for lounging on the sofa, watching TV. Each morning, he promised to call the real estate agent who kept sending him listings for condos and houses. He knew he needed a home, but never had time to see any of the properties.

The DA's main floor was quiet, and no one else was there. David sauntered past the empty metal desks and went to his office to eat his donuts and plan his strategy for the day. Last night he fell asleep after finishing his ribs from The Smoke House and tossed and turned until he woke fully at four am. He ran on the treadmill in the hotel's fitness center for half an hour, showered, and dressed in a black suit, white shirt, and black loafers. David didn't expect anyone else to arrive in the office until seven or eight am. He figured he'd get at least one hour of peace.

Settling behind his wooden and gray metal desk, he polished off one donut and drank half the coffee while waiting for his computer to boot up. New York State was not supplying ultramodern equipment to any of its staff. The legal pad with the list of action items he'd scribbled down was beside his keyboard. First, investigate AK Stone and Kevin Green. He should have immediately requested a background check when the boss lady told him she was a formidable foe. Maybe then he would have known Alicia was AK Stone before she could blindside him with that information. He was also curious to see a photo of Kevin Green.

David logged in and searched the Westchester County Library System database for news articles related to Alicia and Kevin. Several popped up, and he opened *The New York Daily News* article headlined EX NYPD OFFICER SLAIN IN HARLEM. A photo of a uniformed officer who looked a lot like him smiled up at him from the middle of the page. Jamal was right. Kevin could be his twin brother. The article, dated July 9, stated that Green was shot on 127th Street during gang-related gunfire, and the gunman and several others had been arrested.

Green left the police force to become an investigator for the Burke and Powell Law firm in White Plains and was newly wed to the attorney Alicia K. Stone. David thought of Alicia, and his heart softened toward her. *It must have been awful for her to receive such horrible news suddenly after taking their marriage vows. No wonder she behaved so oddly in the garage. She probably thought she saw a ghost!* Heat rose in his body as the memory of her sitting in his car and his desire to kiss her resurfaced in his mind. *Knowing who she is now, I shouldn't feel anything for her beyond compassion. But there is something special about her. I felt it the moment I saw her. A weird, warm, squishy feeling. Something I never felt for Elizabeth.*

A knock on the door interrupted David's thoughts, and he quickly lifted his head when Eddie pushed the door open. "Morning," he said with a goofy grin. "I've got good news."

"Really?" David sat straight up in his chair, giving him his full attention.

"The police sent over some security video footage from the penthouse building on the night of the murder. A car from the Devine fleet left the parking garage at midnight."

David stood up. "Show me."

Eddie appeared animated and excited as he led the way down the hall to the electronics room. "You can't clearly see who the driver is, but I think it'll be enough to break Jerri's alibi of being home all night alone."

David had never seen Eddie show this much enthusiasm for this case. He was glad because he was getting tired of doing all the heavy lifting on case preparation and could use some help. Eddie was familiar with the local officers and had an established rapport with them. It made sense that he would be the conduit between their law office and the police department. They entered the electronics room, and the video was already cued to the point of interest. Eddie pressed play, and the video showed a black SUV slowly pulling out of the garage and turning left toward 8th Avenue.

"The Devines have four black Chevy Suburbans registered under Raymond Meeks. A zoom-in on the license plate confirms this SUV was one of theirs. With no traffic at night, the drive from the New York City to Katonah would take about an hour." Eddie pressed fast forward on the video player and then stopped it. "This portion shows the vehicle returning to the garage. Timestamp, three am."

"This is excellent, excellent." David put his hand out for a high five, and Eddie's hand slapped it up high.

"The police also tracked down Bryan James. They camped out on his doorstep all night and caught him when he arrived home early this morning. Said he's been in Memphis for the past few days visiting his sick mother."

"When did his flight leave?"

"October 8th at four pm. He was long gone before the murder took place." Eddie sighed. "I know DeLeo thinks this guy is involved somehow, but I think this pretty much clears him."

"I know. Do you have a full copy of the police interview notes? I want to read them to see if they glossed over anything."

Eddie nodded. "Yes, they're on my desk." They left the electronics room and headed back toward their offices. When they reached Eddie's doorway, David waited in the hallway while Eddie retrieved the notes. Eddie's office was a mess to David. Papers, files, and books strewn across the desk and haphazardly stacked on the floor. Handing the notes to David, Eddie said, "I know we got off to a rocky start. My fault completely. I want you to know I'm fully on board and proud to be your co-counsel on this case."

David took the folder in one hand and gave Eddie a firm handshake with his other.

"Welcome aboard. Let's get this video officially into evidence." He stroked his mustache with his thumb and forefinger as he looked up at nothing in particular. "We should take another crack at Jerri in light of this new evidence. Schedule an interview with her for Monday afternoon."

"Okay, I'll take care of it." Glancing down, Eddie shuffled his feet. "I think I might have another item of interest for you." He went back into his office and returned with another folder. "Full dossier on Alicia Katherine Stone. DeLeo keeps a current file on all the leading competition."

David took the folder. "Thank you. Great work. Let's keep it up." He wasn't sure what had lit a fire under Eddie, but he was grateful for it. Once back in his office, he read Alicia's file. She would indeed be a formidable foe. *Most likely, Alicia is into playing head games and being a pretender like Elizabeth. That's why she never mentioned being an attorney when I met her. It's part of her defense strategy. I cannot let my attraction to her get in the way. I need to focus on cracking Jerri's alibi to prove she is guilty.*

Chapter 6

As Alicia finished her morning routine of coffee and prayers, the phone broke the silence. Diana was on her way to her place with the dossiers. Alicia preferred to work from home on Saturdays whenever possible. Dressed in a comfortable gray sweatsuit, she anticipated a long day ahead as she and Diana had a lot of ground to cover. But this day would not include the preparation of a motion brief to dismiss the charges. Without solid evidence, it was foolish to even request such action from the judge.

When the doorbell rang, Alicia had barely finished cooking bacon and flipping the French toast. Diana let herself in, carrying a box with folders. She, too, sported a casual ensemble clad in blue jeans and a black sweatshirt with the Nike slogan, *Just Do It*, on the front.

"Lots of good reading to do. Mm, girl, it smells good in here. How'd you know I'd be hungry?"

"Because you're always hungry?"

"Sure, you right," Diana laughed. She placed the box on the floor by the table and fixed herself a plate. "We can read while we eat." They sat across from one another at the kitchen table with their breakfast plates and coffee mugs. Diana removed a folder from the box and handed it to Alicia. "I know you want to read this one first."

Alicia knew it was the dossier on David without even looking at the tab. She didn't want to appear too eager to read it and nonchalantly placed it on the table beside her plate. "Before we get started on this, tell me. Did you go to the cabin yesterday?" Alicia hoped Diana had turned up something, anything of interest.

"Yeah, girl, I went up there." Diana's eyes got wide as she spoke. "People need to stop playing, calling it a cabin. It's made from wood and stone, but it is no cabin. It's a big old farmhouse surrounded by acres of green countryside. Absolutely beautiful." She stopped talking long enough to take a sip of coffee. "Unfortunately, you ain't gonna find nothing on those grounds without dogs sniffing a scent. It's very spread out. I perused the perimeter of the house and examined the inside, but there was nothing of interest. And the neighbors are Martha Stewart and Ralph Lauren. Their properties are a good distance away, and I'm sure they didn't hear a thing, so I don't think we need to question them." Diana smirked as she reached into the box and pulled out a folder.

That news disappointed Alicia. "Wow, sounds like quite a place." Picking up David's folder, she asked, "Who are you starting with?"

"Raymond Meeks."

"That should be interesting." Alicia opened the folder and slowly began reading. She gleaned from the dossier's Family Fact Sheet that David was 34 years old, the same as her. Brooklyn born and bred. Eldest of three brothers, father deceased, mother, Mary, still alive and living in Brooklyn. *Raised in public housing by a single mom. Hmm, rough upbringing.* Enlisted right after graduating high school. Left service as an army MP and went straight to NYPD Officer. Injured while on duty and went out on disability. *How was he injured? Is he still suffering from it?* Started college at NYU and earned his bachelor's degree in Political Science and Government. *He must have tapped his GI bill benefits to finance his education.* David had articles published in the NYU Law Review and had graduated cum laude with honors. *Quite the student whizzing through NYU, both undergrad and Law School, in seven years.* She flipped through the numerous newspaper articles on various cases David had successfully prosecuted as an ADA under the Manhattan District Attorney, Robert Morgenthau. But what caught her eye was the article from *The New York Times* Society Page, announcing the engagement of David Edward King to Elizabeth Gayle Harrington. There was a photo of the happy couple. Alicia looked at the date of the newspaper. *December, less than a year ago. Is it still on?* She closed the folder and asked, "Anything interesting on Raymond Meeks?"

"Not really, and I'm glad 'cause I think he's kind of cute." Diana flashed the 5x7 glossy photo of Ray from the folder. "He was a star college athlete whose future career got sidelined by an injury. But he graduated from Mississippi State with his BS in Business, and he's been running with Jake ever since. No criminal activity, never been married."

"Because he's in love with his sister-in-law."

"So you say. Anyway, I called Ray this morning. He agreed to gather the band members and meet me at the office later this afternoon. I promised to serve food, and I'm ordering lots of pizza. You want to join us?"

"I do, but I'll just monitor the private interviews, watch their body language as they tell their stories." Alicia hoped something of interest came out of those interviews.

"And tonight, I'll go to Pearl's Supper Club to do some sleuthin. I hope Ray shows up and notices me. It'll let him know I don't trust him, you know, keep him on his toes." Diana swirled her last piece of French toast in a glob of syrup and popped it in her mouth. "The bad news," she continued as she chewed, "is Bryan James will not be joining us. He's in Memphis. Something about his mother being sick."

Alicia reached into the box and pulled out the folder labeled Bryan James. She handed Diana the folder labeled William J. Whitmore. Alicia found the glossy 5x7 photo of Bryan surprising. Shoulder-length blonde hair, piercing blue eyes, firm jaw, brilliantly white smile. Very handsome. She'd assumed Bryan was black. *He looks awfully young, too.* Alicia flipped to the Family Fact Sheet and calculated Brian's age to be 28. Born in Bartlett, TN, apparently to a young single mom. No father listed on the birth certificate. Dawn Hayes, the mother, was arrested several times for drug possession and prostitution, and authorities placed the baby in foster care. She died of a drug overdose shortly after. The James family adopted Bryan at age five and still resided in Bartlett.

She was reading a short article from *Rolling Stone* magazine on Bryan, Jake, and Jerri when Diana said, "This is interesting. In this picture, he looks like a drunk, but Billy was a Navy Seal." Holding up the photo for Alicia to see, the middle-aged man had a dirty blond mop of hair with gray strands, stubble over his thin lips and chin, and bags under his squinty blue eyes. "It's not easy becoming a Seal. They go through one of the most brutal training regimens in the military because they engage in the most dangerous and often covert operations. Says here Billy took part in the invasion of Grenada and served in the Persian Gulf war in Iraq."

"Really?" Alicia put down Bryan's folder and got up to stand behind Diana. Peering at the folder over Diana's shoulder, she ignored Diana's finger, pointing out the Military Service portion at the bottom of the page. Instead, Alicia scanned the top of the page and saw Bartlett listed as Billy's birthplace.

"And somehow, he's related to Bryan James. They're both from the same town in Tennessee." Alicia went back to her seat. "Is Billy included in this afternoon's meeting?"

"I asked Ray to include him, so, yeah, he should be there." Diana paused before asking, "What are you thinking?"

Alicia shook her head. "Don't you think it's strange Jerri didn't mention a relationship between Billy and Bryan? She only referred to him as a part of the management team."

"Yeah, well, you know you can't only go on what Jerri said. I asked Ray who was at the rehearsal when Jerri pulled out her gun because I wanted to speak to everyone there. She left off a name when you interviewed her. Billy Whitmore."

"A Navy Seal would know how to pull off a covert operation, like framing someone for murder. And Jerri said Jake never liked Billy, but she didn't know why." Alicia got excited that they'd finally ferreted out a potential suspect. "You have cell phone records in his file?"

"No," Diana said. "I only brought the parts which were done so that we could get started. The team is still compiling information, like phone records."

"Let's be careful with Billy's interview today. Don't mention that we know about his military background. I don't want to spook him, and he flees before we discover more about him." Alicia pulled two more folders from the box and handed one to Diana. "We need to finish these dossiers on the other band members and compile a list of key questions to ask this afternoon."

"Yup," Diana said as she took the folder from Alicia's hand, "I'm going to need another cup of coffee." She got up and refilled her mug. "Did you find anything interesting in David's file?"

"He's no slouch, that's for sure. His record as an ADA is impressive." Handing Diana David's folder, she pointed out *The New York Times* article. "And it's possible he's engaged."

"She's gorgeous." Diana examined the photo. "I'll consult the grapevine on Monday, but I have a feeling this engagement is over. You know nosy Negros would have said he's off the market, and all I hear is he's Westchester's most desirable, eligible, black bachelor."

"He's not interested in me anyway. It doesn't matter." Alicia sighed and got up for another cup of joe. "I met him late last night at The Smoke House. He was not pleased when I told him I was AK Stone and he should drop the charges against Jerri."

Diana's face twisted up. "You did what?"

"I figured it was best to get everything out in the open." Alicia sat back down at the table.

"Drop the charges? Based on what, pray tell?

"The fact Jerri is being framed."

"We think Jerri is being framed. It has not yet been established as a fact."

"I was trying to get him on our side. He didn't believe me anyway, and he got quite cocky. He thinks he's got this case locked down." Alicia sipped some coffee. "He didn't bat an eye when I told him I would file a motion brief for dismissal with the judge on Monday."

"Why would he? He knew you were bluffing." Diana shook her head. "David may look like Kevin, but he is not Kevin. David is not on your side and probably never will be."

"You're probably right," Alicia replied, shrugging her shoulders. "Let's do a quick review of The Devine Music's financials and see what we deduce from them." After a long, silent perusal of the documents, Alicia got a quizzical look. "There's quite a few large withdrawals made out to Jake. The only notation is 'personal.' What do you think it means?"

Diana pursed her lips before responding. "Large, routine withdrawals of money could indicate a drug problem or a gambling problem. Guess we'll have to ask Jerri and Ray which one Jake had."

Chapter 7

The band interviews were scheduled for four pm. Diana and Alicia arrived a half hour before, carrying paper plates, cups, and napkins. As they made their way to the conference room, Alicia couldn't help but notice Carlton's office door ajar, a rare sight for a Saturday.

Setting up the table, Alicia caught Carlton observing through the long glass window. He sauntered to the doorway. "Hello, ladies."

They each said hello before Alicia turned to Diana. "Can you call and alert Tom at the front desk that we're expecting a large pizza order? We forgot to mention it when we came in."

Diana went for the phone as Alicia strolled toward Carlton. "What brings you into the office on a Saturday?"

Carlton smiled. "I was hoping to see you here. As your co-counsel, I'd like an update on Jerri's case."

"Oh," Alicia stumbled, "I didn't know you were acting as co-counsel."

"You thought I would let you handle this alone? This case is crucial for the firm and its reputation. I have complete confidence in you, of course. But as you know, anything could happen during a case, and until we have a verdict or a deal, someone must be ready to take over if necessary." Carlton paused as he gauged her reaction. "You don't have a problem with this arrangement, do you?"

"No, of course not." Alicia responded casually, but inside, she was a bit miffed he'd be looking over her shoulder. "I just assumed you turned the case over to me because you didn't want to be involved. Since you are involved, shouldn't I be your co-counsel?"

Carlton grinned and said, "Let us not forget, the client requested you be her attorney. Besides, I truly am stepping back from the details of casework these days, but I think I can still be a valuable advisor."

"Yes, of course." Alicia turned and gestured toward the table. "Well, today, we're conducting interviews with the band members. The police neglected to speak to any of them. You're welcome to join us if you'd like."

"No, no. You go ahead. I'll be here for a while. You can update me afterward." Carlton flashed her a smile and sauntered back toward his office.

Shortly after, Ray entered the office with three men in tow. Diana rushed to greet them at the door and usher them to the conference room. "Gentlemen, this is AK Stone, Jerri's attorney." Gazing at Alicia, she said, "I know you've already met Ray."

Ray stepped forward to shake Alicia's hand. "Nice to see you again. Billy's coming up with the rest of the guys." He turned to his companions. "This is Matt McCray, our drummer." The wiry, dark-skinned man with a short afro waved his hand. "This is Walter Grant, our sax player, and Joe Harris, our trumpet player." The two older light-skinned gentlemen with salt and pepper hair mumbled a greeting, and Walter, the smaller and rounder of the two, extended his hand to shake Alicia's.

Alicia smiled, shook his hand, and pointed them toward the table. "Pleased to meet you all. Have a seat and make yourselves comfortable. Pizza is on the way, and we'll begin soon."

Billy arrived moments later with the rest of the band. Guitarist Victor Bennet and percussionist Felix Ortiz were both short and appeared to be Latino. A tall, light-skinned man with a large afro was the bassist, Ronald Parker, and a medium-height, thin white man with a long black ponytail was the pianist, Alex Hayes.

Once the introductions were complete, Diana positioned herself at the head of the table. "I am the lead investigator for this law firm, working with Ms. Stone to prove Jerri's innocence. As you all know, Jerri is facing a murder charge. Anything you can tell us about Jake or Jerri, their relationship or behavior, or anything at all, no matter how small it may seem, could go a long way toward forming a successful defense."

Walter adamantly piped in, "I know Jerri didn't kill Jake. I been with them from the start, and ain't no way she coulda done that." The rest of the band members nodded and agreed on Jerri's innocence.

Diana brought the group back to order with a loud, "We agree. We want to prove she's innocent." In a softer voice, she continued, "I'll speak to each of you privately in another office. Please stick around until I speak to everyone in case I need to ask a follow-up question." The pizza deliveryman arrived carrying five large pie boxes and a case of soda. "Please, everyone, help yourselves to the food. Mr. Parker, I'll start with you. Would you please follow me?" The tall man with the big afro rose and left the room with Diana.

Alicia observed the remaining men in the conference room as they helped themselves to the pizza and soda. Billy was sitting alone, looking sleepy, while the others had clustered together in casual conversation. She picked up a slice of pepperoni pizza and sat by Ray. "How's Jerri doing?"

Ray looked at her with sad eyes. "Bout well as can be expected. Still drinking too much and a whole lot of crying, asking why."

"I understand she is grieving, but I wish she wouldn't drink so much. A clear head is necessary to remember details about events that could help her case."

"I know, believe me, I'm trying to talk to her." Ray shook his head as he spoke. "She's not the only one suffering. I lost my brother, my best friend."

Ray's eyes were getting watery as Alicia patted his arm. "I'm very sorry for your loss."

Fortunately, Walter called out, "Hey Ray, do you remember the time we played down in Jackson, Mississippi, at the Harlem Inn?" The other band members groaned, "Not again," which told Alicia they'd all heard this story. As Walter droned on, Ronald Parker strolled back into the conference room. Diana was behind him, shaking her head, signaling that nothing interesting was uncovered during the interview.

Diana lifted her hand and called out, "Matt McCray? You're up next." Alicia watched as they walked down the hall and then turned her attention back to Walter and his story.

A few moments later, Diana nodded as she followed the drummer back into the conference room. She was somber as she said, "Walter Grant, you're next. Alicia, I think you should join us."

"Oh, watch him now," Joe Harris called out. "Walter may have a heart attack alone with two beautiful women." The other men laughed, and Walter waved them off as he followed Diana from the room. Alicia hopped up and trailed behind Walter down the hall.

They entered a small windowless room with bare gray walls. Diana took her seat behind the small wooden desk, and Walter sat across from her in a steel folding chair while Alicia sat in one like it, off to the side. Before Diana could ask a single question, Walter grinned and asked, "What did I do to deserve this special attention?"

"Well," Diana began, "you did say you've been with Jake and Jerri from the beginning. I believe that gives you the best insight into their relationship."

Walter continued grinning and started to blush. "I guess I do."

Diana started with the standard questions she and Alicia had agreed upon; how long have you been with the band? Did you have any issues with Jake? Jerri? Did you know Jerri carried a gun? Ever heard Jerri threaten to kill Jake?

Walter chuckled at the last question and leaned back in his chair. "Jerri, naw. Now, Jake, he threatened to kill people all the time. He could be a real hot head if he wasn't gettin his way."

Diana then added a new question. "I understand you had a rehearsal the day Jake was killed. What do you recall about that?"

"Aw, shucks, Jake had one of his fits that day. Came in yellin and cussin. Tole Ray they had to talk and tole everyone else to get out."

"Do you know what Jake was angry about?"

"No, God only knows. I heard him yellin through the closed door, 'I'm gonna kill 'im' on my way out." Walter shifted in his chair and leaned toward Diana. "Ya know, Jake would get himself worked up over all kinda things, like folks showin up late for rehearsals, clubs cancellin shows. That wernt the first time he got pissed and canceled rehearsal. But Lord knows it'll be the last."

"Was it a full rehearsal with everyone?"

"No. Bryan and Jerri were workin on the leads, not sure where. That's why I was shocked to see Jake come to our rehearsal. He usually oversees Bryan and Jerri's sessions. He's so jealous over her, he didn't ever leave her alone with any man, other than Ray."

"Jake was jealous?"

"Oh, yeah." Walter leaned back in his chair. "Can't say I blame 'im. Jerri is a beautiful girl with a sweet, gentle spirit."

"But Jake did mess around with other women."

"That's true, but he'd always go back to Jerri. I think he did all that skirt chasin to prove he was a big man who could do anythin. But he loved Jerri, and if anyone tried to get too close to her, he'd go crazy. Jake fired a few playas in the band over the years for tryin to step to Jerri." Walter leaned in again and continued in almost a whisper. "There's chemistry between Bryan and Jerri. Everybody can see it, but nobody says nothin bout it. But I think that's what makes the music magical, the connection between them two."

Diana leaned toward Walter. "You think the chemistry went beyond the stage?"

"I can't speak for Bryan, cuz I don't know him real well, but Jerri would never leave Jake. She loved that man. Even after all the stuff he put her through, she stuck by his side."

Diana glanced at Alicia. "Bryan and Jerri weren't at the rehearsal that day. What about Billy? Was he there?"

Walter leaned back in his chair. "Yea, Billy was there. He took me home after Jake shut down the rehearsal. Usually, Ray takes me back and forth, but he asked Billy to do it since Jake needed 'im. I don't know what took Billy so long to get to the car. He had me waitin outside a good fifteen minutes. Said he had to hit the can. Musta been some shit to take that long."

Diana chuckled and got to her final question. "Where were you the night Jake was shot?"

"I was home. Had a few beers, watched the boob tube, and went to bed. My nosy neighba, Olivia Woods, will tell ya. That lady stay in my business."

Diana escorted Walter back to the conference room and pulled Alicia aside. In a low voice, she said, "I think this blow-up Jake had is key." Alicia concurred. "We should split the interviews with the remaining guys so we can get to Billy and Ray. I'll take the piano and trumpet guy, and you can interview the guitar player and percussion guy in your office. You've got a tape recorder set up there, don't you?" Alicia nodded.

Within half an hour, Alicia and Diana had divided and conquered. Now only the two primary persons of interest remained. As they stood outside the door, Alicia said, "I hope I can trust you to interview Ray without getting too distracted because I want to talk to Billy. Think you can handle Ray like a professional?"

"Come on, girl. Stop playing. I'm always a professional when it comes to my job. Now, after hours, that's another story." Diana entered the conference room and said, "Guys, thank you for your cooperation and patience." The pizza boxes were empty, and folks were looking sleepy. "We're going to chat with Ray and Billy, and then you're all free to go. Ray, come with me. Billy, you're with Ms. Stone."

Behind her, Alicia could hear the shuffle of Billy's feet. She still couldn't reconcile how Billy appeared in person with what she learned about his past. Billy glanced at the whiteboard as they entered Alicia's office. She quickly took an eraser to the red letters and sat behind her desk as he flopped into the chair across from her.

"Tell me, Billy, how long have you been with The Devine Music?"

"Little over a year. I signed on with Bryan, you know. We were like a package deal." Billy's speech was slow and had a southern twang. "I been managing Bryan's career going on two years now. He was doing okay when we first got together, playing small club gigs and selling a few songs he'd written. But I knew Bryan could be a star. The boy's really talented. He just needed the right connections, you know?" Billy avoided making eye contact with her. He gazed around the room with squinty eyes, as if the light was bothering him.

"You connected Bryan with Jake?"

"Not Jake directly. I had a friend who had a friend who knew Ray. I think they played college ball together. Anyway, Bryan's always been a huge fan of The Devine Music, and I knew he'd jump at the chance to play with them. So, I had this friend arrange a meeting between Ray and me, and I gave him a demo tape of Bryan's music. Ray and Jake liked what they heard, and the rest is history."

"But you're more than just a manager to Bryan, aren't you? I mean, who else's career have you managed besides Bryan's?" Alicia picked up Billy's dossier and flipped it open. She wanted him to stop pretending to be a country bumpkin. She peered down at the folder and then stared at Billy. "Says here you're from Bartlett, Tennessee, the same place where Bryan was born. That's not a coincidence, is it?"

Billy perked up in his seat, trying to see what Alicia was reading. "Uh, no, no, ma'am, it's not."

"Are you related to Bryan in some way? Is that why you've taken such an interest in his career?" Alicia cocked her head, gazing at him. Finally, eye contact.

"Yes. I'm Bryan's uncle."

"How's that?"

"Bryan's mother was my baby sister, Dawn."

"Oh, you're related to his birth mother, not the mother who raised him. Why are you so concerned about Bryan now? Where were you when your sister was drugged up and the boy was taken away from her?" Alicia slapped the folder closed.

Billy's face reddened, and he glared at her. "I don't see what that has to do with Jake's murder. Are you going to ask me a relevant question, or are we done here?"

Alicia softened her tone. "Where is Bryan? Is he still in Memphis? We need to talk to him."

"About what? He wasn't here when Jake got murdered. He's got nothing to do with it."

"I'd like to hear it from him. When's he due back?"

"Later tonight. I'll tell Bryan to call you when he gets back in town. Is that it?"

Alicia shifted back into tactical mode. She reopened the folder and firmly answered, "No." She pretended to read from the dossier. "You were at the rehearsal studio with the band the day Jake was murdered. What do you recall about that day?"

Billy sighed and leaned back in his chair. "Jake burst in, yelling and screaming. He told everyone to get out. Rehearsal's over. So we left. I took Walter home, and then I went home. When I got home, I got a call from Nathaniel James, saying Connie, Bryan's adoptive mother, was in the hospital with heart trouble. She had a heart attack a couple of years ago. I called Bryan, and he said he wanted to be there for her. I booked him a flight to Memphis and drove him to the airport."

"Do you know what Jake was angry about? Walter said he was threatening to kill somebody."

"I have no idea; Jake was always blowing up about something."

"Where'd you go after dropping Bryan at the airport?"

Billy sighed loudly, "I went home, cleaned up, and went back out around seven to O'Reilly's Pub for a burger and a few beers. I met up with a lady friend, and I spent the night at her place."

Alicia gave him a skeptical look. "Your lady friend has a name?"

Billy looked at the ceiling and grumbled, "I already talked to the police about this. I'm sure you have her name, phone, and address in that file of yours. Are we done here?"

Alicia closed the file. "You were the last person to speak to Jake before the murder. When did he call you to say he wanted to see Jerri?"

"About one in the morning. Woke me up out of a dead sleep. That little lady worked me over, you know." Billy gave her a sly grin.

Alicia rolled her eyes. "Mm, I bet." She scowled at him. "How did Jake sound? Was he upset, yelling?"

"No, he sounded like he always does. Bossy."

"Why didn't you immediately pick Jerri up and drive her to the cabin when he called?"

"Because Jake said he wanted to see me, Jerri, and Ray first thing in the morning. He said he'd been trying to reach them but couldn't."

"That's all he said?"

"Yes, ma'am. You know, Jake wasn't one of my favorite people, and he was not my biggest fan. I am a part of The Devine Music to protect Bryan's interest, not to make friends. It was strictly business between Jake and me." He went back to squinting. "Will that be all?"

"For now. Thanks for your cooperation."

Billy got up and stomped down the hall as Alicia followed. He stuck his head into the conference room door and barked, "Come on, guys, the party's over." Ray and the other guys looked bewildered but got their coats to follow Billy out the door.

Diana hurried around the table, trying to shake some hands, and said, "Thanks, guys, for coming. We appreciate your help," as they filed out the door.

She had a long handshake with Ray before he exited. "Let me know if there's anything else I can do," he said in a seductive tone.

Once alone, Alicia and Diana looked at each other and began cleaning up the mess the men had left behind. Alicia asked, "How did it go with Ray?"

"First, I asked about the large withdrawals of money from The Devine Music accounts to Jake marked personal. Ray admitted Jake had a bit of a gambling problem, a habit he was trying to break him of. When I questioned him about his whereabouts the night of the murder, he stuck to his story about meeting Jake at the cabin around nine after tucking Jerri in. When I asked him about the rehearsal and why Jake got angry and canceled it, his eyes started shifting around, and he got nervous. He said Jake was upset about a deal for a performance at the Madison Square Garden Theater that went south." Diana threw the last empty pizza box into the trashcan. "I think he's lying. I asked him if he knew where Jerri and Bryan were working together, and he said they always worked at a smaller studio not far from the penthouse. He gave me the name and address of the place. I'm going to check it out. He also said we're welcome to look at the fan mail anytime." She paused and asked, "How'd you do?"

"Well, I broke Billy out of his quiet, drunk routine. He's got quite a temper. He's Bryan's uncle, the birth mother's brother, but he didn't want to talk about it. He takes credit for the collaboration between Bryan, Jerri, and Jake; said he brokered a deal with Ray." Alicia sat down at the table. "He made Jake's outburst at the rehearsal seem trivial, and he swears Bryan has nothing to do with Jake's murder since he was in Memphis with his sick mother. Once I had him riled up, he wanted to end the interview. He, too, stuck to his alibi about being with a woman. We're going to have to track her down."

Diana headed towards the door. "Shouldn't be too hard to do. I'm going to the kitchen to find something to wipe down this table. You should go see Carlton."

Alicia sighed. "Yeah, you're right. Thanks for the great work today. I'll submit the interview recordings to the transcriber team on Monday morning. Go home when you're done here and get some rest."

Diane laughed as she walked out. "Girl, please. I'm going to Pearl's Supper Club tonight."

Alicia went to her office to gather herself before updating Carlton. Abruptly, her desk phone rang. "Good evening, counselor." It was David.

"I hope you're not still working on your motion brief for a dismissal of the charges." Before she could answer, he went on. "We have some new evidence regarding your client's alibi. I'd like to meet with both of you Monday afternoon, say around two?"

"What new evidence?" Alicia asked, concerned he might have something substantial. "Will I be privy to this evidence before our meeting?"

"This is a courtesy call. A formal request for an interview in our office will be forthcoming. I'll be happy to share it with you when I see you. I'm looking forward to it. You have a nice evening." And he hung up before she could say anything else.

Chapter 8

Sunday was typically Alicia's day of rest, but this Sunday would require extra work. Despite being in the dark about the recent evidence, she couldn't afford to relax. Jerri needed to be prepared for the Monday interview with the ADA.

As usual, Alicia attended the eight o'clock service at Mount Olivet Baptist Church. It was always best to attend the early service because Pastor Evans had to wrap up his sermon by ten am to allow the saints to prepare for the next service at eleven. The eleven o'clock service could last until two or three in the afternoon. Alicia believed it was important to participate in corporate worship, but Pastor Evans tended to belabor the point of his sermon if given sufficient time. She didn't feel it was necessary to spend three or four hours in church for the Lord to know how much she loved Him.

Normally after church service, Alicia would drive to Ossining to have brunch with her sister, Faith. Alicia had promised her mother and Nanny Kay she'd watch over her younger sister once they passed. Faith was a fledgling middle school English teacher and dedicated most of her time to her students. She loved her job but struggled financially on a teacher's salary. Sunday was the only day that suited both sisters' schedules, and brunch was their time to catch up. Alicia welcomed the opportunity to spoil Faith a little, splurging on brunch and often a shopping trip to the mall afterward.

She hated to cancel their date, but Faith was very understanding when Alicia called her. Her next call was to Jerri.

Jerri answered with a cheerful tone. "Alicia, I'm glad you called. I was going to call you in a moment. Bryan is here, and I know you wanted to talk to him. Can you come by the penthouse today?" They agreed to meet at one pm.

The news of Bryan being at the penthouse startled Alicia. She had expected to receive a call from Billy at some point during the day to arrange a meeting with him and Bryan. A nagging feeling grew in her belly. *Was there something to the chemistry Walter had mentioned? Could Bryan have sanctioned Billy's actions? No. If he's in love with Jerri, he'd want Jake dead but Jerri in the clear and free.* Bryan was an enigma Alicia needed to get her arms around immediately.

Alicia changed from her gray wool church dress into a comfortable pair of jeans and a red cowl neck sweater. She cooked scrambled eggs with cheese and a packet of instant grits and jotted down questions to ask Bryan as she ate. She also had to prepare formal remarks on her progress on the case for the upcoming partner meeting on Monday morning. Each week, the lead attorneys would engage in a roundtable with Carlton and Bruce Powell, the firm's other senior partner, to give an update on their cases. She had informally discussed her strategy with Carlton on Saturday evening, and he agreed Billy should be the focus as a primary suspect.

With her notes completed, Alicia looked up at the clock and it was eleven thirty. Driving from Peekskill to Manhattan on Sunday afternoon would only take fifty minutes. She called Diana to see if anything interesting had happened at Pearl's Supper Club, but she only got her voicemail. She decided to head out a little early since she was too antsy to sit at home.

The doorman greeted Alicia as she entered Jerri's building. "Good afternoon, Ms. Stone. You can go right up. Ms. Devine is expecting you."

Alicia took the elevator up, but there was no security guard when the doors opened. Not sure which way to go, she called out, "Hello?" and started down the hall toward the study, stopping when a cackle of laughter came from the opposite direction. She turned and followed the voice. Rounding a corner into the living room, she gasped. Bryan and Jerri were standing together, and he was nuzzling her neck and fondling her breast. Jerri's floral silk robe gaped open as she softly laughed, caressing his bare back.

Alicia shocked them when she loudly cleared her throat. "Good afternoon!"

Jerri quickly pushed Bryan away, pulling her robe closed. "Alicia, you're a bit early, aren't you? No matter, come on in, please, have a seat." Bryan casually picked up his denim shirt from the sofa and put it on. "This is Bryan James. Bryan, this is Alicia, my lawyer."

While buttoning up his shirt, Bryan walked over and gave Alicia a big smile and a firm handshake. "Pleased to meet you. I heard you were eager to interview me about Jake's murder. I don't know anything, but I'll do whatever I can to help Jerri out of this mess."

Alicia gazed at Jerri, sipping on a glass of wine. "Why wasn't there any security at the door?"

"I told them they could leave," Bryan said. "I can protect Jerri."

The living room was a sharp contrast to the dark study, with its walls painted a bright golden yellow, and an enormous royal blue sectional dominating the center. Gold records hung on several of the walls, and several glass tables, trimmed in brass, were adorned with luscious bouquets of pink roses and white lilies. The pulled-back vertical blinds allowed the sunlight to pour through the wall of windows. Alicia stood there taking in the lovely partial view of the West Side skyline and the Hudson River, trying to overcome the shock she'd received.

Walking over to her, Jerri said, "The views used to be better, but someone's always building something bigger, getting in my way." She sat on the sofa, gesturing for Alicia to sit beside her.

As he filled Jerri's glass on the coffee table, Bryan asked, "Would you like some wine?"

"Sure," Alicia replied as she sat and took out her notepad and pen. She didn't normally drink with clients, but after what she'd just witnessed, she could have used something stronger than wine to drink.

Bryan retrieved another glass from the curio, but when he went to pour Alicia's portion, only a dribble of white wine came from the bottle. Jerri started to rise, but he stopped her. "Sit, relax. I'll go to the kitchen and get another bottle. I hope you like Riesling, Miss Alicia."

Once Bryan had left the room, Alicia gave Jerri a stern look. "What was that?"

Jerri sipped her wine and replied, "Comfort."

"This will not bode well for your defense. You told me you loved Jake. How could you do this now?" Jerri turned to gaze out the window as Alicia continued to scold her. "If people find out you're having an affair with him, it will only make you look guilty and strengthen the prosecutor's case."

Bryan strolled back into the room with an opened bottle of wine. He filled Alicia's glass and his own and settled across from her and Jerri. "So, Miss Alicia, what do you want to know?" Like Billy, Bryan's speech had a Tennessee twang to it.

"How's your mother doing? Everything all right with her?"

"Yeah, thank you. I left Momma resting at home with Dad. She gave us a real scare. Doctors initially thought she had another heart attack due to a malfunction of her pacemaker. But after they did some tests, it turned out that her pacemaker just needed some new programming."

"Oh," Alicia said, "how lucky." Jerri seemed captivated by Bryan's words. She barely touched her wine.

"Yeah, it was because as soon as I heard about Jake, I wanted to return here as soon as possible. I knew Jerri would need me." He gazed lovingly at Jerri before continuing, "Soon as Momma was home, I caught the next flight out of there."

Alicia took a big sip of wine. "Yesterday, I received a call from the District Attorney's office. They claim to have new evidence to break Jerri's alibi. Any idea what that evidence could be?"

"No," Bryan answered. "But the police were waiting on my doorstep when I arrived home yesterday morning, asking where I've been and what did I know about Jake's murder."

"You arrived home yesterday morning?"

Bryan nodded.

"And what did you tell them?"

"I told them pretty much the same thing I just told you. I don't know anything about Jake's murder."

"Did Billy know you got home yesterday morning?"

"No, he didn't, and I didn't call him because I knew he'd tell me not to see Jerri. But I talked to him this morning, and guess what he said." Leaning forward, he focused on Alicia intently.

Befuddled, Alicia shook her head.

Bryan laughed, "Don't go to see Jerri." He took a sip of wine and gazed at Jerri. "He also told me you wanted to talk to me, but she had already told me." He took another long, slow, sip while his eyes stayed on Jerri.

"Jerri told me you two had lunch the day Jake was murdered. But Ray said you were rehearsing a new song at a nearby studio. Was Jake with you, too?"

"Yeah, he was there. We finished working on the song pretty quickly because my girl here is such a pro. Jake said he was going to a meeting with some guys from Madison Square Garden because he was trying to get us a gig there. He told us to go to the penthouse and that he'd catch up with us later. So, I came back here with Jerri, and we had lunch." Bryan gave Jerri another sultry look. "Right after lunch, Billy called me about my momma."

Alicia realized she needed to break this lovefest up. "I think that covers all of my questions for you, Bryan. Do you mind if I speak to Jerri alone for a few minutes?"

"No problem." Rising from the sofa, he went to Jerri, took her hand, and kissed it. "I'm going to the kitchen and fix us something to eat. Holler if you need me."

Jerri picked up her wine glass for a sip, and Alicia finished her drink. She turned to face Jerri. "Who else knows about your affair with Bryan?"

"No one."

"Are you sure? Because it sounded to me like Billy knows. Did you know Billy is Bryan's uncle?"

"Is he?" Jerri said. "I had no idea." She shook her head, murmuring mmm, and sipped some more wine. "It doesn't matter. I told Bryan no one, absolutely NO ONE could know 'cause if Jake found out, he'd go crazy, and there'd be hell to pay for both of us." Jerri took another sip of wine, and a far-off gaze crossed her face. "A long while back, I got caught up with a bass player, Teddy. I told him we had to keep our thing a secret, but he started making stupid comments and dropping hints to Jake. One day, Jake followed me to me and Teddy's meeting place. He saw us kissing, and he went ballistic. Pulled his gun on the poor guy and threatened to kill him. Thank God he didn't shoot Teddy, but he did pistol whip him and left him lying on the ground. Then, he took me home and beat me. The next thing I knew, we had a new bass player, and I never saw Teddy again. Neither did anyone else." Jerri looked at Alicia. "Bryan understands. He won't tell anyone."

"Okay." Alicia paused to process Jerri's story and her line of thinking before continuing. "The Chief Prosecutor wants to interview you tomorrow regarding this new evidence. Do you have any idea what the evidence could be?"

"No."

"Well, whatever it is, I'm certain he's going to push you to change your plea to guilty and offer you a reduced sentence."

Jerri shrieked, "No, no. I didn't shoot Jake. Do I have to talk to him? Can't you just tell him I don't want a deal?"

"Unfortunately, no. Not until we know what cards he's holding."

Jerri started to sob, and Alicia searched her purse for her Kleenex pack and handed her a few. "Listen," she said softly, "you don't have to say anything tomorrow. Let me do all the talking. Whatever they ask you, you talk to me quietly off to the side, and I will relay your answers." She waited a moment for Jerri to calm down before saying, "It's going to be all right. We're not changing your plea and we are not accepting any deals." Jerri wiped her tears, nodded, and drained her glass. Alicia stood and gathered her things. "Hey, Bryan," she called out. He quickly came into the room. "Jerri needs to meet me at my office tomorrow around one o'clock. Can you see to it she gets there? We have to meet with the Assistant District Attorney."

"Yea, yea. I'll make sure she's there, Miss Alicia," he replied.

Alicia looked at Jerri. "Please don't worry about this too much. Everything will be fine. Get some rest. I'll see you tomorrow."

Jerri lowered her head. "Okay, thanks for coming."

Alicia's body tingled, sensing something was off as she walked to her Jeep. She sat there, mentally replaying what she'd just heard, as her truck warmed up. After a few minutes, she shut down the engine and exited the Jeep to return to the building lobby.

The doorman greeted her. "Hello again, Ms. Stone. You going back up?"

Alicia smiled. "No, I actually would like to speak to you. What is your name?"

"Franklin, ma'am."

"Franklin, where's the service elevator?"

"On the backside of the building. An emergency door on 16th Street leads to it and the stairwell, but most of our tenants access it from the parking garage. It's not used often, only when someone moves in or out or receives new furniture."

"But is it left open? Can anyone access it at any time?"

"Oh no, ma'am. Tenants must notify the management of their need for the service elevator and make arrangements."

"Everyone? Even the penthouse tenants?"

"Mr. Devine was an owner, not a tenant. He had a key and could access the service elevator anytime."

"Thanks for your time, Franklin. You have a good afternoon." Alicia returned to her Jeep and said to herself aloud, "I think I know what Jake was angry about." Taking out her phone, she tried to reach Diana again, but her phone still went to voicemail. "Hey Di, I need you to look for another potential suspect. His name is Teddy Vaughn."

Chapter 9

Sunday morning dawned and David sprung from his bed, feeling as rejuvenated as a racehorse at the starting line. Gratitude filled his heart as he thanked the Lord for the deep uninterrupted night's rest, a rare treasure he hadn't experienced in weeks. Everything was going well on the case, and he could finally relax. His notes were prepared for the Monday morning meeting with the boss lady. He expected DeLeo to be delighted with how the case was progressing.

After reviewing the police notes from Bryan's interview, he contacted the hospital in Memphis. Sure enough, the hospital had admitted Bryan's mother to the emergency room on October 8th. His team examined the passenger manifests from all flights from Memphis to any New York airport in the area: JFK, LaGuardia, Islip, Newark, Westchester County, and Stewart International. There was no record of Bryan leaving Memphis and sneaking back to New York between October 8th and the 11th, when he returned home and met with the police officers. Bryan had not secretly returned to New York on the day of the murder. David knew DeLeo had a hard-on for this kid, but nothing pointed toward Bryan as a suspect. Hopefully, this information would convince her he had nothing to do with Jake's murder.

He called his mother, who was living with his youngest brother, Darius, to check on her, and thankfully she was well. David, along with his brothers, Damian and Darius, had vowed to take care of her after their father, Devon, affectionately known as Deacon, had a sudden heart attack that sent him home to the Lord a few years ago. All the brothers followed in their dad's footsteps by serving in the military. After his discharge, their father worked as a janitor at the local high school and often bragged about his army days. He got the nickname Deacon due to his unwavering dedication to service in the church. It was Deacon who instilled in David the trait of bearing responsibility without showing emotion. Frequently, his dad's sage advice echoed in his brain, "Don't lose control, boy. You can't walk around wearing your emotions on your sleeve." Other times it was his favorite saying reverberating in his ears., "Don't let me see you crying those crocodile tears. Ain't nothing to be wailing about. Be a man!"

Assured of his mother's well-being, David checked his messages. He responded to the call from Rachel Saunders, the realtor, and set up a meeting for later in the afternoon, before heading to the gym for a full workout with free weights and the treadmill. Not in a rush to be somewhere for the first time in a long while, he relaxed in the sauna after his workout. Sweating in the hot air, he rubbed his mustache, imagining the shock on Alicia's face tomorrow, with Jerri crying and confessing her guilt. He was about to save the taxpayers the huge expense of a trial and receive national accolades. This would bring him one step closer to his ultimate goal, judgeship.

David whistled on his way back to his suite and sang in the shower. Clad in black jeans and a t-shirt, his favorite Air Force One kicks, and a Negro League Baseball bomber jacket, he was ready to soothe his hunger pangs. Within minutes, he arrived at the nearest diner, Olympia's. The gray-haired cashier at the entrance greeted him and offered him the takeout menu.

Grinning, David said, "No, no. Nothing to go today, Sarah. I'm going to eat in. May I have a booth?"

"Sure, counselor, no problem. Follow me." With a waddling step, Sarah led him to a corner booth by the window. "Glad you could join us today. You're always on the go."

"Yeah, well, I had a big breakthrough in my case and decided to reward myself with a little R&R."

"Good for you," Sarah said. "I think you'll find the food's even better when you eat it while it's hot. Your waitress, Linda, will be right over to take care of you."

David returned to the diner entrance and bought a local newspaper from the vending machine. He ordered the Hungry Man Special: scrambled eggs, bacon, sausage, pancakes, home fries with orange juice, and coffee. Sarah was right. The food was better when you ate it hot. He devoured everything on his plate as he perused the newspaper. Once he finished, he held up his coffee cup for a refill. Linda filled his mug, and he sipped his coffee as he went to read the comics section. He laughed out loud at the Boondocks cartoon. Amidst the chatter of patrons and the aroma of freshly brewed coffee, he found solace in the simplicity of the moment, briefly liberated from the weight of the world. Eventually, the peaceful reveling ended, as it was time to meet the realtor.

Rachel Saunders greeted David with a firm handshake and a big smile. "I'm so happy you finally have time to find a home. Based on our first conversation, you were looking for a two-bedroom, two-bath condo near your office. Has anything changed?"

"No, that's still exactly what I need."

"Great, based on that information, I have printed out some listings I think you will love. Three are vacant, so we can see them now if you like."

Eager to find a home, David replied, "Let's do it."

Rachel gathered her purse and keys. "It's best if I drive since I know the neighborhood."

David concurred and followed her out to her silver BMW sedan. He hadn't paid attention before, but Rachel was an attractive woman. Her forest green suit fit her nicely and complimented her milk chocolate complexion. He appreciated her natural beauty with minimal makeup and a neat, short afro. Observing her swaying hips, he considered attempting to establish a connection with her. Suddenly, Alicia's face appeared in his thoughts. He shook his head to rid himself of the image.

As they rode, Rachel carried on most of the conversation, pointing out sites of interest in the city. Parking in front of a red brick high-rise building, she announced, "This is the place." They stepped out of the car. "What do you think?"

Glancing around, the large gray courthouse loomed in the distance. Plenty of people were out on the street for a Sunday afternoon, and a shopping mall was only two blocks away. It brought back memories of his days in Brooklyn. "Neighborhood seems nice. Let's go in."

As they climbed the narrow steps leading to the second floor, David's heart began to race as beads of sweat formed at his temples. Abruptly, he was in the stairwell of an apartment building in Harlem, responding to a report of domestic abuse. A woman's voice shrieked loudly as David instinctively put his hand on his hip, reaching for his gun holster as he searched for the scream's source. The muscles of his entire body tensed as Rachel moved toward the apartment door. As she struggled with the lockbox, David gripped the stairs' handrail and took a deep breath. *There is nothing behind that door. An angry man will not be wildly waving a gun around when she opens it.*

The door swung open and with a perpetual brilliant smile, Rachel gave him a tour of the apartment as his heartbeat returned to an average pace. Her infectious enthusiasm re-energized David's commitment to the home search. Noticing Rachel wasn't wearing a wedding ring, he entertained the notion of inviting her to dinner. Once the tour was over, she asked, "Well, David, what do you think? Do you love it?"

"The location is great, but this place is a bit too small. Anything roomier on your list?"

"Sure, no problem. Let's take a look at another condo."

They got back into her car, and David mentally checked off any condo that was a walk-up as a no-go. That panic attack had utterly taken him by surprise. Turning to Rachel, he asked, "Any nightlife around here?"

"A few taverns on Mamaroneck Avenue have happy hours and whatnot, but no real nightclubs with music and dancing." Rachel glanced over at David. "You're so busy anyway. When do you have time to go clubbing?"

"Now that you mention it, I can't remember the last time I went out with the fellas. But I'm hopeful that will change eventually, and I'll have more time to do some things. What do you like to do for fun?"

"Me? Oh, I have fun with my kids. I've got three of them. They keep me very busy when I'm not working." Rachel pulled in front of another brick, high-rise building. "Here we are. Let's see if this is more suitable to your tastes."

Relief washed over David as Rachel swayed her way to the front door, grateful she had brought up her three children because he'd almost asked her on a date. *Women with kids are a nonstarter. I don't want a ready-made family. I want to create my own. I thought Elizabeth wanted the same thing. Maybe she does, but not with me.*

Fortunately, this building had an elevator. The condominium was on the fifth floor at the end of the hall. As they walked in, they entered the living room with a big window letting tons of sunlight in, and it was open to the kitchen with cherry-wood cabinets and black appliances. "This is an open floor plan," Rachel said. "Does this feel more spacious to you?"

Walking to the center of the room, David turned around. "Yes, I like it. How large are the bedrooms?"

Rachel led him to the left of the living room, and there was a large bedroom with an entire wall of closets. "This is the master. Right through that door is your master bath."

Opening the door revealed a nicely renovated washroom. He stepped into the shower stall to check the height and width. Rachel poked her head in, "Nice, right?"

Nodding his approval, David replied, "So far, so good."

They walked back through the living room to the other bedroom. The second full bathroom was at the end of the hall alongside the bedroom door. It was a little smaller than the master bedroom, but he could envision his office there. He turned to Rachel. "I think we've got a winner here."

"Great. I'm glad you're happy with this one, but before you decide, there's one more condo that I'd like to show you."

They discussed closing costs, condo fees, and amenities as they drove to the next place. While impressed with the third condo, David told Rachel the second one was still the best and he wanted to put in an offer on the fifth-floor condo. They returned to Rachel's office, and she drew up the paperwork. By the time they finished, David's hunger pangs returned, and he wished there was someone he could call for a dinner date. Because of his work schedule, he did not have time to make new friends in the area. The only local people he'd met had been his colleagues. *And Alicia, who I should not be thinking about. She's on the wrong team.*

After thanking Rachel for all her work, David drove back to the building which would be his new home. After parking, he walked around to get a lay of the land. Discovering a Chinese restaurant on the next block, he ordered takeout. Next, he drove to his office, and when he arrived in ten minutes, he smiled at the prospect of having such a short commute. Unable to find an apartment in Brooklyn on short notice when he moved out of the brownstone he'd shared with Elizabeth, he took up residence in his brother Darius' basement. When he first took the job in Westchester, he commuted from Brooklyn for a few weeks, but the trip was long, and the traffic was brutal. He quickly realized it wasn't working and moved to the Springfield

Suites. Elizabeth had purchased most of their furnishings, so he only had a few items, like his desk, a recliner, and numerous books, record albums, and clothes stored at his brother's house. David figured he'd have time to shop for furniture before he closed on the condo in a few months.

When he returned to his hotel suite and opened the door, David found a manila envelope lying on the floor. *Someone must have slipped it under the door while I was out.* Before he touched it, he called the front desk and asked if anyone had stopped by to see him or left a message. The clerk told David there was no one. He donned a leather pair of gloves before picking up the envelope. It was blank; no address or postal marking on it. Using a kitchen knife, he opened it, and two photographs fell out. One was a bit blurry, but there was no mistaking it was Jerri Devine and Bryan James in the photos, kissing. David stared at them, incredulous, and said, "Now, who could have taken these?" Alicia's voice echoed in his head, saying, "Your evidence was awfully easy to find."

Taking the envelope and photos, he placed them in a plastic bag. Tomorrow, he would turn them over to the police. Hopefully, they could pull some fingerprints off. He was curious as to who had given him this gift. Regardless of how they were obtained, David planned to use the photos to strengthen his case. DeLeo's gut had been right after all.

The next morning, David and Eddie met with Janice DeLeo in her war room. As usual, Janice DeLeo had her porcelain face perfectly made up, and she wore a black suit with not a single hair out of place on her auburn bob. David showed her and Eddie the photos.

"Well, this surely ups the ante," DeLeo said. "Revenge wasn't Jerri's only motive, and this gorgeous young man looks like he is worth killing for." She examined the photos in the plastic bag again as a smirk crossed her face. "Between these photos and our surveillance footage, I think we've got her. Press Jerri hard for a guilty plea today, David."

"Will do." David handed the plastic bag to Eddie. "Please have the police dust these for fingerprints. I want to know who took these pictures and was kind enough to share them with me."

Chapter 10

The weekly Partner Meeting began promptly at 7:30 am in the conference room. Carlton opened the meeting with a reminder that the Westchester chapter of the American Bar Association's Gala was being held on Saturday. "I expect all our attorneys to be there and support the judges running in the upcoming election. Respectably schmooze, as you are representing Burke and Powell at this event. We'll now start the case reviews with our most important one, the Devine case."

Alicia was relieved to be first up in the roundtable, and her strategy to point the jury to Billy Whitmore as the culprit garnered positive feedback. As the other attorneys discussed their cases, she became distracted, thinking of David and the mysterious evidence he'd provide later until Valerie Upton began speaking.

Valerie, Alicia's former boss in the firm's Matrimonial and Family Law division, began with a grimace on her well-made-up face. "I would like to welcome Ms. Stone back to the Partner Meeting. However, due to her transfer back to the Criminal Law division, I've had to juggle our caseload amongst my remaining staff." Her tone told everyone she was not pleased about her juggling act. She glared at Carlton and Alicia while explaining her new hierarchy and progress on her key cases. After completing the roundtable, Valerie saddled up next to Alicia as she walked back to her office. Each of them wore Chanel, Valerie in red with a mid-length skirt, and Alicia in royal purple with a knee-length skirt and a slit opening in the back. Valerie always dressed impeccably and kept her long brown weave tight.

But outfits weren't the only thing dueling this morning. In a salty tone, Valerie said, "It would have been nice to hear it from you that you were leaving my department."

"Valerie, I apologize, but when Carlton asked me to take the Devine case, how could I refuse?" Alicia gave her a quick side glance.

Valerie smirked. "Oh, is that why you were so eager to take it? I assumed you wanted the chance to spend time with David King."

"What? Don't be ridiculous."

"Ridiculous? Tell me, dear, how was your cozy dinner at The Smoke House?"

"That was strictly business, not that it's any business of yours." They arrived at Alicia's office, and she opened the door. "I'm sorry if you feel you've been slighted, but the Devine case takes precedence over any of your cases. After all, the firm's reputation is paramount to all our careers."

"You're not deepening any alliances in the firm with this move," Valerie said. "Robert Hayes is livid he didn't get the Devine case. For the past two years, he has busted his ass running the Criminal Law division, and you just waltz back in and take his place. If you ever expect to make partner here, you'll need more friends than Carlton."

Alicia gave her a hopeless look. "Listen, I didn't ask for the case. The client requested me. If you, Robert, or anyone else have a problem with me, I suggest they take their grievance directly to Carlton. Now, if you'll excuse me, I have work to do." She entered her office, sat behind her desk, and started rifling through her files. Alicia ignored Valerie as she continued to stand in the doorway, glaring at her with a twisted, angry face. After a minute, Valerie walked away, and Carlton took her place.

"Why is the Chief Prosecutor demanding a meeting with Jerri Devine today?" Carlton asked as he came in and closed her door.

"Apparently, there is evidence he thinks will break Jerri's alibi."

"What evidence?"

"I'll find out this afternoon," Alicia answered. "I had a meeting with Jerri yesterday, and she's clueless about what the evidence could be.

To make matters worse, she's having an affair with Bryan James."

Carlton's eyebrows shot up. "What? Did she tell you that?"

"No, I caught her and Bryan about to do the nasty in the penthouse." She hesitated before continuing. "I know it sounds like a blow to our case, but after some thought, I decided we could use it to strengthen our case against Billy. Seems he does not approve of Bryan and Jerri's relationship."

Carlton exhaled loudly. "How do you know Billy disapproves?"

"Bryan pretty much said it when I interviewed him. He didn't say exactly why Billy disapproves, but take your pick. Jerri is married. She's forty, and Bryan's twenty-eight. She's black, and he's white. Billy is old school, so his feelings are understandable. It makes sense why he not only killed Jake to protect his nephew. He framed Jerri to eliminate her from Bryan's life."

Carlton contemplated Alicia's theory momentarily and asked, "Do we have any physical evidence against Billy yet?"

"No."

"Well, we're going to need it. There's too much physical evidence that points to Jerri. To convince the jury of her innocence, we'll need more than circumstantial evidence against Billy."

"Billy was meticulous in his actions, but he had to come up with this plan quickly once he overheard Jake threatening to kill Bryan. I'm certain, in his haste, he made at least one mistake. Diana is all over this. We'll get something solid soon." Alicia sighed. "What's troubling is that Jerri and Ray are not fully cooperating. She concealed her relationship with Bryan from me until she couldn't, and I believe Ray lied about the reason Jake was so angry to Diana. I think a talk about the need for truth and transparency from my co-counsel is in order."

"What time will Jerri arrive here today?" Carlton asked.

"One. The meeting with David King is at two."

"I'll speak to her then." Carlton arose to leave. "I'll expect a full report on your meeting immediately afterward." Alicia nodded in agreement, and he left her office.

Two minutes later, Diana entered Alicia's office, and she was not her usual bubbly self. "Good morning," she grumbled as she flopped down into the chair. "I'm sorry I didn't return your calls yesterday." Dressed in all black with a baseball cap pulled down low, Alicia couldn't see her eyes.

"Well, I'm glad you're okay. I was getting worried."

"I went to Pearl's Saturday night and spoke to most of the waitresses and bartenders. They all confirmed Ray's alibi. Ray didn't seem intimidated by my presence at all. He sat at my table, bought me a few rounds and we had a nice, non-Jerri-related conversation. I left the club at two am, went home and I don't remember what happened next, but I slept until eleven pm on the sofa yesterday." Diana glanced up from beneath the lid of her cap. "I think I was drugged."

"What?" Alicia shrieked.

"Although my apartment wasn't vandalized, it was evident that someone had gone through my files on the Devine case. I went to the police this morning to report I may have been drugged, and my home invaded. Their forensics team took blood for analysis and they're at my house now dusting for fingerprints."

"Oh, my lord. You think Ray drugged you?"

"Not unless he knows of a strong potion with a long-delayed reaction," Diana said. "If he had put something in my drink, I don't think I would have made it home. No, I think someone was stalking me and he wanted to know how much we know about him."

"But how could someone drug you without you seeing them?"

"I don't know. First, I need the lab to confirm I was drugged and

I'm not coming down with the flu. When I woke up Sunday night, I had a throbbing headache and pain in my neck and shoulders. Once I know what I was drugged with, maybe I can figure out how it was administered." Diana paused before continuing. "You need to be careful and stay alert. I suspect it was Billy, but whoever did this may attack you next."

Alicia began developing a headache of her own. She hadn't slept well last night, stressing over the mystery evidence, then Valerie's attack on her this morning, and now this news from Diana wasn't helping. She started rubbing her temples with her thumbs as Diana asked, "I heard your message about finding Teddy Vaughn. What's that all about?"

"Teddy Vaughn is an old bass player from The Devine Music. He had an affair with Jerri years ago, and Jake pistol-whipped him when he found out and fired him from the band. I need to be certain he's still alive."

"You think Jake may have killed him?"

"Jerri didn't know what happened to Teddy, but if he is alive, he may be the one who killed Jake."

"Any idea on where to start looking for him?"

"I'm guessing Clarksdale, Mississippi, where Jerri and Jake are from."

"Okay, I'm on it. Anything else?" Diana asked as she rose from her seat.

"Jerri and Bryan are having an affair. I think Jake found out, and that's why he was so angry at the rehearsal studio. Billy must have overheard Jake threatening to kill Bryan and sprang into action."

"Oh, my God," Diana whispered.

"And David has summoned Jerri for an interview this afternoon. Claims he has new evidence to break Jerri's alibi."

"That's not good."

"No, it's not. Jerri will be here at one for some more prep before the interview, and we meet with David at two. You should go home and see what the forensic team comes up with. I'll call you after the meeting."

"You sure? I'm not full strength, but I can work."

"Yes, I'm sure. Have your team start looking for Teddy Vaughn and check on their progress on those phone records on your way out. We need them as soon as possible. And add Nathaniel James to the list of phone records needed. He's Bryan's father in Memphis."

Diana nodded and left. Alicia picked up her picture of Charlotte Ray. "Charlotte, what would you do next?" She waited a moment, hoping to hear an answer, but received none. Placing the picture back on her desk, she quietly prayed for wisdom and guidance on the Devine case and that David's new evidence would not be too devastating.

With renewed resolve, Alicia meticulously typed up her notes on what she believed to be Billy's actions, hoping to find a loophole where he could have made a mistake and left physical evidence as the killer. Once done, she reviewed them and began prioritizing how to address each issue. The phone records were critical for a couple of answers. Hopefully, she would get them today. In the box with the initial discovery material from the DA's office were the crime scene photos, and she went over them with a magnifying glass, but nothing jumped out at her. Since David was presenting new evidence today, an update on discovery material should also be forthcoming. She rummaged through the files, seeking an autopsy report. There was only a statement from the coroner showing the cause of death as gunshot wounds. A complete autopsy would include a full physical exam of the exterior body for wounds, scars, cuts, and bruises and a full toxicology report on his blood. She'd be sure to ask David about it at their meeting today. Alicia's confidence level rose, knowing she had a plan of action. She hated being treated as a victim, like her client, and believed David was trying to do that by making her wait to review his mystery evidence. She wanted him to know his little power play would not intimidate her. By asking for the full autopsy report, she would leave him questioning whether he'd thoroughly examined his evidence.

After Carlton gave Jerri the talk about telling the truth, she would question her again about Jake and Billy's relationship. She prayed Jerri would show up sober and with a clear head so she would remember more about events on the day Jake died.

Her stomach started growling, and Alicia realized she hadn't eaten anything. She'd left extra early to arrive on time for the partner meeting and only had a cup of coffee during her prayer time. Checking the clock there was time to go out for a salad before Jerri arrived. A walk to a corner cafe was in order since her feet wore comfortable black pumps with low heels and she could use the fresh air.

Moments after Alicia returned to the office refreshed with a full belly, Jerri and Ray arrived. Jerri dressed simply in jeans, a light blue cotton shirt, and a leather coat, topped with a wide-brim hat and sunglasses, and Ray wore a black suit. They were sitting in Carlton's office, chatting with the door wide open. Paralegals and secretaries casually walked past the door to get a glimpse of the R&B star in person.

Swiftly, Alicia entered Carlton's office and closed the door. After the greetings, she gave Carlton a look to let him know it was time for the talk. He wrapped up the chit-chat and got down to business.

"Jerri, you requested AK Stone to represent you. For her to do her best job for you, I need you to promise you will be truthful with her about everything she asks. The same goes for you, Ray." Jerri and Ray glanced at each other, bewildered. "It's come to my attention Jerri, you concealed a love affair with Bryan, and you, Ray, lied to my investigator about a conversation you had with Jake. This stops now, today. Alicia's trying to help you, and it is vital you fully cooperate with her. Otherwise, I advise you to seek legal counsel elsewhere." Carlton gave them a stern look and waited to hear if there would be any rebuttal.

"Carlton, I apologize," Ray said as Jerri looked down at her feet. "We don't want to find another lawyer. Whatever you say goes. But are you all making any progress with her defense?"

"Yes," Alicia said. "And we'd be making more if you didn't send us on wild goose chases by not telling the truth. There are a couple of people whom we are zeroing in on as alternate suspects for the murder, but a defense strategy takes time to develop. After today's meeting with the Chief Prosecutor, we should get some more key information we can use to our advantage. At the proper time, I will review the details of our strategy with you both."

"We will vindicate Jerri of all charges," Carlton said, "And your full cooperation will go a long way to achieving that outcome. Does everyone understand?" Jerri and Ray nodded in agreement. "Ok then, I turn you over to AK Stone."

Alicia led Jerri and Ray down to her office. Once they were seated, she focused on Ray. "Jerri told me a very interesting story about a bass player named Teddy. Do you know who I'm talking about?"

"Yeah, I know. Teddy Vaughn."

"She said Teddy disappeared after Jake pistol-whipped him. Do you know what happened to Teddy, Ray?"

"Jake didn't kill him, if that's what you're asking. He told me where he left Teddy. Me and a couple of my boys took him to a clinic, got him cleaned up, and I filled his pocket with a grand. I told him to catch the first bus out of town and never return. Teddy took the money and disappeared."

"Do you know where he is now? It's possible that Teddy has a long memory and wanted revenge on Jake. I'd like to talk to him."

"I have no idea where that two-bit playa is, but it isn't him. He doesn't have the balls to step to Jake."

Jerri was quiet and nervously fidgeting with her hands, checking her palms and fingernails. Alicia asked, "Jerri, anything you want to share or ask before we go to the meeting?"

"No. I just want to get this over with."

"All right, let's be on our way. Ray, you can wait here in my office until we return."

Alicia and Jerri rode over to the DA's office in silence. It was a short trip, and they arrived ten minutes before two pm. David was waiting in the conference room with another ADA. He instructed Alicia and Jerri to sit at the long wooden table across from them.

"This is Eddie Smith, my co-counsel. Ms. Devine, would you please remove your sunglasses?" Jerri complied with the request.

"Ms. Devine, you stated you were alone in the penthouse sleeping when your husband was shot. However, the video you're about to see tells a different story." David gave Eddie a nod, and he played the video footage of the SUV leaving the penthouse.

"This surveillance video is from your building. Isn't that you leaving the penthouse at midnight?" David asked.

Jerri's mouth opened, about to answer, and Alicia grabbed Jerri's arm underneath the table. "I can't even see who is driving in that video," Alicia said. "How do you know it was Ms. Devine driving?"

"The license plate belongs to a Suburban registered to Raymond Meeks. Ms. Devine said she was home alone in her statement to the police, so who else could it be?" David said.

Jerri leaned over and whispered in Alicia's ear. "My client says the keys to the SUV are hanging in plain view in the kitchen, and the security team that works for them has access to those keys. Ms. Devine doesn't drive herself anywhere. She is always chauffeured."

"Ms. Devine, don't you have a valid NY driver's license?" David asked. "Even though you say you don't drive, you could if you wanted to, right?"

Alicia answered quickly, "Ms. Devine keeps a valid license solely for identification purposes."

David frowned, and then he dropped the photos on the table. "What do you know about these pictures?"

Jerri gasped. "Oh my god!"

Alicia asked, "Where did you get those?"

"An anonymous source provided them to me," David replied.

"An anonymous source? Gee, that's convenient. We have a right to know who gave those photos to you. Don't make me do a motion brief for full disclosure of information."

"Oh no," David said, "not another motion brief threat. Instead of focusing on how I got them, I would like to hear Ms. Devine tell us what's happening here in these photos."

Jerri leaned over and whispered to Alicia. "My client says it's a friendly kiss. No big deal."

David glanced at Eddie and asked, "Does this look like a friendly kiss to you?" Eddie shook his head no. "Good, because it does not look like a friendly kiss to me, either. That kiss looks deep and passionate. Ms. Devine, are you having an extramarital affair with Bryan James?"

Panic crossed Jerri's face as she leaned over to whisper to Alicia. "If she is, what bearing does it have on this case?"

"It gives her a motive to murder her husband." David turned his attention to Jerri. "Ms. Devine, you shot Jake to be free of him, so you could marry Bryan James. Why don't you tell us the truth about what really happened that night? I bet you were drinking, and you got to thinking about how much better your life would be without Jake. All he did to you all those years finally got to you. Then you drove to the cabin and shot Jake." David softened his tone as he looked at Jerri. "Everyone knows Jake beat you and cheated on you. He wasn't even writing music for you to sing anymore. You had a new man who loved you and treated you better than Jake ever did. You knew Jake would never willingly let you go, so you had to do what you had to do. Anyone could understand how desperate you were."

Jerri started sobbing, and Alicia spoke for her. "Ms. Devine loved her husband and is devastated by her loss. She maintains her innocence and will not take a plea deal of any sort. Is there anything else you'd like to share today, counselor?"

David gave Alicia a terse look. "No, there's nothing else."

Alicia said, "I have a question for you. Have you received a full autopsy report yet? I didn't see one in the discovery material."

"No, I haven't received it yet. You will receive a comprehensive update on our discovery material tomorrow morning."

"Thank you." Alicia and Jerri arose to leave. Directing Jerri to wait for her down the hall, Alicia shook David's hand while pressing a small piece of paper into it. She whispered, "Here's a gift." Aloud, she said, "Till we meet again." With purpose, she strutted to Jerri's side, and together they left the DA's office.

Ray was patiently waiting, reading a newspaper, when Alicia and Jerri returned to her office. Overwhelmed, Jerri burst into tears and ran into his arms. While Ray held her whispering, it's all right, Alicia called her co-counsel and invited him to her office. Once Jerri regained her composure, Alicia told Ray and Carlton about the SUV footage.

Alicia asked Ray, "Do you keep records on who's using the Suburbans, like a log?"

"No, there was no need for that," Ray said. "I have one that I use all the time, Billy has one, and Jake had one. The fourth Suburban is for the security team for Jerri, who use it to take her around when I'm not available."

"The prosecutor also had two photographs of Jerri and Bryan kissing, which they received from an anonymous source," Alicia stated. She glanced at Ray. "Any idea who had access to Jerri that could have taken those pictures?"

Bewildered, Ray stumbled over his words. "Besides me, there is the security team, Billy, and the band members. I didn't take the pictures, and the band members don't come to the penthouse often, so it must be one of the security guys or Billy."

Carlton said, "The good news is all of this new evidence is circumstantial. They can't prove Jerri drove the SUV, and they can't use photos obtained anonymously other than to talk about them to the jury, as part of their theory of Jerri's motive to murder Jake."

Jerri began sobbing again, prompting Alicia to ask, "Carlton, would you mind taking Jerri to your office? I have a few more questions for Ray." Once Carlton escorted Jerri out., Alicia focused her attention on Ray. "Tell me the truth about what you and Jake argued about the day he canceled the rehearsal. It wasn't about losing a gig at Madison Square Garden, was it? It was about Jerri having an affair with Bryan. Jake was so mad he wanted to kill him."

Eyes to the ceiling, Ray sighed loudly. "Yes, that was what we argued about."

"Did you know about Jerri and Bryan before Jake told you?"

"I didn't know for sure, but I suspected something was going on from how they would look at each other whenever they performed together." Slapping his hands on his knees, Ray glared at Alicia. "Look,

I'm the one who calmed Jake down and told him he couldn't kill Bryan. We needed Bryan to continue to write music for Jerri. I told him to go to the cabin and think about what was best for Jerri and the band. Hell, our entire business. When I went to see him later on at the cabin, he had calmed down and agreed that we needed Bryan's music. We decided to draw up a new contract agreement where Jake would be an exclusive purchaser of Bryan's music for the next couple of years, and Bryan would no longer perform with the band. We would promote him as a solo artist. I figured Billy would go for it because he never liked working with Jake. That way, Billy and Bryan get paid, and he wouldn't have to deal with Jake anymore."

Cocking her head, Alicia asked, "Is it possible Jake took those pictures? Did he tell you exactly how he found out about Jerri's affair?"

Looking down at his hands, Ray sighed heavily. "I suppose it's possible. Jake was as suspicious as I was about Bryan and Jerri. He made Bryan and Jerri think they'd have plenty of time alone at the penthouse after their rehearsal. Jake said he told them he had to go to a meeting with some folks at Madison Square Garden, and the two of them should go on to the penthouse for lunch, and he'd catch up with them later." His eyes met Alicia's stare. "Then he took the service elevator up, which opens in a room behind the kitchen, and saw them having sex in a guest bedroom. He said they didn't even notice him, and he quickly left the same way he came in." Shaking his head and looking down, Ray continued. "Jake could have snapped those photos, but I doubt it because he never showed them to me. I'm pretty certain he was so hurt and angry he hustled out of there and came to find me at the rehearsal studio."

"Why did Billy have such a problem working with Jake? You don't seem to have a problem working with Billy."

Looking up at the ceiling, Ray replied, "Let's just say two know-italls working together does not work at all."

Satisfied, Alicia folded her hands on top of the desk. "Thanks, Ray. Why don't you go on and take Jerri home? Let her get some rest. I'll be in touch."

Ray went to get Jerri and left. Alicia gathered her Billy Theory notes and wondered how much she should share with her co-counsel. She'd taken an enormous risk in giving David the note, but she once again wanted him on her side. The DA's office had many more resources available to them through the police than she had here at the firm. Her investigators could not legally search Billy's residence or put out an APB for Billy's whore. If she could convince David that Billy was a viable suspect for the murder, he could use those police resources to prove Billy truly was the killer. *Better to keep the tip to David to myself and not tell Carlton.* She was about to add the SUV and picture evidence to her Billy Theory, but then her last bullet point, WHO ATTACKED DIANA, jumped out and she picked up the phone instead.

"Hey, girl," Diana answered. "It's official. I got drugged, but there were no fingerprints found in my apartment."

"How are you feeling? You okay?"

"Yeah. The doctor said the full effects of the drug should wear off soon. It was Detomidine, a horse tranquilizer. Thank God our boy knew what he was doing, or I could be dead. If the drug is not administered in the right dosage, it can kill a person. And he used a tranquilizer dart to administer it. The doc found a needle mark on the back of my neck."

"Oh, my lord."

"The bad news is it's legal to own a tranquilizer dart gun, and Detomidine is widely available. Veterinarians use it all the time." Diana sighed. "We need to get into Billy's apartment and search it."

Alicia said, "I'm working on a plan to get more information on

Billy. Meanwhile, I have good news. David's evidence turned out to be pretty inconsequential." She relayed the meeting details and asked, "Any word on when I'll get phone records?"

"Yup, they're ready. I'll come in, and we can review them together."

"No," Alicia said. "I'll start reviewing tonight, and you can help me finish in the morning. I need you full strength tomorrow. Now I need to talk to Carlton and update him. I'll see you tomorrow."

"Okay, but remember what I said. Please be careful. Billy is dangerous."

Grabbing her Billy Theory notes, Alicia went to Carlton's office.

"Sounds like you handled the Chief Prosecutor well today," Carlton said.

"There's more that I couldn't discuss with you in front of Jerri and Ray. Diana was drugged, and her apartment searched. She believes Billy did it, but we can't prove it."

Carlton's eyebrows shot up. "What? Is she all right?"

"Yes, she's fine, but the horse tranquilizer dart he used could have killed her." Alicia handed Carlton her Billy Theory notes. Once he perused them, she continued. "I'm going to start reviewing Billy's cell phone and landline records today. As you can see, quite a few things can be made crystal clear with a phone record review. Is there any way we can legally get a copy of Connie James' hospital records?"

"The DA should have it. Has there been an update in discovery material yet?"

"No, David said they will be sending it over tomorrow."

"Let's hope it's in the update. Anything else?"

"Well, after the new evidence, I now suspect Billy has a copy of Jake's service elevator key. I think he snuck into the penthouse, took those pictures, and anonymously sent them to the DA's office. He also could have used the key to go down to the parking garage to drive the SUV out at midnight and return it to the garage without being seen. I'm sure he knows where the security cameras are in the garage, and his exit would be filmed and time-stamped. This guy is a real piece of work, and if he's the one who drugged Diana, who knows what he'll do next to cover his trail."

Carlton gave her a terse look. "You and Diana need to be vigilant. Did she file a police report? Maybe we should ask for police protection for her."

"Yes, she filed a report, but no on the police protection. They'll only get in the way."

"Well," Carlton replied, "I agree with your theory so far. Keep up the good work. We'll get him. Everybody makes mistakes, and Billy's no exception, even if he is an ex-Navy Seal."

Alicia went to see Parker, a young tech-savvy member of Diana's team, picked up the phone records, and took them to her office. They were clearly labeled, and Alicia added them to each appropriate dossier. Billy's phone records were not as large as she expected. There were no calls to Nate James in Memphis on October 8th, as she had hoped, but she did decipher that Billy had not received a call from Jake at one in the morning on the 9th. Jake's phone records verified he never called Billy. She was eager to hear Billy explain that. Billy had lied to the police, and she would be certain to point it out to David. She figured Billy probably used a payphone to call Nate James, so it couldn't be traced. But he forgot that Nate James wouldn't use a payphone to receive the call. She quickly went to review Nate's records, and there it was. Nate received a call from an unknown caller at one pm. Then a call from Nate to Billy at two pm, the call to let Billy know Connie was in the hospital. There was a call from Billy to Bryan at two fifteen pm. Alicia picked up Bryan's dossier to look at the police interview notes for Bryan's flight information and realized she didn't have any notes. Something else for her to hope would show up in the updated discovery material.

Alicia wondered how David was processing her gift. She recalled the day they'd met and their first conversation. He'd said he wanted to ensure laws are equally and properly enforced. Billy had lied to the police, which should warrant at least one more interview where David could confront Billy with this new information.

Chapter 11

David's hand slipped into his pocket as Alicia sauntered away, rocking her purple suit. Heat surged within him and that weird sensation swarmed his body. *She is good all right, a formidable foe.* Instead of crumbling, Alicia countered every challenge with effortless grace. *She delivered it with such style, I wanted to kiss her.* Yeah, Jerri had cried plenty, but it wasn't from fear or guilt. She seemed most disturbed when he talked about Jake and how he'd treated her during their marriage. *Jerri was genuinely mourning that bastard.* This interview had not gone as planned.

Heading down to Janice DeLeo's war room, David found Eddie already there, speaking to the DA.

"What happened?" DeLeo asked. "Jerri Devine did not change her plea. Did you really press hard on her?"

"Looks like AK Stone is determined to go to trial," David said. "She was unphased by the evidence I presented and had an answer for everything. We can't prove Jerri was driving the SUV, and as for the photos, Jerri called it a friendly kiss."

"A friendly kiss? Are you kidding me?" DeLeo said, "I don't know what kind of friends she has, but that's not going to walk with a jury. I want you to interview everyone Ms. Devine claims had access to those SUV keys. If no one else takes responsibility for the midnight ride, then it was her. No ifs and or buts about it."

"Ms. Stone demands full disclosure of how we got the photos, and we can't use them as evidence until we can provide an answer," David said. "She also asked for a full autopsy report, which we don't have yet. We all know Jake died from gunshot wounds. What does she expect to find in a full autopsy?"

"She's reaching, that's all. Remember, the burden of proof is on us, not her. She's just looking for a way to muddy up the water." DeLeo glared at Eddie. "Anything from forensics on the photos or envelope?"

"Not yet," Eddie said.

"Okay, gentlemen, let's keep pushing. We're going to nail Jerri eventually."

David and Eddie left the war room together. En route to his office, David asked, "Please call police forensics and check on those pictures and contact the coroner to find out when the autopsy report will be ready. I'll draft up the formal request to defense counsel to provide the names of said authorized personnel for the Devine fleet."

"You got it."

David went into his office and closed the door. He was itching to read the paper in his pocket. He pulled it out and read, "Billy Whitmore, for justice's sake." Bafflement washed over David. *Billy Whitmore? He wasn't even on the radar as a suspect.* David sought out Jamal. "Please request a full background check on William Whitmore for me."

Returning to his office, David sat in his chair for a few minutes, stroking his mustache, wondering what Alicia was up to. Finally, he picked up the phone. With a low husky voice, he said, "Okay, counselor. I'm unsure what to make of this gift you gave me."

"Have you ever been to Bear Mountain?" Alicia asked in a cheerful voice.

"Uh, no."

"It's a beautiful state park, and the foliage there is amazing right now. How about you meet me there for leaf peeping? If we get there by five, you'll also see the most glorious sunset over the Hudson River. What do you say?"

After some hesitation, David said, "Sounds amazing. How far away is this place? It's already four."

"It's a 45-minute drive. Can you leave now? Sunset is at six. I'll wait for you by the inn."

"I'm on my way."

David used his GPS to guide him to Bear Mountain, stroking his mustache as he mused about seeing Alicia. She looked so gorgeous today. It pained him that he couldn't truly acknowledge her at the meeting as anything other than the enemy. The change in the landscape, as he drove further north from White Plains, had more trees and fewer houses along the roadside. The parkway narrowed from three car lanes for each direction of traffic to two. There were also more traffic lights as he passed through the small villages of Briarcliff and Ossining. Then the highway opened again to three lanes alongside the Hudson River in Croton. The view was superb as the sun twinkled off the water. It was getting close to rush hour and traffic was building. *Where the hell is this place?* The road narrowed to two lanes and up a steep incline. The river became obscured by large mountains colored in bright yellows, reds, oranges, and even more giant mountains looming in the distance. The GPS showed he was getting close as the road got curvy, and a Jeep was stopped at the traffic light for the left turn ahead to the Bear Mountain Bridge. He slowed behind the Jeep, flashing his headlights.

Alicia acknowledged his flashing light by waving at him through her rearview mirror. He followed closely once they got the green light. They were now on a road with one lane for each direction of traffic and only large stones acting as guard rails against the mountain slopes.

As they ascended the winding road, he slowed to match Alicia's speed. Mature trees and boulders bordered the left side of the road, and a mountain loomed over the right side. A sign ahead cautioned FALLEN

ROCK ZONE. There was no room to pull over since the road was terribly narrow. As they approached another curve, a tractor-trailer came around the corner from the opposite direction, and it appeared to be headed straight for him.

"What the hell?" David yelled as the truck passed him on his left side and continued down the mountain. Mercifully, his car hugged the road, handling each quick bend superbly. He realized why she was driving so cautiously and was grateful for it. They rounded another curve and the Bear Mountain Bridge appeared in the distance like magic. It was a remarkable sight, majestically spanning the Hudson River, but David hoped this ride would be over once they crossed it. Shortly after they crossed, he followed Alicia into the Bear Mountain State Park entrance, and they parked side by side near the inn, which resembled a large dark brown wooden ski chalet.

David's legs wobbled a bit as he got out of the car. "Jesus, that drive was certainly something else. I haven't encountered a road like that since I left Germany."

Alicia grinned. "Thanks for meeting me here. Glad you enjoyed the ole goat trail, as it is lovingly known around here." Standing so close to her caused heat to rise within him. "When were you in Germany?"

"A long time ago, when I was stationed there during my army days." There were acres filled with mature trees, lush green lawns, and a sizeable lake. "How did you ever find this place?"

"I live nearby. I wanted to be sure no one from either one of our offices would see us together. Come on, let's go into the inn."

A few people mingled inside the inn amongst the small faux wooden tables and chairs, talking and drinking coffee. They found a spot to sit, and David went to the coffee bar. He returned with two steaming cups and handed one to Alicia.

"This time, it's my treat." Smiling at her, enthralled with her beauty, he wanted to tell her how good she looked, but thought it better not to. "Well, here we are. So, tell me, where does Billy Whitmore fit into this case?"

"He's the one who murdered Jake Devine."

David's eyebrow went up. "And you have evidence to prove this?"

Alicia nodded. "Circumstantial, but yes."

"I'm all ears."

In a confident tone, Alicia relayed to David her theory of Billy committing the crime.

Once she was done, David rubbed his mustache with his thumb and forefinger, wearing a thoughtful expression. "It's a plausible theory, but you may be giving Billy too much credit. Just because someone is trained to kill does not mean he has the where with all to plan and organize. I'm ex-military myself, and I know from my experience there are soldiers and generals. Many of those guys wouldn't know when to tie their shoes unless given the order. This is not enough to drop the charges on Jerri, but since Billy lied to the police, it's worth looking into to find out why."

"And will you talk to the woman who supported his alibi, too?"

"Assuming we can find her, yes." David gulped down the remainder of his coffee. "I believe you promised me leaf peeping and a sunset. Come on, let's go take a walk." He held his hand out to Alicia, and she took it as she rose from the table. Her hand was soft and gentle to the touch. That weird, warm, squishy feeling flared up, overwhelming his body. When she stood up, they were face to face and David gazed intensely into her eyes. "I didn't get a chance to tell you how amazing you look today," he said in a low, husky voice. "I've tried to mentally demonize you because you're my opponent, but I can't."

"I'm glad you don't see me as evil."

David was still holding her hand as they left the inn together. Alicia pointed at the vibrant foliage with her free hand as they stepped onto one of the walking paths. "Isn't it stunning?" The leaves created a magnificent yellow, orange, red, and green mosaic.

"I agree. I haven't been in such lush woodland in years. I'm a city boy at heart, but I appreciate nature's simple beauty."

Grinning, Alicia's eyes sparkled. "In the summer, the lake is open for paddle boats, and there is a small zoo with black bears, coyotes, and other animals native to this area. Perhaps we could come back here when it's warmer and enjoy all the park offers."

"I like the sound of that idea, assuming we haven't killed each other in court by summer." Still gripping her hand, David didn't want to let go. What he wanted was to touch more than just her hand. He wanted to kiss those lush lips and caress her full, round bottom. Being so close, he caught a whiff of her sweet musky perfume, igniting a fire of desire within. He hadn't been this close to a woman since the break with Elizabeth, and he didn't want the feeling to end, but the sun began to set.

"The park's closing soon. Would you like to get dinner?" Alicia asked.

"Since you've delivered on your promise, sure, I could eat. This is your territory. Is there a good place nearby?"

"Yes," she said, "at the bottom of the ole goat trail. I'm certain you didn't notice it as we drove up here since you followed me."

David grinned. "And again, I will follow you down that crazy road." They each went to their vehicles and made the trek down. The sun continued to set, transforming the blue sky into a lush pink and orange hue among the clouds. The Hudson River view was sparkling from the sun's rays. David relaxed behind the wheel once they were almost down the mountain road but instead of completing the descent, Alicia's blinker came on as she made a right turn onto a small gravel road. David slowed and cautiously followed. The short gravel road led to a large two-story stone and natural wood building with a panoramic view of the Hudson River behind it. A sizable weather-worn sign read Monteverde Restaurant and Inn.

They parked side by side in the lot and entered the restaurant. A few guests were scattered about the large, open dining room, which was elegantly decorated in a nautical theme, with ship wheels, fishing nets, and lighthouse pictures strategically placed on the walls.

Once seated in a corner by a window with a river view, David said, "Nice place. And they have rooms here, too? Why didn't we just meet here instead of up on top of the mountain? This place is far enough out of the way, and we won't be spotted. You must believe it too. Otherwise, we wouldn't be here."

"Where's the adventure in that?" Alicia said. The waitress came to take their drink order. David ordered a scotch, neat, and she ordered a glass of Chardonnay. "Scotch? I'm surprised. I figured you'd be a martini man, like James Bond."

"Why?"

"Because underneath your diplomatic, black suit exterior, I think you enjoy intrigue, like a secret agent. I was counting on it when I slipped you the note that you would be too curious to ignore it."

"Which brings me to my question," David said. "Why are you doing this? Confiding in me? You know you're exposing your defense strategy. I could use this information to thwart your plans."

"I remembered our first conversation when you said you believed in fair representation on both sides of the justice system. I don't think winning this case is an ego trip for you. It's about the truth. You want to prosecute the killer, not necessarily Jerri Devine. Now, your boss, she's a horse of a different color. DeLeo has an enormous ego, and I'm not sure justice is always her motive, though as DA, it should be."

They opened their menus as David asked, "What's good here?"

"I recommend the Surf and Turf. Lobster Tail and Ribeye Steak. That's what I'm having." The waitress delivered their drinks, and they both ordered the Surf and Turf with baked potato and salad. "What happens next, counselor?"

"I will corroborate the information you've given me. If it's true, Billy will be brought in for questioning to find out why he lied to the police. And we'll bring in the woman who supported his alibi." David hesitated before saying, "It's funny. DeLeo had this gut feeling Bryan was at the crux of this murder. We all assumed she was right when Jerri and Bryan's affair came to light and solidified a motive for Jerri to murder Jake. Now Bryan may be the crux, not for Jerri, but for his uncle Billy's motive to murder Jake. DeLeo will not like it when I tell her we have another viable suspect to investigate, but at least she can console herself knowing her gut was still right."

"Be cautious with Billy. He's very cagey and dangerous, and I suspect he's behind another crime." Alicia filled him in about Diana's drugging incident.

"That's why you want the full autopsy report? To see if Jake's body has a similar wound?"

"Yes, along with a tox screen to see if Jake had the same drug in his system."

David calmly stroked his mustache again. "I'm not sure they'll find that drug if they are not looking for it. It's not a part of an ordinary toxicology exam."

"Me neither, but you can ask them to look for it. After you are convinced, Billy truly is a viable suspect, of course."

The restaurant's dim lighting made Alicia appear even more lovely to David. "Okay," he said. "Enough talk about the case. How about them Yankees? You know, I'm a huge baseball fan."

Alicia's eyes widened. "You are?"

They discussed the NY Yankees' odds of winning the upcoming World Series until the waitress brought their food. Examining the luscious plate, Davide nodded his approval as he tasted his steak. "I must say, you do have a way of choosing the best restaurants. This is delicious."

As they ate, they conversed about the weather, the impending cold that was bound to come with winter, and Hurricane Isabel, the largest storm to make landfall in the southeastern part of the country in years. Only a month had passed since the storm had ransacked North Carolina and Virginia. Alicia was animated as she talked about the hurricane's devastating effects on Virginia, her old home state. She still had uncles, aunts, and cousins living in Norfolk who had shared the damage to their home and neighborhood with her. While she did most of the talking, David quickly devoured his food. Once his plate was clean, he focused on Alicia as she finished her meal and indulged in a kissing fantasy. Tenderly observing each time she carefully scooped some of her potatoes into her mouth and how her lips moved as she slowly savored the taste. Oh, how he wanted to kiss those lips and savor her taste. His desire for her rose within him with each bite.

Putting her fork down, Alicia asked. "Are you ready for dessert?"

"Oh no, I'm full, but I would like coffee. How about you?"

"Coffee sounds good," Alicia ordered as the waitress cleared their plates. She gazed at David. "May I ask a personal question?"

"Of course."

"I heard you're engaged. When is the wedding?"

Puzzled, David gave her a tense gaze as he rubbed his mustache. "Where did you hear that?"

Alicia giggled. "Okay, I didn't hear it. I read it in your dossier."

His eyes widened. "That was in there?"

"Yes, your dossier included an article from the *New York Times* society page, announcing your engagement to an Elizabeth something or other."

"Ha. Guess my dossier needs updating. There isn't going to be a wedding. The engagement ended months ago." David leaned back with a smirk on his face.

"What happened? You both looked so happy in the newspaper photo."

"After the engagement, we moved in together, and after cohabitating for a while we both decided we weren't a good match. Nothing dramatic, just a parting of ways."

"I'm sorry things didn't work out for you."

"Why be sorry," David said. "I'm not. I'm glad we found out before we got married. Besides, I wouldn't be sitting here right now if I were engaged. And right now, I'm where I want to be. Here, getting to know you better." The waitress brought the coffee, but David's eyes never wavered from Alicia's face. He raised his mug for a sip of coffee. "Is it my turn to ask a question?"

"Sure."

"Tell me something about yourself that isn't in your dossier."

Alicia smiled. "Ah ha. You've read mine as well, have you?"

"Of course."

Alicia was thoughtful momentarily before saying, "My dossier says my father was convicted of breaking and entering and attempted murder charges. He was sentenced to twenty-five years at Sing Sing Prison. My mother moved us here to New York from Virginia to be near him, but my father was murdered by another inmate after serving five years. What the dossier doesn't say is he was innocent. I know every convict says that, but it's the primary reason I became a lawyer. My father was in the Bronx visiting his family when he was picked up because of a misidentification. I never want to hear about that happening to another person, though I know it happens far too often, especially in the Black community." She turned to the window with a faraway gaze. "I spent several years trying to clear his name with no luck."

"What a horrendous story. I'm so sorry the justice system failed you and your family."

"Yes, me too. So, you'll have to forgive me if I don't have much faith in the police or prosecutors, not even one as handsome as you." She gave him a small smile.

Reaching over, David took her hand. "Listen, you trusted me enough to share crucial information today. You must have had some faith that I would help you, or you wouldn't have done it."

"True."

"What else would you like to know about me?" David asked.

"Why did you become a lawyer?"

"I was raised in a New York City housing project, surrounded by crime. I never understood why no one was doing anything about it. We rarely saw policemen patrolling our neighborhood to prevent crime. They always came after the crime. At first, I became a police officer, thinking I could make an impact. But we often would bust people for petty crimes like drug possession for a tiny bag of marijuana or dealing with domestic abuse cases. I was shot in the leg by an enraged husband threatening to kill his wife. I still suffer from occasional PTSD from that incident. I realized I wasn't making a dent in the crime problem during my recovery. I decided to become a lawyer, hoping to make a difference in the courts in a way I could not accomplish patrolling the streets."

"And how's that working for you?" Alicia asked, cocking her head to the side "Do you feel like you're making a difference?"

"Yes, absolutely. Many dreadful people belong behind bars, and I'm putting them there. Unfortunately, some people, like your father, get swept up in the system based on false information. And I know people of color often don't get the justice they deserve, but we can't change it if there are no people of color within the justice system to take notice and campaign for innocent victims."

"Innocent victims like Jerri Devine?"

"I'm not certain Jerri is innocent. But I'm willing to entertain the thought. I don't ever want to prosecute the wrong person."

"And I don't defend persons I believe are guilty," Alicia said. "Some lawyers are only about the money. They take cases based on the fee and will do unscrupulous things to let criminals go free. I interview all potential clients before I commit to their service. If I'm not convinced of their innocence, I do not take up their case."

David's eyebrows raised. "And your boss allows you to be so discriminating?"

"Yes. That's the beauty of private practice. You can choose whom to represent. My boss can always assign the case to another attorney if he disagrees with my assessment."

"You know criminal law can be dangerous," David said, rubbing his mustache. "Do you carry a gun?"

Alicia shook her head. "No, I've never felt the need to."

Leaning back, David crossed his arms. "You should consider it. Even though I'm no longer on the police force, I practice with my weapon regularly. I faced multiple threats as an ADA in Manhattan. You've never been threatened by a client?"

"I have, but, back then, I had protection. My husband…" Alicia dropped her eyes from his gaze and silently sipped her coffee.

"How did we get back to all of this legal speak?" David said. "I asked you to tell me something about you that wasn't in your dossier. I mean, what happened to your father is awful, and I know it impacted you. But I wanted something a little more personal. Like, are you dating? Anyone special in your life?"

"No, no one special in my life now. After my husband passed away, I threw myself into my work. That's when I switched to matrimonial law and devoted the majority of my time studying to prepare myself for the change. As a result, I never had much time for dating."

David leaned in and stared into her eyes. "If the right man came along, could you make time?"

A demur smile formed on her lips. "Yes, if the right man came along."

"Does it bother you that I look so much like your late husband?"

The question caught Alicia off guard. Hesitating, her eyes fluttered before focusing on his. "No. I find it rather attractive because he was a wonderful person I deeply loved. But I do realize you are your own man, and I don't expect you to be just like him."

"Good because I find you very attractive, too, but I don't want to feel like I'm just filling in for a love you've had before. I'm sure he was a good man, or you wouldn't have been with him. But as you said, I am my own person and want to be appreciated for who I am, not for looking like someone else."

"Am I anything like Elizabeth?"

"Oh no," David chuckled. "Elizabeth is a socialite. Her father, a judge I used to clerk for, introduced us. Elizabeth was raised with money and influence. She has an interior design business, but I swear she only does it to be nosy and see what other people have in their houses. Her interests lean toward superficial things. You know, being with the right people, living in the right neighborhood, things like that. I think her father thought I could bring her head out of the clouds and back to earth, but we were just too different. The more time we spent together, the more I realized it wouldn't work." David didn't want to discuss their breakup in detail, so he gave Alicia the short version.

"Well," Alicia said, "we seem to have much more in common. Like you, I didn't come from money. However, we are on opposing sides of this case, so I don't think right now is the best time to think about dating one another."

"I understand you're being cautious, but you know it's not illegal for opposing counsel to be friends. If the relationship is really serious then disclosures must be made, but we're just getting to know one another."

"I know, but it's just the optics. Would you want to be defended by a lawyer who is intimately involved with the person pressing charges against you?"

"Just think about us getting to know each other better. No one else needs to know." David gave her a sly smile. "All this mutual attraction, something is happening here, and we both know it. We'd have to keep it on the down low, at least until this case is over. But I want to see you again. Like this. As a person, not attorney to attorney."

"I do know a few out-of-the-way places," Alicia grinned. "I'll think about it."

"Good. That's all I ask."

The waitress came, and David paid the check for dinner. As they walked to their cars, he asked, "Are you attending the ABA gala on Saturday?"

"Yes."

"Do you think we could get together in another secret place afterward?"

"We'll see, Mr. Bond," Alicia laughed. But David wasn't laughing. He gazed at her intensely, taking her hand before she could reach for the car door.

"There's something I've been wanting to do all evening," he said in a low, husky voice.

"What is it, counselor?"

"This." He leaned in and kissed her gently on the lips. Alicia's lips parted and allowed his tongue's slow, smooth entry. He enjoyed the sweet taste of her mouth as she kissed him back, and the kiss deepened. Their tongues danced around one another briefly, and a surge of warmth flowed through David's body from his head to his feet. David loosened his grip on her as he felt himself stiffen in his boxer briefs because he didn't want her to know what her kiss was doing to him. He opened her car door, and she slid into the Jeep. "Get home safely," he said as he closed the door.

David had trouble focusing on the road as the GPS guided him back toward White Plains. Alicia's face kept floating before his eyes instead of the asphalt while his fingers glided across his lips, remembering the soft touch of her lips. He had continued to stay aroused even after Alicia had gone, his need was so enormous. *I'm letting my emotions get away from me. I'm losing my head around Alicia, doing the very thing I said I wouldn't do. Her mystical charm has created a magnetic pull I cannot resist. And her lips, ... that kiss.* The speedometer reached 70 miles per hour as he eased his foot off the gas pedal, putting both hands on the steering wheel. He forced himself to remember she was still technically his opponent, and she hadn't agreed to another intimate face-to-face. But he was confident she'd felt the passion in their kiss, and he believed she was just as eager to share more with him as he was.

Chapter 12

Driving home, Alicia attempted to compose herself. Initially stunned by David's kiss, it felt so good she eagerly kissed him back. Alicia tightened her grip on the steering wheel. David's proposal lit a fire in her core. A secret affair. Pursing her lips, she flicked the blinker to turn onto Hudson Avenue. Her blood tingled as she remembered the crush of his kiss. *Had Kevin ever kissed me like that?* It had been a long time since she'd kissed anyone like that. Years, in fact, and she wanted more. Pulling into her driveway, her mind raced with the possibility of having more of those kisses and eventually making love. She entered the house, threw off her coat, and flopped down on the sofa, her head swirling with dizzying thoughts. *Should I allow my feelings to show and agree to a secret affair?*

On the one hand, she was glad he'd confirmed he was attracted to her and developing feelings for her, but on the other hand, she knew it was entirely unprofessional for her to act on it. Carlton would be so disappointed in her if he ever found out she was having a relationship with David. And David could lose his job if DeLeo discovered their romance. There was too much at risk for a heated moment of passion. But desire rose within and she wanted to. David's kiss awakened her need for love and intimacy. It felt good to be touched, held, and kissed. She wanted to experience it again with him.

From her perch on the couch, Kevin smiled at her from his silver frame on a corner table near the fireplace mantle. Walking over, she picked up the photo. His face was dusty. *Has it been so long since I've seen you? I used to look at you every day.* Memories of Kevin kept getting stirred up a lot lately. First, meeting David, his twin, and then Jerri discussing her dead husband. Now she was trying to do a job they used to do together and wasn't sure she was succeeding. Wiping the dust from the glass of the picture frame with the sleeve of her suit jacket, her eyes welled up with tears. She fought hard against them, lifting her head and squeezing her eyes closed, but they began to roll down her face anyway.

There was an instant attraction between them the first day Kevin came to work at Burke and Powell. They quickly progressed from being co-workers to being a couple. It seemed they were always together, yet she never got tired of his company. In a matter of months, she left her home with her mother and sister and moved into his apartment. Kevin surprised her on her birthday the following year by placing a torn-out magazine picture of a diamond ring on her plate beside two strips of bacon and one egg over easy-on toast.

As he laid the plate in her lap, she asked, "What's this?"

Kevin knelt by the bed in his gray sweatpants, bare chest, and muscular arms glistening. Taking her hand, he gazed intently into her eyes. "I don't want another year to go by without making us official. Leeshe, will you marry me?"

Alicia's eyes widened. As the shock wore off, she smiled, pulled his hand to her lips, and kissed his rough knuckles. "Of course, I will if you buy me a real ring. I mean, what am I supposed to do with this?" Giggling, she waved the magazine clipping around in the air.

Kevin climbed into the bed, taking the glossy page from her hand. "I want you to choose your ring. Lord knows, I probably wouldn't pick out the right one."

Alicia lightly smacked him in the head with a pillow. They both laughed as he tried to stave off her attack, and the plate of bacon and eggs went flying. When he wrestled the pillow from her grip, he bopped her on the head with it, still laughing.

"I love you so much, Mrs. Green."

The plate didn't matter. She wasn't hungry anyway, at least not for food. They kissed and played with one another until it slid into some serious lovemaking.

The memory brought a small smile to her lips as she wiped the tears away. For months, she was mad at God for suddenly taking her husband. It became hard to pray and believe that God would answer any of her requests because He'd turned his back on her. Slowly, she began to heal and feel God's comfort, eventually accepting Kevin's death was God's Will, and He wasn't punishing her for some unknown sin.

Within the silver frame in her hands, Kevin smiled up at her with his fine self, sporting a mint green suit paired with a green paisley tie. A diamond stud sparkled in his earlobe. Now she could easily distinguish David from Kevin. Their physical features were very similar, but there were differences. Both men were gentle giants, but Kevin had a thuggish edge to how he carried himself, and people knew when they saw him coming not to mess with him. His voice boomed when he spoke, and he didn't take any shenanigans off anybody. Well-versed in street slang, Kevin could easily converse with gang bangers and hookers and code-switch to proper white folk speak when appropriate.

David was much more refined. She was confident he could hold his own if confronted, but he never came off as aggressive as Kevin. Constantly stroking his mustache with his thumb and forefinger in thought, he chose his words carefully when he spoke in that soft, husky tone. One would never know David was raised in the hood. He appeared as if he'd been born with a silver spoon in his mouth. Yet, he seemed sensitive to other people's circumstances and feelings, and after talking with him, she knew he had not forgotten where he came from.

Placing Kevin's picture on the table, she whispered, "Goodnight, my love." There was no going back. As she walked to her bedroom, a vision of David's face filled her head. *Perhaps God knew it would take someone like him to force me out of the cocoon I've surrounded myself in.* No longer numb after David's kiss awakened her sexual desire, she was fully alive again. And Kevin was not going to be able to satisfy those needs anymore. No, David was not Kevin, and it was time to move on. She went to sleep with David's face floating through her mind, thinking of all the possibilities ahead.

Chapter 13

Early Tuesday morning, David wasted no time verifying Alicia's information. Fortunately, Billy and Jake's dossier already had phone records included, and David confirmed there was no call between them the night of the murder. Armed with this vital information, he gathered up his reports and headed straight to Janice DeLeo's office.

As he approached, there were murmurs from behind the closed door. Ignoring any hesitation, he knocked and was greeted by a visibly shaken Eddie.

"David, good morning. I didn't expect to see you here so early," Eddie stammered, clearly startled by David's arrival. "I was just updating Janice on the latest developments in the case." He looked down at his dusty brown loafers as he opened the door wider.

David entered and greeted his boss before turning his attention to Eddie. "What's the latest news? Did I miss something since yesterday afternoon?"

Adjusting his glasses, Eddie hesitated before responding. "The full autopsy report came in after you left. Since you didn't return to the office, I figured I should review it with Janice this morning."

"Yes," DeLeo said. "As you know, time is of the essence. What pulled you away from the office so early yesterday?"

Not missing a beat, David fabricated a story. "I had a meeting with a realtor. I had put in an offer on a condo over the weekend, and my offer was accepted, so I needed to complete the paperwork to get the sale rolling."

"Oh, well, congratulations," DeLeo said as she gave him a firm handshake. "Glad to hear you're putting some roots down. Guess that means you'll be staying with us for a while. Eddie, give him a copy of the autopsy report."

DeLeo and Eddie waited silently as David read the report. "We didn't see anything earthshaking. What do you think?" she asked.

After perusing the document, David said, "I don't see anything out of the ordinary. As requested, I'll pass this on to the defense, but I don't think it will give AK Stone any juice. I sent a request to Ms. Stone for the names of the Devine security team. With any luck, we'll get an answer today, so we can conduct those interviews."

"We also expect the forensic results on the photos today. Hopefully, they will have some good news and identify our anonymous source." Eddie said.

"Sounds like we've got another busy day ahead. Great work, gentlemen." DeLeo dismissed them, and David retreated to his office, uneasy about Eddie's haste in presenting DeLeo with an autopsy report that revealed nothing new. It made him apprehensive about bringing up his possible new suspect theory with them both.

In solitude, he reviewed the autopsy report again. The cause of death was confirmed as gunshot wounds, and Detomidine was not listed on the toxicology report. However, a puncture wound was found on the exterior of Jake's body, along with minor bruising under the arms. His police training told him it could indicate the body had been dragged. Not wanting to make a big deal of it in front of Eddie, he opted to save it for later when he could speak to DeLeo privately. An in-person visit to the coroner was necessary to request they test for the presence of the horse tranquilizer and get his professional opinion on what the puncture wound and bruise marks meant.

As David prepared to leave, he received a call from Rachel. His offer had indeed been accepted on the condo, and she needed him to sign additional paperwork. It eased his conscious a bit about lying to DeLeo regarding where he had gone since now it was kind of the truth. David promised to stop by Rachel's office later in the evening, and then he headed out to see the coroner.

Stopping for a coffee in a delicatessen before completing his walk to the coroner's office, David picked up a local newspaper. He almost choked on his first sip, seeing the photo of Jerri and Bryan's kiss splashed on the front page, under the headline, *DID SHE KILL FOR LOVE? Why hadn't anyone mentioned this earlier this morning? Surely DeLeo has seen this story in the news. Is she the one who allowed it to be leaked to the press? Alicia and Jerri must be freaking out over the photos going public.* David could do nothing about it, and the story would keep public opinion on the DA's side. *DeLeo does love publicity in her favor. I hope Alicia does not see this as a betrayal, holding me responsible for the leak.*

The coroner, Paul Gregg, was a big, burly white man with graying brown hair on his face and atop his head. Wearing a white medical coat over his jacket, he greeted David with a firm handshake.

"Happy to meet you, Mr. King. How are you enjoying the new job?" David glanced around the sterile white exam room with a gurney and glistening metal instruments atop. Dr. Gregg was standing behind his large metal desk with a color picture of the human anatomy hanging behind him on the wall. Stacks of medical files lay on his desk. "Please have a seat."

"The job is going well. Thank you for seeing me," David said as he sat across from Dr. Gregg. "I wanted to ask you a few questions about the autopsy report on Jake Devine. Any idea what would have caused a puncture wound on his back? And those bruises under his arms?"

"The wound could be an insect bite, though I do have my doubts. It seemed more prominent than an ordinary spider or mosquito sting, but I don't have a definitive answer."

"Could it be from a tranquilizer dart?"

"It's possible," Dr. Gregg replied. "As for the bruising, it's indicative of someone dragging the body. Do you believe Mr. Devine could have been drugged before the shooting?"

"I would like you to do another tox screen to see if any tranquilizers were in his blood. Specifically, Detomidine."

"Detomidine? That's the second time I've heard that drug come up this week. Highly unusual. Do we have a madman with a tranquilizer gun running around town?" The doctor said it with sarcasm but bore a severe expression.

"Not sure, but I know about the young lady who was drugged this weekend. She's an investigator working on the Devine case, and I believe it could be related to Jake Devine's murder. Could be the same person shooting darts."

Dr. Gregg agreed to do another toxicology screen and get the results to David as soon as possible. David returned to his office, picked up William Whitmore's dossier from his desk, and proceeded to go speak with DeLeo. Fortunately, she was alone, and David dropped the newspaper on her desk. "We have a leak either here or in the police department. Did you know about this?"

Glancing at the paper, DeLeo pushed it aside. "Yes, I saw it this morning. I don't know how the press got a hold of the photos." She looked David in the eyes as she pushed a wisp of hair behind her ear. "What I don't understand is why you seem upset about this. If we can't use the photos in court, we'll get plenty of mileage out of this news story. You do see this helps our case, don't you?"

"Yes, I do, but if this kind of information is being leaked, how do we know what else the press knows? The next headline may not be in our favor."

"Don't worry about that. Is that the only reason you came to see me?" DeLeo asked.

"No, it's not. I've been doing a deeper dive into other possible prime suspects. We're going to need the police to pull in Billy Whitmore again. I reviewed the phone records for Jake Devine and Mr. Whitmore. There is no record of a phone call from Jake to Billy at one in the morning on the day Jake's body was found. He lied to the police, and I want to know why."

DeLeo was astonished. "What? I can't believe the detectives let that slip by them. Absolutely. Please demand they get Billy Whitmore to explain it. Good catch, David."

"And we should also have them pick up the woman who verified Billy's alibi, Lena Martin. She claimed to have overheard the call while Billy was with her."

"Agreed. I hope they can find the little strumpet." DeLeo said, obviously irritated by the police's lack of due diligence. "If Billy Whitmore is our man, do you have any idea what his motive would be to kill Jake?"

"Billy and Jake were in business together, so I'm going to guess it was about money."

"But we looked at Devine Music's financials, and there wasn't much money."

"Maybe Billy didn't know it. Jake had us all fooled, living the high life. The important fact is Billy is an ex-Navy Seal which makes him capable of committing the murder and framing Jerri for it." David handed DeLeo the file labeled William Whitmore.

DeLeo took a moment to peruse the dossier. When she finished, she said, "Let's find out why Billy Whitmore lied and where he really was that night. Are you doing a deeper dive into Raymond Meeks as well? His alibi seemed a bit weak to me."

"Yes, I'm also looking into him, but I haven't uncovered anything about him so far."

"Well, once again, great work, David. Keep me posted on what the police find out."

Pleased that DeLeo agreed to a second interview, he wanted to call Alicia to share the good news, but he didn't. He assumed her hands were full, doing damage control for her client after the news broke about Jerri and Bryan's affair. Instead, he went to talk to Eddie about getting the police to order Billy Whitmore to come in for questioning.

Chapter 14

Alicia returned home from her morning walk to the sound of her house phone ringing incessantly. When she finally answered, Diana yelled, "Girl, turn on the TV! Now! Channel 5!"

Throwing down the phone receiver, she grabbed the TV remote and turned it on. The female reporter was discussing Jerri, suggesting her motive for killing Jake was to be with her young lover. A blow-up of the photo of Jerri and Bryan kissing was plastered on the wall behind her.

Picking the phone back up, Alicia shook her head. "Diana, are you still there? I can't believe this. Jerri is going to have a heart attack when she sees this."

"I know, girl. It's all over the place, in newspapers and on TV. You think David did this?"

"No, this looks more like DeLeo's handiwork. Since she can't use the photos in court, she allowed them to be leaked to the press and let them run with it. She's such a media hound. I'm sure she loves this attention. I better call Jerri and try to get ahead of this mess. I'll see you at the office."

Alicia was about to call Jerri, and then she put the phone back down. *Crap, what am I going to say to her? How do I put a positive spin on this?* She decided to go and have a talk with God and pray He'd give her the words. If Jerri had seen the news, she would have been calling her, but she didn't have any messages on her answering machine. Alicia knelt beside her sofa, bowed, and called upon the Lord.

When Alicia arrived at the office, Carlton stood in his doorway, waiting for her. "Good morning. Jerri Devine called me frantic a few minutes ago."

Alicia strode past him into his office, removed her leather coat, and tossed it into one chair as she sat in the other. "What did you tell her?"

Carlton closed the door and walked to stand behind his desk. "I told her not to panic and that you'd be there this morning to strategize addressing this news."

"Good, because that's exactly what I'm going to do."

Carlton sat, folding his hands atop the desk. "And what exactly are we going to say to the press?"

"That it's true, but the relationship was brief and only started after Jerri learned of Jake's death."

"You really think the press will buy that story?"

"Yes, if Jerri sells it right." Alicia stopped talking. Carlton was slightly shaking his head in disagreement. "Look," she continued, "we have no choice. There's no denying what's in the photo. We may have escaped the prosecutor's clutches with the friendly kiss story, but in the general public's eye, it won't work." Rising from her seat, she paced around behind the chairs.

"When I asked Jerri why she was messing around with Bryan, she called it comfort. And that's how we'll sell it. A moment of comfort, but they're not having an ongoing affair. And I will tell Jerri she needs to cool it with Bryan. I will tell both of them. I'll talk with her and Bryan, and we'll devise a joint statement they can each read to the press from separate locations." She looked to Carlton for support.

"Maybe I should go with you to see them," Carlton said with concern. "I need to know what you're going to say before we go public with a statement."

"I promise I will consult with you before we do anything. Please, let me talk to Jerri."

Carlton reluctantly said, "All right."

Alicia went to her office and called Jerri, who answered the phone sobbing. "Please, Jerri, stay calm. I'm on my way to see you. Is Bryan there with you?"

"No. No one's here. I'm alone."

"Please call Bryan and ask him to meet with us at the penthouse. We need to come up with a statement for the press, and it needs to be from both of you."

"Okay, I'll call him, but please hurry." Jerri was still sobbing as she hung up the phone.

Alicia called Diana next. "Hey, girl, what's up? How's Jerri?"

"A mess, as you would expect. I'm going to see her once I finish speaking with you. Where are you?"

"On my way into the office."

"I need you to tail Billy today. The police are going to pull him in for questioning. I'm afraid he will get spooked and do something, possibly try to run."

"How do you know the police are picking him up?"

"Because I dropped a tip on him to the Chief Prosecutor."

"You did what?"

"I met with David last night." There was a long silence on the phone. Alicia asked, "Diana, are you still there?"

"Yeah, I'm here, but I'm in shock. What possessed you to meet with David and tell him who our prime suspect is? Are you crazy?"

"No, I took a gamble, and it's paying off. I don't want to go to trial if I don't have to. I didn't get a chance to tell you about it, but I got a solid slip-up on Billy's part." She explained about the missing phone call.

"Is that it?" Diana asked. "Is that all you told him?"

"Essentially, yes. I'll give you all the details later. For now, please focus on Billy. I expect the police will at least consider him to be a person

129

of interest, but I doubt if they will hold him after questioning. I'm certain he'll come up with some kind of lie to buy himself some time. Be at the police station so you can follow him after he's released. I want to be sure he doesn't try to leave town."

"All right, but I don't like this, you dealing with David. You must give me all the details of your meeting with him later."

Alicia drove as swiftly as the law allowed to the penthouse to meet Jerri. A throng of news reporters gathered at the entrance, and Franklin was out front shouting at them to get back. As Alicia approached, she was recognized by one of the reporters, who rushed into her path and shoved a microphone in her face.

"Ms. Stone, what can you tell us about Jerri Devine's affair with Bryan James?" The other reporters surrounded Alicia as she tried to reach the front door.

"We'll be issuing a statement later today," Alicia said. "Right now, there is no comment." She nodded at Franklin and entered the building to take the elevator up.

The two security guards were back on duty when the elevator doors opened. "Good morning, Ms. Stone," the taller one said.

"Good morning. The last time I was here, I didn't get your names. You are…"

"Chris Jones." He put out his hand and gave Alicia a firm handshake. Alicia extended her hand to the shorter, rounder, dark-skinned brother.

"Mars Bellamy," he volunteered, shaking her hand.

"Has Ray had a chance to speak with you about your involvement in Jerri's case?" Alicia asked.

They both got dumbfounded expressions.

Chris sputtered, "Involvement in the case? We ain't had nothing to do with Jake's murder."

Alicia explained, "The police took surveillance video from the parking garage. Someone drove one of the Devine's SUVs on the night of the murder. Were either of you on duty that night?"

"We both were, but Mars and I left about eleven, long after Ray had put Jerri to bed. Neither one of us drove anywhere that night."

"The police are going to want to question you about that night. Please cooperate and tell them the truth. Are there any other security team members, or is it just the two of you?"

"It's just us, Ms. Stone," Chris said. "Ray didn't mention anything about being questioned by the police when he stopped by this morning. I don't feel comfortable talking to them about anything. I've been hassled and roughed up by Five-O before over some BS, you know. You sure that's all they want to talk about?" Mars was standing by, listening and nodding in agreement as Chris spoke.

"Yes, I'm sure. Just stay calm and answer their questions. You'll be in and out of there in no time."

"All right then," Chris said, "we'll cooperate. You can go on into the living room. Jerri's waiting for you in there." He lifted his arm to point the way.

Alicia went down the hall into the living room. Jerri was standing in front of the windows taking in the view. "Hi Jerri, how are you?"

Jerri turned around, her face streaked with tears, her red and white silk floral gown flowing around her. She shrieked at Alicia, "Why is this happening? Who gave that picture to the newspapers?"

"I don't know, but we will fix this together." Alicia sat down on the sofa and pulled her notepad out. She jotted down the names of the security team, so she could get it to David this afternoon. "Did you call Bryan?"

"Yes, he's on his…" Before Jerri could finish answering, there was a loud yelling in the hall.

Billy stormed into the room with Bryan lagging behind him. "What did you do?" His face was an angry red.

Alicia stood up, unsure if the question was directed at her or Jerri, but she raised her voice to answer it. "What are you yelling about? I had nothing to do with the picture going public."

"I'm not talking about pictures. I'm talking about the police. They just called me saying I need to come down to the station to answer more questions. What did you tell them? I know it was you that said something," Billy hollered as he stepped closer, invading Alicia's personal space. A musty odor emanating from his army jacket assaulted her nostrils.

"I have no idea what you're talking about." Alicia stared into his squinty eyes, unafraid.

Billy raised his hand and pointed his finger in Alicia's face. "You better not be trying to pin Jake's murder on me to save her sorry ass. I'm not going down for this." He turned and pointed at Jerri. "She did it."

Jerri began to wail as Bryan jumped in front of Billy, making space between him and Alicia. "Hey, hey, calm down. I didn't hear anyone accuse you of anything." Billy backed up, and Bryan glided from Billy over to Jerri, taking her into his arms. "And Jerri did not kill Jake. You know that." He held Jerri, stroking her hair as she stifled her tears, and moaned into his denim-clad shoulder.

Alicia focused on Billy. "I don't know why the police want to question you, but all you have to do is go to the police station and answer their questions. You say you didn't do anything wrong, so what are you so worked up about?"

"I don't trust you," Billy said in a low growl. He paced around the room like a caged animal, running his hand over his hair.

"I'm here to work with Jerri and Bryan on creating a statement they can give to the public to address all the drama the photo in the news is causing. I don't care if you trust me or not. I'm not representing you. I'm here for Jerri and her alone."

"Why don't you just go to the station and talk to the police," Bryan said. "The sooner you do it, the sooner you'll know what they want. I'll stay here, and you can come back to get me when you're done."

"You shouldn't even be here!" Billy shouted at Bryan. "If you had listened to me from the get-go and kept your hands off of that woman, we wouldn't be involved in this murder mess at all. How are you going to explain kissing on another man's wife? I told you messing around with her was going to cause trouble. She's no good for you."

Bryan released Jerri and stepped back over in front of Billy. "Okay, enough. You need to go somewhere, calm down, and then speak to the police." Bryan guided Billy toward the elevator door and continued to talk to him in a low voice. He returned to the living room shortly after, alone. "I know it's early, but I need a drink after all that," Bryan said. "Ladies, can I get anything for you?" He headed over to the bar and picked up the brandy bottle.

Jerri asked for brandy, and Alicia asked for water. Bryan brought the drinks, and the three settled around the coffee table to discuss their statement for the press.

Chapter 15

The lead story on the evening entertainment news was Jerri Devine's statement. Elegantly dressed in a black wool sweater dress accessorized with a dazzling rhinestone necklace, matching earrings, and black leather boots, she addressed the crowd of fans and reporters assembled at the corner of 8th Avenue.

"It's with great regret I stand before you today, confessing that, in a moment of weakness, as I mourned the loss of my husband, Jake, I took comfort in the arms of my friend and musical partner, Bryan James. In what I imagined to be a private moment, he gave me solace by holding and kissing me, but that's as far as it went. We were not intimate, and we are not a couple. Bryan and I developed a close working relationship as we collaborated on our music and produced my latest album, *Ms. Devine Rocks*! Bryan loved Jake too, and we comforted one another as we grieved. That is all. I want to thank all of my fans who have supported me through my journey, and I pray this incident does not cause any of you to lose faith in me. I loved my husband, Jake, and I did not murder him. Rest assured, the truth will prevail, and I will be vindicated of all charges. Thank you."

The reporter noted Ms. Devine did not take any additional questions after making her statement. Meanwhile, across town on 3rd Avenue, Bryan James echoed similar sentiments. Clad in denim jeans, jacket, and cowboy boots, Bryan addressed a smaller group of supporters and journalists. "The coward who invaded a private moment between friends, comforting one another in a moment of shared grief, should be ashamed of themselves. Jerri Devine is a wonderful woman who was a loving, devoted wife to Jake Devine for twenty years. We are not and have never been lovers. Our bond is purely platonic, rooted in friendship and a mutual passion for music. The photo shown in the news completely misrepresents our relationship. Jerri Devine is incapable of committing murder, and I could never motivate her to go against her sweet, loving nature to commit such a heinous act. I stand by her innocence wholeheartedly and know that eventually, justice will prevail and she will be found innocent in a court of law. Thank you all for your continued support."

The reporter surmised that the photograph did not necessarily translate into an affair and that seeking comfort during the grieving process was normal.

Carlton and Alicia gave each other a high five after watching the news report together on television. "Great performances by Jerri and Bryan," Carlton said. "They've completely diffused the love affair motive for the murder story. Great job, Alicia. I knew you could do it!" He went to his credenza and pulled out a bottle of scotch and two glasses.

Alicia raised her hand. "None for me, thanks. I'm glad everything worked out for Jerri, but I still have work to do. I'm going to head to my office and get to it."

"Anything I need to know about?"

"The updated discovery material from the DA's office arrived, so I need to go through it. We'll talk later." She left Carlton's office and went down to her own.

First, Alicia sent David an email with the names of the Devine security team, as he'd requested. Her phone rang just as she pressed the button to send.

"Hey, girl." It was Diana.

"Hi. Did you follow Billy?"

"Yeah, I just watched him go into his apartment building. He doesn't appear shaken by his police interview, but I'll sit here a while and make sure he doesn't come back out with a suitcase."

Nodding, Alicia replied, "Sounds good."

"He did make a few stops after he left the police station before heading home. First, he went to 8th Avenue and 40th Street. He must have been looking for Lena, his hooker girlfriend, cause that's her territory, but he came up empty. Then he went to a storage facility on 11th Avenue and hung out there for almost half an hour. I'm going to double back there later and see if I can figure out which storage unit is his."

"Interesting."

"Yeah, you know, these covert military types often use a storage unit as their base of operations rather than their living quarters. That way, if their place ever gets searched, the police won't find anything. Who knows what I may find if I can get into his storage unit."

"Maybe a tranquilizer dart gun?"

"Right, among other things. I'll call you later with an update."

"All right. Be careful." Alicia hung up and turned her attention to the folders of updated discovery material on her desk. First, she took out Connie James' hospital record, which stated she'd been rushed into the emergency room at 1:30 PM, complaining of chest pain and dizziness. Further tests showed her symptoms may have been caused by a malfunction of the pacemaker Connie had implanted two years ago. However, the cause of the chest pain was not definitive. Doctors monitored her heart rate for two days and reprogrammed her pacemaker as a precaution before releasing her from the hospital. It confirmed her suspicion that Billy coaxed Nate and Connie into having a fake emergency to get Bryan to leave town quickly.

Next, she read the full autopsy report. Jake did indeed have a puncture wound on his upper back, which made her glad, but the absence of the tranquilizer in his blood disappointed her. There were bruise marks under the arms, but no bruises anywhere else. Alicia trusted that David asked the coroner for an explanation for the bruising as well as a second toxicology report to see if Detomidine was present. She was also curious as to how the questioning with Billy had gone. Thinking of David, she instinctively ran her finger across her lips, remembering the kiss from the night before. Alicia kept pushing the memory of the kiss away, but it continued to resurface. She hadn't decided whether to accept David's proposal of a secret affair, but she knew when they spoke again, he would ask. The phone's ring brought her back into the present moment.

"Good afternoon, counselor," David said.

"Good afternoon. I was just thinking about you. How are you?" Alicia became flush with a warm sensation at the sound of his voice.

"It's been a busy day. I didn't have much luck with your boy, Billy."

Alicia frowned, not surprised. "What did he say?"

"When I presented him with the phone records indicating the missing call, Billy produced a prepaid cell phone. He claimed his cell phone was giving him trouble, and he bought this prepaid phone as a backup so he wouldn't miss any important calls. That phone showed a call received at 1:05 AM from an unknown caller, still listed in the call log."

"That could have been from anyone. What about the fact Jake's phone doesn't show any outgoing calls at that time?"

David let out a long sigh. "Billy had an answer for that, too. He said he showed Ray the new prepaid phone, and Ray was so fascinated, that he wanted to know where he could get one for himself and Jake. Billy said Jake could have used a similar phone to make the call."

"Well, I expected him to come up with something to cover his tracks, but this story is truly genius. Any luck finding Lena Martin?"

"Nope. And since I'm satisfied with Billy's answers, I can't press the police to keep searching for her."

"Great, just great. I'm going through the latest discovery material now. Did you get my email on the Devine security team?"

"Yes, we just dispatched a Westchester County officer with contacts in the NYPD to go down and interview them at the Devine's penthouse. No need to drag them into the station for a few simple questions. Besides, as DeLeo would say, time is of the essence, so this way, we get immediate answers instead of waiting for them to make their way to White Plains."

"Good for you," Alicia said. "Just so you know, they didn't drive the SUV that night."

"That's the testimony I was expecting. And that means, as far as we're concerned, Jerri was the driver."

Alicia was about to argue it wasn't Jerri, but without something to stick to Billy, she didn't bother. "I read Jake's autopsy report. Did you ask the coroner about doing a follow-up tox screen?"

"Yes, I did. Dr. Gregg was familiar with the incident involving your investigator, so he didn't make any fuss. I should get those results tomorrow." David paused before continuing. "Even if it does show up, you still have no way of tying the tranquilizer to Billy. Your case against him is getting weaker, counselor."

"I know."

"DeLeo is amped up, and we're about ready to go into full trial preparation mode. We should be getting the official start date for the trial any day now. I don't think I'll be able to help you out anymore with Billy."

"I understand, and I do appreciate your efforts. It's okay. I've got more than one trick up my sleeve, so don't count me out yet."

"Great job, though, on the damage control," David said. "I watched Jerri and Bryan's statements on the news. Looks like you dodged a bullet in the court of public opinion."

"For now, anyway."

"I hope you know I had nothing to do with that photo being leaked to the press."

"I never suspected you. I know it was that darn woman you work for, though she'll never admit it. Guess that means your source remains anonymous."

"Yes, I just got the news. The forensics team couldn't pull any fingerprints from the photos or the envelope, so we can't use it in court, but now we don't have to."

They listened to each other breathe a moment until David said, "I haven't stopped thinking about you and our dinner last night. Have you given any more thought to my proposal?"

"I have."

"Will I see you after the gala? If you say yes, I promise we won't discuss the case. We'll just focus on getting to know each other better."

"I'd like to, but is it wise?"

"Probably not, but I want to see you anyway. Come on, Miss Adventure. Don't you want to rendezvous with the infamous Mr. Bond?"

Alicia hesitated. "I'm going to have to get back to you, counselor. Right now, I'm tired, and I'm hungry. I'm not in the right mindset to make a good decision."

David sighed loudly. "Fair enough. You know how to reach me. Have a good night."

"You, too."

Alicia continued to stare at the phone after she put the receiver down. *What am I going to do about my feelings for David? Can I ignore them and my newly rediscovered womanly needs? I want to fully explore a relationship with David, but I need to keep my head screwed on straight.* The kiss had left her reeling. If they got any closer, she wasn't sure she could go after David like every other prosecutor she had come up against. As much as she'd pressed to get Jerri's charges dismissed, it appeared she would have to defend her in court. David was right, the trial date would be set and announced any day now. *How can I fight for Jerri and defend her best if I'm falling in love with my opponent?*

Her stomach growled and broke her train of thought. She got up, put on her coat, and went out seeking sustenance.

Chapter 16

Lowering his head, David frowned as he hung up the phone. He wanted Alicia to be willing to explore what was happening between them. She'd already confessed her attraction to him and he believed it was worth the risk. After all, they were both intelligent people. Surely, they could find a way to be together without the whole world finding out. Frustrated, he got up from his desk and sought out Eddie.

Eddie was not in his office, but he'd left the door open. David entered and quickly surveyed the organized chaos, as Eddie called it, shaking his head. He couldn't understand how anyone could work like this, and then he spied his name scribbled on a yellow legal pad. Curiosity piqued David ventured a closer look. He pushed aside a folder covering the full sentence Eddie had written on the legal pad and read it. *David requested a second toxicology report from the coroner.* His head jerked up after he read it, wondering why Eddie would make a note of that. *How did he even know about it?* The same uneasy feeling he'd had this morning overcame him again. *Was Eddie's early morning meeting with DeLeo about more than the autopsy report? Is Eddie spying on me for DeLeo?*

Hurrying back to his own office, David slammed his hands onto his desk in frustration. *DeLeo doesn't trust me. That's where Eddie's sudden enthusiasm for the case came from. She must have told him to report my activities and promised Eddie something if he came up with any dirt.* David was furious that he was under the microscope, his every move being monitored. He'd assumed DeLeo had confidence in his ability to prosecute the case, but apparently not. Not wanting to believe DeLeo's actions had racial undertones, he couldn't help wondering if she did this with all her other new ADAs. *This type of treatment is reserved for rookies.* Suddenly, he needed fresh air, put on his coat, and left the building.

Sitting in his car, David grappled with his emotions. Alicia and the Smoke House came to mind, offering solace. Nothing would make him feel better right now than a good plate of ribs, collard greens, and macaroni and cheese. Checking his GPS, the address for the restaurant was still on it. Thinking about Alicia as he drove calmed him down. It was a pleasant surprise when her Jeep sat parked in The Smoke House lot.

Entering The Smoke House, David scanned the patrons in the dining room. Spotting Alicia standing under the takeout sign in the left-hand corner of the restaurant, he walked over as she gave her order to the clerk and stood behind her. When she'd finished and turned, her eyes widened as her lips formed an "o." "David, what are you doing here?"

David smiled, gazing into her warm brown eyes. "What can I say, counselor? Great minds think alike. I got frustrated at work and decided some good food would make me feel better. So here I am."

Recovering from shock, Alicia smiled back at him. "Frustrated with what?"

"Oh, just a certain lovely lady who's avoiding my advances. I spoke with her on the phone, trying to get a date, but alas, she's unwilling."

"How sad," Alicia teased, feigning pity.

"Do you have to rush back to the office, or can you spare some time to keep a lonely man company?" David asked.

"Is that a good idea? One of my colleagues saw us here before and already suspects something is amiss."

"Ah, come on. Where's your adventurous side? You can always tell your colleague we were hammering out a plea deal. It's just dinner. Even lawyers have to eat."

Relenting, she said, "You're right. Go find a table, and I'll tell them to bring my order over."

Victorious, David strode to a booth on the other side of the restaurant. It was as if God had answered an unsaid prayer, finding Alicia here. He needed someone to talk to and to laugh with to get him out of his feelings about Eddie and DeLeo. When she sauntered over, David couldn't help but acknowledge again what a fine woman Alicia was. As she shed her leather coat, David admired her shapely figure in her blue paisley silky dress.

"You look stunning," David said as she sat across from him.

"Thank you, counselor. You don't look too bad yourself. What's got you frustrated? Problems with the case?"

"No, the case is fine. I guess I'm having a little trouble adjusting to how my new boss likes to do business. I know I'm the new kid on the block in the DA's office, but I didn't expect to be treated like a newbie. I'm an experienced attorney who has successfully prosecuted some pretty big cases."

"What did DeLeo do?"

"Let's just say my assigned ADA on the case seems a bit more interested in my methods than following my orders."

"Maybe he's watching you closely so he can learn from you. I'm certain several other ADAs wanted to get the Devine case. Maybe he's trying to figure out why they selected you."

"Maybe," David conceded. The waitress came over and took David's order, and they explained Alicia's meal was already in the works. After she left, David looked at Alicia and said, "I'm surprised you didn't jump to the conclusion DeLeo is up to something nefarious. You clearly do not like her."

"Nope, and I know she doesn't like me. Everybody's entitled to their opinion. DeLeo may not do things as I think she should, but she is the

DA. She didn't get there without doing the work, and someone thinks she's doing a good job. Otherwise, she'd be canned."

"It's true. The county has had a sterling reputation under DeLeo's administration. I checked it out before I took the job. I guess I have to get used to her methods. Anyway, I don't want to waste my time with you talking about her." David gave her a smoldering gaze. "How are you doing?"

"I'll be a lot better once they bring me some food. I'm starving, and smelling all this barbecue is not helping much."

Alicia seemed nervous, fussing with her dress. He wondered if he was making her feel unsteady with his eyes. Her relief was evident when the waitress returned with glasses of water and a basket of hot cornbread.

"Thank goodness," she said, reaching into the basket for a piece of bread. "This ought to take the edge off."

David watched silently as Alicia closed her eyes, softly moaning as she bit into the warm cornbread.

"Lord, I am hungry." She wiped some crumbs from around her mouth, grabbed her glass of water, and took a big sip before taking another bite. David imagined that soft moan was what he'd hear when he held her and filled her up. He didn't think she was intentionally trying to be erotic, but the way she slowly chewed the cornbread really turned him on. *How will I wait until Saturday for the chance to kiss her again?*

"Have you been to the crime scene?" Alicia asked after she'd finished her piece of bread.

"Yes, of course. Why?"

"I haven't, and I'd like to go up there and look around. Think you could do a walk-through with me tomorrow?"

"You know, you don't need me to go with you," David said. "I can just let the police know you're going to examine the scene."

"I know, but I'd like you to go with me. I'm interested in hearing your insights about what happened there the night Jake was murdered."

David hesitated. Only a moment ago, she was so concerned about being seen with him in public. "Is that proper?"

"It's not unheard of," Alicia replied casually. "Do you think you could do it tomorrow afternoon?"

With DeLeo and Eddie watching him closely, David was uneasy about escorting Alicia to the crime scene. His action would surely be reported back to them. "Honestly, I think we should be a little more discreet. Why don't you meet me at the Kittle House restaurant after you view the crime scene, and we can discuss it there? It's not far from the Devine cabin. I had lunch there once with Eddie, and they serve gourmet food in an elegant atmosphere. I think you'll like it and it's out of the way. Most people with an interest in the case have already been to the cabin. I'm surprised you haven't been there yet."

"It's been a hectic week. I'd planned on going to the cabin today, but then the press and Jerri happened. And you're right, we should be discreet," Alicia said. "I'll go to the cabin with my investigator and pass on the restaurant. No need for us to meet later. I wouldn't want anyone to think you're sharing your legal strategy with me, or vice versa."

The waitress brought over David's barbecue rib platter and Alicia's beef brisket sandwich with a side of coleslaw. They were both hungry and focused on their plates eating in silence. David was halfway through his platter when his cell phone rang, and he instinctively answered it.

"Oh, hi, Rachel. I'm so sorry, I forgot I promised to come to see you this evening. Can you give me, say, half an hour? I'm just finishing up dinner with a friend. Okay, thanks, I'll see you soon." David put his phone away and explained, "That was my realtor, Rachel. I'm buying a condo and need to sign some paperwork at her office."

"How exciting. Congratulations. Where is the condo?"

"Right here in White Plains. I want to be close to the office."

"Wow, you must be paying a pretty penny for it. Condos in White Plains are expensive."

"I've got some money saved up, and I desperately need a place. I'm tired of living in a hotel and commuting from my spot in Brooklyn was not working. So, I decided to buy myself a home. Real estate is always a good investment, right?"

"True. I didn't know you were staying in a hotel. I can see that getting old real fast. I'm sure you'll be very happy in your new home. White Plains is a great place to live, and you'll be close to work."

"I could still use someone to show me around," David grinned, "I've been so busy working I haven't done much exploring on my own. Know anybody who could help me?"

"Yeah, sure. Maybe after the case is over."

The waitress stopped by their table to check on them, and David asked for the check and to-go boxes.

"Sorry, I've got to wrap this up, but I need to meet with Rachel."

"No problem, I understand. It's not like we had a date or anything." When the waitress brought the to-go boxes, David quickly packaged up his leftover food and placed a fifty-dollar bill on the table to pay the bill.

Alicia pointed at her food. "You go on ahead. I'm going to stay and finish this. Thanks for dinner."

David gave her another smoldering gaze. "I'm glad I bumped into you. Have a good night." He gently caressed her hand before walking to the door. He wanted to kiss her, but he knew it wasn't possible, and he settled for a touch.

Chapter 17

Once David was gone, Alicia chided herself. *Did I just try to get another date with David for tomorrow? What am I doing? I used to work with Kevin on cases; I am not working with David on this case. Why should I care about his insights at the crime scene? Kevin used to be the one who would do a crime scene walk-through with me, never the prosecutor. Thank goodness David thought better of my request and backed out like a gentleman. Like a lawyer with integrity. And here I am allowing my feelings for David to get in the way of being a professional.*

Jealousy ran through her when she heard him say 'Rachel'. *I'm getting jealous over a man who isn't even mine. This is ridiculous. I can't do it. I can't have a secret affair with David and be the best defense attorney for Jerri at the same time. He throws me completely off my game, and Jerri deserves much better. I need to take the same advice I gave Jerri about Bryan; cool it! I will review the crime scene with Diana tomorrow and forget about spending Saturday evening with David.*

Diana offered to pick Alicia up and drive them to the cabin in Katonah the following day. Dressed comfortably in jeans, a white t-shirt, a jean jacket, and sneakers, Alicia was waiting out front when the silver Toyota Camry pulled up and quickly slid into the passenger seat.

"Hey girl, how are you feeling this fine morning?" Diana asked as she put the car in drive and headed toward the highway.

"I'm good. We've got a lot of catching up to do."

"I know, so spill. What's going on with you and David?"

"After he interrogated Jerri on Monday, I met with David privately and told him Billy had lied to the police."

"And where did this private meeting take place?"

"Bear Mountain. I didn't want to risk being seen with him, so I chose an out-of-the-way place. Valerie Upton got wind of my earlier meeting with David at The Smoke House and accused me of wanting the Devine case so I could cozy up to him."

"Which isn't entirely untrue, but, of course, that wasn't the sole reason," Diana chuckled.

Alicia was offended. "That wasn't the reason at all. I took the case to help Jerri Devine because she asked me to. Period."

"Okay, okay. So what else happened at this private meeting?"

"We had dinner afterward at Monteverde. I told him what happened to you and my suspicion that Jake was drugged with the same tranquilizer. I asked him to get the coroner to take a second look at Jake, and again, he agreed. The results should be in soon."

"That's the big payoff for confiding in David?"

"Yes, but the Billy interview didn't go so well." She relayed the prepaid cell phone story. "The good news is if the tox screen shows Jake was drugged, David will have to admit Jerri didn't do it."

"Hmm, I don't know if I reach the same conclusion, but it helps our defense case. Is that it? What else happened at dinner?"

"We talked and got to know one another a little better. David really is a good guy, and he's no longer engaged."

"Girl, I already got that tea off the street. I didn't tell you?"

"No, you didn't, but he did. He also said he's attracted to me."

"And you're attracted to him?" Diana asked. Alicia didn't respond to the question or look at her. "You do realize he's not Kevin, and you don't actually know him. He could use this attraction to gain an advantage over you with this case."

"I know." She turned in her seat and faced Diana. "But I can't help it. I am attracted to him. And he kissed me."

"What?" Diana's head fully turned as she glared at Alicia.

"Keep your eyes on the road." Alicia turned to face the front, gazing through the windshield. "He's a great kisser. It reminded me it's been a long time since I've been with a man and of feelings and needs I've been ignoring. But worst of all, it made me crazy, and those feelings are already throwing me off my game. I want to know more about David and see if this could lead to something, but I won't do anything about it now, even though he wants to."

"Listen, I'm not surprised he wants to pursue you," Diana said. "Why wouldn't he? You're beautiful, intelligent, and successful. But now is not the time. I'm glad you're being sensible because it's a bad idea. You know these things never stay secret for long."

"Yeah, just look at Jerri and Bryan. They thought they were doing something secretly, and it blew up in their faces. Now the whole world knows about it, and a man is dead. I bet if they knew the cost before they had their affair, they wouldn't have ever done it."

"Hindsight is always twenty-twenty, right?"

"Right. Anyway, I'm sure the test will show Jake was drugged. Now we have to tie Billy to the tranquilizers."

Diana shot Alicia a sideways glance. "I've got someone watching Billy today."

Alicia raised her eyebrows. "You do?"

"Yup. Billy followed me, so now I'm tailing him. The storage facility he went to is self-serve, and I've got eyes on him to find out which unit is his next time he makes a visit. Once I find out, I will figure out a way to search the place."

"Even if Billy has the dart gun and vials of the drug, it's still circumstantial evidence. We can't prove that is the weapon used on you and Jake."

"I'll settle for circumstantial. I'm pissed Billy violated me and my home, and I'm pressing charges against him."

"That's your right. Finding those things will also help our case." Alicia paused before saying, "I know you don't agree, but I do hope David will realize Jerri couldn't have drugged Jake and drop the charges against her."

"You have got to stop trying to win David over to our side. Unless we get solid physical evidence or Billy confesses, this case is going to trial. It's not up to David. It's Janice DeLeo's call, and she wants Jerri bad."

"I suppose you're right."

Diana snorted, "Umph, you know I'm right." She turned onto a gravel road with the signpost 'Private Property'. "And we're here."

Two police officers stood guard at the entrance to the cabin's driveway. After showing ID, Alicia and Diana were permitted to drive to the cabin. As the building came into view, Alicia was in awe of the beautiful old stone and wooden farmhouse, surrounded by lush green lawns, wildflower gardens, and manicured fruit trees. "Boy, you weren't kidding. This is not a cabin. This place is amazing."

Diana parked the car in the circular driveway by the front door. They both put latex gloves on, and Diana started narrating as they approached.

"The police report states there was no sign of forced entry, so the perpetrator had a key or was let in the house by Jake."

They walked through the open doorway into a large foyer decorated with a hunting theme. Large buck heads and antique rifles were mounted on hall walls, and forest green carpet led to a large living room. The living room had ornate chairs, and a sofa upholstered in a green vine pattern, facing a large fireplace with an enormous wooden decorative mantel. Over the fireplace hung a large painting of a beautiful black horse, with a gold nameplate underneath "Apollo." Several framed photographs of Jake with a black stallion graced the walls nearby. It didn't look like the type of room anyone ever used. It was all too beautiful and immaculately clean.

They passed through it into the large kitchen, modernized with granite countertops and shiny black appliances. On the other side of the kitchen was a more comfortable-looking great room with sectional dark blue sofas, oversized recliners, and wooden accent tables strategically placed throughout. Large glass windows and French doors led out to the patio, a large swimming pool, and an endless green lawn. Toward the back of the great room was a wooden staircase.

Diana pointed towards the staircase. "Let's go to the bedroom where the body was found."

"The autopsy report stated Jake had bruises under his arms," Alicia said as they climbed the stairs. "After Billy drugged him, he must have dragged Jake to the bedroom and positioned him in the bed."

They entered the bedroom, and there were still drops of blood on the hardwood floors next to the bed. The mattress had large blood stains as well, but the bedding had been removed by the police to be tested and analyzed for blood type and fibers. Alicia tried to visualize the moment when Jerri came in and found Jake's body. There was an evidence marker on the floor near the bed, and Alicia surmised from looking at the crime scene photos it was the spot where they had found the gun.

"Billy would have had to undress Jake before he put him in the bed. When the body was found, he was only wearing boxer shorts. I wonder what he was wearing before that?" Alicia poked her head into the open mahogany wardrobe, rifled through the hanging shirts, and examined the backs of the shoes on the floor. Not a single pair had any sign of scuffing on the back. Concluding her investigation, Alicia whirled around to Diana, who was nosing around a large mahogany dresser across the room.

"Where do you think Jake was when Billy fired the dart at him? The puncture wound was on his upper back, near the left shoulder blade, so he hit him from behind." Alicia asked.

"He was probably down the hall in the media room. There are only two other bedrooms up here, which were untouched."

Alicia followed Diana down the hall to the media room. The media room had light blue walls, an authentic bear skin rug on the floor, and a large white screen opposite the door. All types of electronic equipment were on a giant steel rack on the far wall to the right, and a well-stocked bar and a small refrigerator were over on the left side of the room. Low-back red leather chairs and glass tables were grouped in a couple of areas of the room, and there were horse racing sheets and reels of audio tapes on one of them. Large speakers were mounted in every corner of the room, and a TV projector was aimed at the white screen. Alicia imagined Jake sitting in one of the red leather chairs, watching TV or listening to music when he was drugged. She walked back toward the bedroom slowly, searching for a scuff mark on the hardwood floor along the way as evidence of the dragging.

"He didn't leave any evidence," Diana said. "I know you like to visit crime scenes to try and visualize what happened, but we're dealing with a professional. Before he dragged Jake's body, he would have removed his shoes to ensure there were no scuff marks."

"I'm going to ask Ray what Jake was wearing when he came by for his visit. Whatever shirt Jake was wearing should have a tiny hole in it to prove he got hit with a dart."

They agreed they'd seen enough and walked back out to the car. Alicia looked up at the windows of the house and the surrounding grounds.

Diana said, "Billy probably parked down the driveway a ways and walked up to the house, so Jake wouldn't hear the car engine or see headlights approaching. A guy with his skill could easily pick the lock on the front door."

"Or Billy boldly came and rang the doorbell, and Jake let him in," Alicia said. "Then he waited for the opportunity to shoot Jake while his back was turned. How big is a dart gun? Could he conceal it under his coat?"

"I guess it's possible. The bottom line, we're not going to find anything useful here. We've got to get into Billy's storage unit." Diana went and got into the car. After a few moments of looking around, Alicia joined her, and they drove back to her townhouse. She told Diana she'd meet her at the office later and went into her house alone.

Chapter 18

David scanned his scribbled list of action items as he sipped coffee and indulged in a glazed donut. Today's priority was to fully outline the prosecution's version of the crime, citing motive, means, and opportunity. The evidence seemed clear cut in David's mind, but Alicia's voice echoed in his head, "Your evidence was awfully easy to find."

It was true. The murder weapon, abandoned at the scene with damning fingerprints, painted a clear picture. The incriminating photographs taken, anonymously delivered, laid bare a scandalous affair. Even the surveillance video, showing the SUV leaving and returning to the penthouse parking lot, seemed perfectly staged. However, all these facts could not be overlooked just because they were convenient. Jerri Devine was not a seasoned killer. It was feasible that she would make these mistakes, except for the photographs. The photographs were one of those nagging loose ends that stopped David from being certain Jerri was indeed the killer.

Another nagging loose end was William Whitmore. There was no denying he was a potentially dangerous man. In addition to his military service, Billy had a few years of mercenary work under his belt, paid to assist foreign governments with coups, hostage rescue missions, and other sordid deeds. Behind his façade of a rustic, whiskey-swilling country boy, lurked a trained killer who had the skill to frame someone like Jerri Devine. David refused to be fooled by his act.

Looming over everything was the autopsy report. David expected he'd receive the results of the second toxicology screening today. *If the test proves Detomidine was in Jake's blood, how could Jerri have administered it? And why?*

A forceful, rapid two-tap knock on his office door brought David back into the present. Janice DeLeo stood in his doorway, looking a bit frazzled. Her coat was open, her hair windblown and out of place, and her cheeks were apple red. She waved a manila envelope she was holding. "Good morning. We need to talk. Now."

David got up immediately and followed her down to her office. Janice threw her coat on her desk and shoved the envelope into David's chest. "Why did you request a second tox screen on Jake Devine?"

Calmly, David met her gaze as he took the envelope from her hand. He had anticipated this interrogation. "After reading the full autopsy report again, I wanted the coroner's opinion on what caused the puncture wound on Jake's back and the bruises under his arms. I went to see Dr. Gregg, and he said the bruises indicated the body had been dragged, which means Jake Devine may not have been shot in the bed where the body was found."

"Blood was not found in any other room." Janice gave him a tight-lipped glare.

"True, so then, the question is, why would the body need to be dragged? I asked about the puncture wound, and Dr. Gregg believes it's not prominent enough to be an insect bite. It's possibly from a needle. If Jake was drugged in another room before he was shot, the killer must have dragged the body into the bedroom and staged the scene before shooting."

DeLeo continued to glare at David with cold, steel-blue eyes but didn't have a rebuttal. He continued, "We need to know if Jake Devine was drugged and with what. I believe this is why AK Stone was so anxious to get the full autopsy report. She will use this drugging incident to deflect blame from Jerri Devine and point to another suspect. We need to be prepared to counter that defense."

"That's going to be tough," DeLeo said, softening her gaze, as she turned from David, picked up her coat, and hung it in her small office

155

closet. "Right now, our theory of the crime doesn't include Jerri drugging Jake."

"We're going to have to adapt our theory to include that," David said.

Pursing her lips, DeLeo looked up at the ceiling. "Or ignore it altogether." Focusing on David, she continued. "Personally, I would have preferred not to have this tox screen because I honestly do not wish to address this issue. But I guess if Ms. Stone already suspected drugs were involved, there would have been a follow-up tox screen anyway. Hopefully, it's the only wrinkle in our case." DeLeo walked around the desk and sat behind it. "I say we build the prosecution strategy without mention of the drugging issue. Let the defense bring it up; it's one piece of the penny anny strategy they're devising, and I don't think it has any real bearing on the case."

David hesitated before responding. "Okay, I won't mention it at all."

"I need an outline for our prosecution strategy as soon as possible. We need to work up a witness list, comprehensive evidence list...."

Raising his hand to interrupt her, David said, "I know how to prepare for trial. Isn't that why you hired me?"

DeLeo smirked. "Get out of here, David."

With a nod, David strode out of the office, swinging the envelope at his side. He suspected the results confirmed Jake's drugging, but he craved firsthand confirmation. Once alone seated behind his desk, he pulled the toxicology report out and read, 'a significant amount of Detomidine was detected in the victim's blood.' Further down in the report, it stated that 'reexamination of the puncture wound reveals it is consistent with a wound caused by a tranquilizer dart.' *Alicia will be ecstatic to get this news.* He yearned to call her and hear her voice squealing with joy. A vision of her face danced in his head, igniting memories of their kiss. He hoped Alicia would agree to a private meeting after the gala, but his hope was fading. *It shouldn't take her so long to decide if she feels the same way I do.*

Shaking off the distraction of emotions, he refocused his attention back on DeLeo. Thankfully, she hadn't made the leap of accusing him of colluding with the defense team. His explanation for his actions only made him seem extremely diligent in her eyes for ferreting out details related to the case. But in his mind, his actions were making him less confident Jerri was the person who should be prosecuted. He didn't like DeLeo's idea of ignoring the drugging issue. There was not one conceivable reason why Jerri would drug Jake, drag him to the bed, and then shoot him. It was another loose thread that didn't make sense. And there was the fact Alicia's investigator had been drugged in the same way. Jerri certainly did not do that.

Not wanting to disagree with his new boss on the prosecution strategy David wrested with conflicted loyalty. Winning this case was crucial to his career in Westchester. Yet omitting crucial evidence was wrong. He was confident he could convince a jury of Jerri's guilt with the physical evidence they had. Resigned, he chose to follow orders and plot the prosecution strategy without mentioning the drugging issue. Alicia would likely alert him to any new physical evidence she obtained tying Billy Whitmore to the crime.

Eddie knocked, opened the door, and stuck his head in. "Trial date's been set for December one."

"Great. Come on in for a minute. We'll need to meet this afternoon to work on our case outline. DeLeo said she wanted it as soon as possible. And here," David said, handing Eddie the envelope.

"What's this?" Eddie's eyes widened.

Calmly stroking his mustache, David replied, "The results from the second toxicology screening I requested. Please see to it a copy gets into the discovery file for the defense."

"Sure thing. Anything else?"

"You don't need to discuss those test results with Janice. I just finished discussing it with her."

Eddie looked down and shuffled his feet. "Okay."

"Let's plan on meeting, say two o'clock? Eat a hearty lunch and plan on being here a bit late tonight." David clapped his hands to emphasize his enthusiasm.

Eddie nervously tapped the envelope against his thigh as he turned to leave. "All right, David. See you then."

David leaned back in his chair, rubbing his mustache. *Now, that little rat knows I'm on to him.* Raymond Meeks' dossier was sitting on the corner of his desk. He'd told DeLeo he was looking into him and Billy Whitmore, but he hadn't even cracked the folder open. Determining there was no time like the present, he picked it up and started reading about Jake Devine's older brother.

Chapter 19

Alicia arrived at the office about two hours after her tour with Diana at the crime scene. She was disappointed it hadn't turned up any new information. Determined, she pulled out her Billy Theory notes and reviewed them to see if there was anything she needed to add. It would be the roadmap of the basis for her defense strategy.

o *Jake blows up and cancels rehearsal. Billy stays behind after the rest of the band leaves and overhears Jake's threat to kill Bryan because of his affair with Jerri. Billy decides he must take Jake out to protect his nephew and meal ticket. Since he doesn't approve, he decides to frame Jerri for Jake's murder to get her out of Bryan's life for good. MOTIVE*

o *Billy calls Nate James and tells him to get Connie to fake heart palpitations and take her to the hospital. Nate James calls Billy once Connie is admitted to the ER. Timing of calls matches timing of ER admittance.*

o *Billy books an airline ticket for Bryan, knowing he'll want to see his mother once he hears she's in the hospital. Billy drives Bryan to the airport. This separates Jerri and Bryan and provides Bryan with a solid alibi.*

o *Billy goes out to a pub and enlists the help of a prostitute to create an alibi for himself. WHERE IS SHE NOW?*

o *That night, Billy goes back to the penthouse, using the street entrance to the service elevator, and steals Jerri's gun while she passed out from drinking. He takes the service elevator down to the garage and drives the SUV at midnight to Katonah. He drugs Jake with a tranquilizer dart, drags his body to the bedroom and kills Jake with Jerri's gun, and leaves the gun with Jerri's fingerprints at the scene. Billy places a*

*call to his own prepaid cell phone at one in the morning, faking a call from
Jake giving instructions to bring Jerri and Ray to the cabin in the morning.*

o *He drives the SUV back to the penthouse, leaves via the
street entrance, and hooks up with his prostitute friend again.*

o *After the band interviews, Billy follows and drugs Diana
with the same tranquilizer dart gun and goes through her files to see how
much we know about him and if he's a suspect.*

Alicia seemed satisfied with her timeline of events, except she still
needed to figure out when and how Billy got a hold of Jake's service
elevator key. Billy and Jake did not get along, so he definitely didn't give it
to him. Was there another key around? Maybe Ray has a key Billy could
have taken, copied, and replaced. But when would he have had an
opportunity to do it?

Another point bothered her as she checked the list. Billy would
have been at the cabin at one am, murdering Jake. *Why wouldn't he just use
Jake's cell phone and place a call to himself on his regular cell phone, so
the call would be on the record? It's a glaring oversight for someone
playing puppet master… And did the police ever recover a prepaid cell
phone that belonged to Jake?*

A knock on the door interrupted her thoughts.

Diana entered with a triumphant glint in her eyes. "I got the call. I
know his storage unit number."

"What's the plan? How are you going to get in?"

"I can't tell you, you being an officer of the court and all." Diana
took a seat across from her friend. "Don't panic. It's just a preliminary
look. If I find anything worthwhile, I'll come up with a way to let the cops
find it, so it's all legal and admissible evidence for court."

Alicia eyed her warily, "You're sure?"

"Absolutely. Believe me, I want Billy to go down. I'm not going to mess this up."

"Okay. Please be careful."

"I will." Diana stretched her neck, trying to see the paper on Alicia's desk. "What are you working on there?"

"My Billy Theory Notes. There are a few holes in it I'm trying to plug up. Here, take a look, and tell me what you think." She handed the notes over to Diana and tried to read her facial expressions as she silently read her theory.

"Looks logical to me." Diana handed the notes back to Alicia. "I'm still looking for Lena. Her official address is a flop house for several hos. She'll show up sooner or later."

"Hopefully, before we go to trial. I would love to subpoena Lena and question her about giving Billy an alibi. The real problem with this theory is the service elevator key. How and when did Billy get it?"

Diana looked thoughtful for a moment. "Hmm, that is a tough one. Maybe he made a copy of the original key weeks ago once he found out about Jerri and Bryan's affair? We have to assume Billy took those pictures."

"Possibly. Anyway, I need to meet with Jerri and Ray and let them in on our defense strategy. I imagine Ray will be quite upset to learn Billy killed his brother. I want you and Carlton to be there when I break the news."

"Of course. Let me know when and I'll be there. Anything else you need me to investigate?"

Alicia sighed, "Any news on Teddy Vaughn?"

"No, but we're still looking," Diana said. "Anything else?"

"No. That's all for now. I need to update Carlton on the case. He may have some follow-up items."

Diana nodded as she opened the door to leave. "I'll call you later to let you know if I turn anything up at the storage unit."

Alicia ran through her notes one last time, gearing up for her meeting with Carlton. His door stood ajar as he gave orders to his secretary, Theresa, to arrange a meeting with Bruce Powers. She waited patiently until Theresa emerged and signaled her to go in.

Carlton sat at his desk with several folders stacked before him. "What can I do for you today?" he asked as Alicia strolled in.

"I wanted to give you an update on the Devine case. Is this a bad time?"

"Never. Have a seat."

She handed her notes over to Carlton and sat in a wing chair. "I think it's time to meet with Jerri and Ray and let them in on our defense strategy."

Carlton didn't answer immediately as he was engrossed in reading her Billy Theory. Once he finished, he looked up and said, "I agree. This looks solid. Since we lack physical evidence, do we have strong witness testimony to support this theory?"

"We have Ray, and one of the band members, Walter. I want to subpoena Lena Martin, who gave Billy an alibi and interrogate Billy himself. I'm thinking I get him to agree to testify about receiving the phone call from Jake, and then I turn on him. Declare him a hostile witness and grill him about his part in the murder and hope he confesses right there on the witness stand."

Carlton picked up his pipe and lit it. He puffed a few clouds into the air and said, "That's rather an aggressive strategy, don't you think? If Billy is really the cold-hearted killer you say he is, what could you possibly say to make him crumble?"

"I've riled him up before. I think I could do it again."

"And what if he doesn't crumble? Will our circumstantial evidence be enough to sway the jury?"

Lowering her forehead into her hand, Alicia shook her head. "Honestly, I don't know."

"Well, I need you to be sure," Carlton said. "You need more than hope. If you don't believe it yourself, you certainly will not be able to convince anyone else your theory is the truth."

Looking up at Carlton her eyes widened. "I told you I wasn't ready to take on a case of this magnitude."

"You are." Carlton rose from his chair. He put the pipe down and walked around to sit in the other wing chair across from Alicia. "Listen, you're doing a great job on this case. Formulating this theory is an excellent start, but you've got more work to do. I think making Billy a hostile witness is a brilliant idea, but you need to know what you will say to trigger the proper response. Getting him riled up isn't enough." He paused before asking, "How's it working with Diana?"

"Diana's great, but she's no Kevin. If he were here, we'd have some solid physical evidence by now."

Carlton shrugged. "Maybe, maybe not. There's no use in even thinking along those lines. You're a great criminal defense attorney. You can do this without Kevin."

"Can I?" Alicia's eyes began to well up with tears, but she refused to cry. "I don't feel like I can. The thought of going to trial without all of the evidence I need to win this case is terrifying."

"I know it is, but you have to work through your fear." Carlton took her hands into his own. "You won cases before Kevin entered your life and will win cases now that he is gone. Diana is a reliable investigator, and I can't imagine she is doing anything less than what Kevin would do."

Theresa knocked and entered. "Court clerk just called. The trial date for the Devine case has been set for December first."

"Great, thanks, Theresa." Carlton stood up. "Call Ray Meeks and schedule a meeting for him and Jerri to come in tomorrow at eleven o'clock." Theresa nodded and left the office. Carlton turned his attention back to Alicia. "As I said, you've got a great theory. Let's use the time we have to tighten up our witnesses and evidence. We're going to get Jerri acquitted." He walked back to his desk and handed Alicia her notes. "When we meet with Ray and Jerri, we should be sketchy with the details on why we think Billy is the killer. The news will be upsetting enough, and we don't want to lead them to change their original testimony."

Taking her notes, Alicia grumbled a low "Okay," as she left and returned to her office. On her desk was a manila envelope from the DA's office. She opened it and pulled out the test results from the toxicology report. Upon reading it, she shouted hallelujah!

Chapter 20

The atmosphere crackled with electricity at Burke and Powers the next morning. Everyone employed there knew their big celebrity clients were due to arrive, and folks gussied up, eager to make an impression. Alicia donned her royal blue Dior suit, aiming to project power, but inside, she felt inadequate. She pinned her hopes on Diana's expedition to the storage unit, praying it would unearth the concrete evidence needed to link Billy to the murder, and she'd get the news before Ray and Jerri's scheduled meeting.

One whole week had passed since she started Jerri's case. Kevin used to always stress how critical it was to get crucial information during the first few days of an investigation, while the details of events were still fresh in people's minds and the evidence gathered was untainted. Though she'd made good progress, doubts lingered about her decision to point the finger at Billy. There were still too many holes in her theory, and she was very concerned about Ray's reaction to the news he would receive today. She hoped he wouldn't try to take revenge against Billy before they could solidify their case. She longed for reassurance from Kevin that everything would be all right.

Sitting in her office, Alicia pored over her notes on the Billy Theory for the millionth time when Diana did a quick knock and entered. The gloomy expression on her face told the story before she even opened her mouth. "There wasn't a damn thing in that storage locker. No dart gun, no vials of the tranquilizer."

Alicia's heart sank. "What was in there?"

"He's got a bunch of guns, ammo, old uniforms, and other memorabilia from his tours of duty. I guess he occasionally goes there to remind himself of his old glory days."

"How about photographs or a camera?"

"Nope, no camera and no recent pictures." Diana loudly sighed. "I need to find a way to search his apartment. He must be hiding something there."

"We've got no reason to request a police search of his apartment. Maybe we can link Billy by finding out where he got the tranquilizer. He'd need a veterinarian's cooperation. Start checking around with local vets and see if anything turns up."

"Will do. How are you doing? Are you ready for Ray and Jerri?"

"No, not really, but I see you are ready to see Ray. Nice outfit." Alicia chuckled. "I think this is the first time I've seen your legs in months."

Diana brushed her hands down her black suede skirt, paired with a red turtleneck and a black suede vest. "Glad you like. It's not often I get a chance to show off my fancier attire here in the office. I'm always out in the field, working."

"The entire office is showing out," Alicia laughed. "All we need is a red carpet rolled out from the front door to the conference room. Anyway, let me wrap up a few things before our celebrity client arrives. I'll see you at the meeting."

Diana left Alicia alone with her thoughts. *How is David processing the news of the second toxicology report? With Jake's drugging confirmed, how does it fit into the prosecution's case?* David and DeLeo should be contemplating dropping the charges against Jerri, as it made no sense for her to drug Jake. But until they reached that decision, she had to press on with her theory.

Alicia's attention snapped to the commotion in the hallway. Rising to investigate, several secretaries stopped Jerri, requesting autographs on the old album covers they'd brought.

Alicia strutted down the hall, intent on intervening, but Carlton blocked her path. "Let them have a moment. I think Jerri could use some love from her fans right now."

Ray straggled past the group and greeted Carlton and Alicia. "I hope this meeting won't take too long. I've got a lot on my plate today." Although his dress was dapper as usual, sporting brown slacks and a tweed jacket, he appeared frazzled, with tired eyes and ungroomed hair. Carlton directed Ray to the conference room, where Diana joined them with a few pertinent files for their meeting and set them on the table. As they sat to talk, Alicia lingered by Jerri as she cheerily chatted with her fans and signed autographs. Once she signed the last album cover, Alicia escorted Jerri to the conference room and shut the door.

Jerri tossed aside her wide brim felt hat and sunglasses at the table's end, pointing an accusatory finger at Ray. "You all need to talk to him." Her purple cape over the black catsuit made her look like she had wings as she threw up both arms in a dramatic pose. "He's making me move from the penthouse. My home. This is the last thing I need right now."

"I already told you," Ray grumbled, "It's out of my hands. Someone else in the investment group wants to move in. They have first rights to the penthouse now that Jake is gone. How many times do I need to explain it to you?"

"Alright now, Jerri, please calm down and have a seat," Carlton said. Jerri flopped down in a chair, and Alicia saddled up in a chair beside her. Turning to Ray, Carlton asked, "What's got you so stressed out?"

"Jake's barely cold, and already the vultures are out looking for their piece of flesh. There are pressing business matters for The Devine Music I need to handle immediately if I'm going to stop us from facing a financial crisis." He explained that Jake was part of a real estate investment group that owned the building, and the other partners were eager to buy out Jake's stake in the group and take full ownership, including the penthouse.

"I have plenty of space for Jerri at my place in Sugar Hill. It'll also be easier to protect her there." Ray looked at Carlton, who was gazing at him with a raised eyebrow. "Not to worry, Carlton. Your legal fees for Jerri's case are not in jeopardy. But I've got a million other things I'm negotiating, like contracts for the now-canceled tour that was supposed to happen after the CD dropped. And now Billy is talking about suing me for breach of contract. He wants to sign Bryan with another producer and record label."

"What?" Diana gasped.

"Yeah, and I am defenseless. With Jerri being on trial and unable to travel, we can't perform." Ray put his head in his hands. "I may need another lawyer to help me with Billy's lawsuit."

"We can't release Bryan," Jerri whined. "I need him."

"You may want to rethink continuing to do business with Billy and Bryan," Alicia said as she stood up and began to walk around the table toward Ray. She picked up a folder from the stack on the table. "We have strong reason to believe Billy is the one who killed Jake."

Ray's head shot up as he glared at Alicia. "What? Billy?"

"No, no, no," Jerri said, shaking her head. "You must be mistaken."

"I don't know how thoroughly you checked him out before you started working with him, but Billy is a trained killer." Alicia handed the dossier labeled William J. Whitmore to Ray.

Ray looked down at the folder but didn't open it. "I knew he was ex-military, but a trained killer?" He cracked a grin. "I don't think Billy could plot his way out of a paper bag, let alone plan a murder and pin it on Jerri. What exactly do you have on him?"

Alicia did a double take. Ray was taking the news so calmly. She loosely recounted her Billy Theory, eyeing Ray and Jerri as they listened. As she reached her conclusion, Jerri shook her head in disbelief as Ray's face hardened and his hands knotted up.

Upon standing, Ray slammed his fist down on the table. "That hillbilly bastard. He done messed around with the wrong one this time. You all won't have to worry about bringing him in. I'm going to kill him."

"Calm down, Ray," Carlton said as he stood. "We don't need any vigilante justice now. That's not going to help Jerri beat the murder charge. We need to get Billy to confess or implicate him as a viable suspect in court to have the charges against Jerri dismissed." Carlton placed his hand on Ray's shoulder. "Please, Ray," he said softly, "sit back down."

"But what about Bryan?" Jerri blurted out. "I can still work with him, right? He didn't have anything to do with killing Jake."

"If Billy is talking breach of contract," Alicia said, "we have to assume Bryan wants to go to a new producer and label."

"But he doesn't. I know he doesn't. Just let me talk to him," Jerri said.

Ray slammed his fist on the table. "No. No more talking to Billy or Bryan." Jerri's eyes widened as she stared at Ray. Then she broke down, softly sobbing. Ray gazed at Alicia, standing across the table from him. "You think you can prove Billy is the killer?"

"I know we can cause enough reasonable doubt in the mind of the jurors that they're not certain if Jerri did the crime or not." Alicia put her hands down on the table and leaned closer to Ray. "And if they're not sure, they can't convict her. But we need Billy alive and cooperating with us. I need to get Billy to agree to be on the witness stand. That means you're going to have to deal with him, Ray."

Ray raised an eyebrow. "What do you mean, deal with him?"

"Tell him there's no need to sue for breach of contract because you're willing to let him out of your deal as long as he cooperates with us for Jerri's defense." Ray eyed Alicia as if she had two heads. Standing straight up, she folded her arms across her chest. "Look, you already admitted that when it comes to the lawsuit, you don't have a leg to stand on. So let Billy think he's won the battle. At least that way, he won't file for breach of contract. It'll be one less headache for you."

"Alicia's got a point," Carlton said. "It will also let Billy continue to think he's getting away with his scheme. After all, we're still investigating. We're working with a strong theory but still collecting evidence to solidify our defense strategy."

"You are really asking for a lot here," Ray said. "How am I supposed to work with Billy's treacherous ass, knowing he killed my brother?"

"You can help us prove Jerri's innocence by staying close to Billy," Alicia said. "He may slip up and tell you something meaningful to the case."

"Please, Ray," Carlton said. "Do it for Jerri. Her life is on the line here."

Alicia walked over to Jerri, who continued to sob with her head hanging down. Handing her a few tissues from the box atop the table while gently rubbing Jerri's back, Alicia attempted to help her calm down. "Jerri, we need you and Ray to work together. I know it's difficult, but you must move in with Ray as he's asked. And please, continue to stay away from Bryan."

Ray got up and went to sit next to Jerri. "It's going to be all right, baby girl. Don't worry. We're going to get through this together. Just like we always do."

Jerri looked up at Ray and stifled her tears. "Okay, Ray," she whispered. She placed her arms around his neck, and they embraced one another.

"Alicia," Carlton said, "Why don't you outline our next steps?"

"As you said, we're still investigating. I will need to talk to you both again about the details of events in the days before the crime. We will need to interview some of the band members again and get them to agree to testify on Jerri's behalf. Also, your security team."

"I'm sure I can get them to agree," Ray said.

"A big issue with our theory is the service elevator's key. Ray, do you have a key that perhaps Billy had access to?"

"I have a key, but Billy never had access to it far as I know."

"Where do you keep it?" Diana asked.

"On my key chain with all my other keys." Ray fished a Playboy keyring holding multiple keys from his pants and laid them on the table. "Penthouse keys and my house keys. There's no way Billy could know what key is for what door. And they're always in my pocket."

"We all have come in and laid our keys down on our desks instead of putting them away immediately," Alicia said. "Isn't it possible you could have laid them down somewhere at some point in Billy's presence?"

Ray sighed heavily, "I suppose so, but I couldn't say for sure."

"It's okay," Alicia said. "At least we know it's possible. For right now, that's all we need. Why don't you take Jerri home? Diana and I will be in touch with you later to set up the interviews."

"I want to know one thing," Ray said as he stood holding Jerri. "When are they going to release Jake's body? I want to plan a service for my brother."

"I'll contact the DA about it and get back to you as soon as possible," Alicia replied.

Carlton escorted Jerri and Ray to the exit. Diana collected the files and left the conference room with Alicia, and they headed toward her office. "That got hairy for a minute," Diana said.

"Yes, it did. Thank God Carlton was able to defuse it."

"Do you think Ray will cooperate with us? And Billy?"

"I don't know," Alicia said. "I think you should keep your eyes on Ray for at least the next few days."

"You have plans for tonight?"

"Besides work, no."

"I think we should go to Pearl's."

Chapter 21

It was a chilly evening, and Alicia pulled the collar of her leather coat together, wishing a button was there. Diana found a parking spot on 128th Street, only two blocks from the club, but the howling wind made the walk to Pearl's Supper Club seem longer.

"Good thing it's Thursday," Diana said. "The club shouldn't be too crowded this early. This place gets mobbed on the weekends." From Diana's buoyant mood, Alicia could tell she was excited about seeing Ray.

The club was at the busy intersection of Malcolm X Boulevard and 126th Street. Plenty of folks were hustling up and down the streets of Harlem. Maneuvering through the crowd, they finally reached the club entrance. Pearl's had a large dining room and a bar on the left wall and another bar on the right wall. A large stage was beyond the tables and chairs, half filled with patrons. Over the buzz from the crowd, Marvin Gaye was singing about sexual healing.

"Hey Tisha, is my table available?" Diana asked the hostess, who was tall and dark-skinned, sporting an enormous afro and wearing a flowing kente cloth dress.

Tisha batted her thick eyelashes. "Yeah, I saved it for you. You know the way."

Trailing behind Diana, Alicia said, "Tisha? You're on a first-name basis with the hostess? How often do you come here?"

"I've only been here a few times, but you know me, I'm friendly. Besides, I had to talk to all these people as part of our investigation. How will they open up to me if I'm stuck up and unapproachable?"

"True." They sat at the table, and Alicia took in the rest of the club's eclectic ambiance. After digging in Ray's financial reports earlier that afternoon, she discovered that Ray was one of the three club owners, not solely a regular patron.

The waitress came over with menus, and they both ordered the fried chicken with sweet potato fries and iced tea. Neither of them had time to eat before leaving the office, and Alicia maintained a strict policy to never start drinking on an empty stomach.

"This table has a great view of the stage, and it's close to the bar," Diana said. "The perfect spot. The band should be starting in an hour, around nine."

As they waited for their food, Ray strolled over to their table. "Good evening, ladies. How are you doing tonight?"

"We're good." Diana gave Ray a big smile and squeezed his hand. "How are you doing? I know we laid a lot on you earlier today."

"Yes, but I'm processing it all," Ray said. "The more I think about it, Billy killing Jake makes sense."

"I'm glad you're on board with our plans for Jerri's defense," Alicia said.

"Hey, I trust you guys know what you're doing," Ray replied. "That's why you get paid the big bucks. I've got to make the rounds, greeting our guests. Hope you enjoy your evening." He leaned down and whispered something in Diana's ear as she giggled like a schoolgirl. Then he moved on to another table.

"What was that about?" Alicia asked.

"He's flirting, that's all. Don't worry. I know he's off limits for now."

A tall, light-skinned waitress stood at the bar and kept a burning gaze on Alicia and Diana. Nudging Diana Alicia asked, "The girl at the bar with the red hair, do you know her? She keeps staring at us."

Diana glanced over and said, "I think her name is Ella. She kind of looks like Jerri, doesn't she?"

"Yes, she does."

Their waitress brought their food, and they ate heartily. "Either that chicken was really good," Alicia said, looking down at her plate of bones, "or I was really hungry."

"Or both." Diana laughed. "Now that our tummies are full, how about a drink? I'm going to go to the bar. I can't wait for our waitress any longer. Rum and coke?"

Alicia nodded. Diana went to the bar and ordered. As she stood waiting for their drinks, the redhead appeared at Diana's side, had words with her, then strolled away.

Once Diana returned to the table with their drinks, she said, "That was weird. Ella wants to talk to me in about fifteen minutes when she goes on her break. I asked her what about, but she said later."

"Was she angry or upset?"

"No, just mysterious. I interviewed Ella before about Ray's whereabouts the night of, and she said he was here all night like everyone else did."

"Do you think Ray may have influenced some of his employees to cover for him? You do know he's an owner of this club, don't you?"

"Yes, but he doesn't seem like the type to do that."

"I think your judgment may be a tad clouded when it comes to Ray. You should have told me that he was an owner."

Diana checked her watch. "Well, we will find out what she wants in fifteen minutes."

The club buzzed with activity as more patrons filled the tables. The band members started coming on stage, fine-tuning their instruments, and doing a sound check. Alicia recognized them instantly.

Ray made another round to their table, standing behind Diana, his hands expertly kneading her shoulders. "Hope you ladies enjoyed the food," he said, oozing charm.

"Yes, it was delicious," Alicia said. "Hey, aren't those guys in Jerri's band?"

Ray nodded. "They are now, but I first met them here when they applied for a gig as the Alex Hayes Quartet. They're a great jazz band, and now I manage them. I also offered them the opportunity to work with Jerri, and they jumped on it. They enjoy the extra work and money doing studio work for her. The plan was to have them be Jerri's opening act on tour and back her up during her performance. Save money on expenses."

"But what about Walter and Joe?" Alicia asked.

"They're too old to be touring," Ray said. "They only do studio work now. It's easy enough to find some local horn players on the road. Their part in the music is repetitive and minor."

"Oh, I didn't know." Alicia marveled at the lively crowd. "You've got quite a turnout tonight. At least the controversy with Jerri isn't affecting your business in this place. I don't see how you're having money issues. Diana says this place is packed on the weekends."

Ray shrugged. "Low-profit margins in the nightclub business. We bring in good money, but the expenses are high. I do this because I love it. Being a club owner was always a dream of mine."

"How's Jerri settling in at your place?" Diana asked.

"It's a downsize for her, but she's adjusting." He nodded toward Alicia. "Thanks to you and Carlton. Got to run." He walked off toward the club door, shaking hands and chatting with other patrons who were entering.

A moment later, a young comedian took the microphone, engaging the audience with a few jokes. Then he introduced the band, and the music started. Diana glanced at her watch and kept checking on the bar area. When Ella appeared and gave her a thumbs-up, Diana got up and followed her behind the bar.

Left alone, Alicia sat enjoying the music, pondering the conversation between those two.

When Diana returned, she appeared flustered. "Looks like you may be right. She asked if I was sleeping with Ray. Said he just dumped her, and she blames me."

"What?"

"Yeah." Diana took a long sip of her rum and coke. "I told her I was not sleeping with Ray, but I could tell she didn't believe me. She changed her story about Ray being here all night and now claims she looked for him around midnight, and he was missing for several hours." Diana took another long sip. "Do you think it's true or that she's jealous and wants to make trouble for Ray?"

"I don't know, but if Ray was missing, that's a problem." Alicia noisily slurped her drink till the glass was empty while gazing at Diana with big eyes. "You need to get to the bottom of this." Putting her glass down, she covered her mouth as she yawned. "It's getting late. I will take the train home so you can stay and talk to Ray. See you in the morning."

Chapter 22

The shrill ring of the phone jolted Alicia from a deep sleep. Glancing at the clock glowing 4:30 in red, she answered it.

"They're taking Jerri Devine to the emergency room at New York Presbyterian Hospital." Carlton's voice came through urgently. "Ray found her unconscious."

"Oh no. I'll meet you there. Did you notify the DA's office?"

"I did. See you soon."

With swift movement, Alicia dressed in jeans and a black turtleneck sweater, threw on her leather coat, and ran to the Jeep. Arriving at the hospital in less than an hour she was greeted by a crowd of reporters gathered outside in the parking lot.

"Ms. Stone," one of the reporters shouted, "what can you tell us about Jerri Devine's condition?"

"Nothing. I just got here. We'll make a statement later. Excuse me."

Pushing through the crowd, Alicia entered the emergency room waiting area, where there was another crowd, including police officers and hospital staff. Carlton was speaking with David in a corner, while Ray sat in a chair nearby, holding his head in his hands. She went to Ray's side. "What happened?"

Tears welled in Ray's eyes as he looked up at her. "When I got home after closing the club, dance music blasted from Jerri's room. I asked Chris, my security guy, what was happening, and he told me Jerri said she couldn't sleep. When I went in to see her, she was on the floor. I couldn't wake her, so I called 9ll. They think she's got alcohol poisoning. They're pumping her stomach right now." He put his hands back on his head and leaned down. "God, please don't let her die," he whispered.

Alicia gently rubbed his back. "I'm sure the doctors will do everything they can. Keep the faith."

Carlton motioned for her to follow him to a quieter section of the waiting area.

"Mr. King wants to classify this as a suicide attempt. They want to put Jerri in protective custody."

"Jerri is not suicidal. She has been drinking a lot, but under the circumstances, it's understandable. I'll talk to him." Alicia scanned the area for David but didn't see him. She turned to Carlton, "We may have another problem. It's possible Ray lied about being at the club all night when Jake was killed."

"What? I thought Diana verified Ray's alibi with the staff. When did this come up?"

Alicia recounted her evening at the club with Diana. "Unfortunately, Diana has developed a soft spot for Ray, and it's influencing her investigating work."

Carlton furrowed his brow. "Am I going to have to take her off of this case?"

"No, but I'm going to have a serious talk with her," Alicia said. "It's my fault too. I took Jerri's word Ray couldn't be a suspect. Neither of us looked deeply into his affairs, but now, that will all change."

David walked back into the waiting area. She was about to speak to him when the tall, thin, light-skinned doctor came out.

"Whom am I speaking with regarding Ms. Devine's condition?" the doctor asked.

Ray rose to his feet. "I'm her brother-in-law, the one who brought her in. These are my attorneys." He gestured toward Alicia and Carlton.

"I'm the Westchester County Assistant District Attorney," David said. "Ms. Devine is technically under my custody."

"Okay," the doctor replied. He turned to a nurse and said, "Please clear everyone else out of the waiting room. We have other patients being tended to, and we don't need all this hubbub going on." As the nurse went to usher people out of the waiting room, the doctor said, "Ms. Devine is still unconscious, but we've pumped her stomach to eliminate any excess alcohol and have her on an IV of fluids to rehydrate her system. She should regain consciousness soon. We need to watch her closely for the next twenty-four hours."

"Can she be transported?" David stepped between Carlton and Alicia to get closer to the doctor. "I want her transferred to Westchester Medical Center, where she can be monitored and receive a psychiatric evaluation." The doctor's face distorted with confusion. "Ms. Devine has been indicted for murder and was out on bail. If this was a suicide attempt, her bail would be revoked. If possible, she must be moved within my jurisdiction."

Alicia asked, "Doctor, was there any evidence Jerri ingested anything other than alcohol?"

"She didn't have any food in her stomach, which is probably why she suffered such severe symptoms and passed out. We are doing bloodwork to determine if there was any other substance besides alcohol in her system. We should get those results soon. For now, I recommend she stay here."

"Is she going to be all right?" Ray asked.

"I believe she'll fully recover," the doctor answered. He headed back towards the treatment room. "I'll keep you all posted."

Ray went back to his seat, and Carlton sat beside him. Alicia caught up with David as he made his way to the door. "Hey, can I talk to you?"

Stopping, David gave her his full attention. "Of course. I was going out to make a call to DeLeo. What's up?"

"Jerri is not suicidal. Why are you trying to put her in custody?

"Just doing my job." David waved his cell phone in his hand. "I'm going to hang here until the blood tests are done. What about you?"

"Yes, I'll wait here with Ray for a while. Anyway, you saw the report that Jake was drugged. Why haven't you dropped the charges on Jerri yet?"

Looking down, David replied, "Our version of the crime doesn't include any drugging. The DA has determined it's not relevant. Anything new on Billy?"

Stunned by that news, Alicia vehemently shook her head with a terse look. "No."

Meeting her gaze, David said, "I've been digging a little into The Devine Music's business affairs. There's something fishy going on there."

Alicia sighed. "I'm well aware of the large cash withdrawals to Jake. Apparently, he had a minor gambling problem."

"That explains some of what I uncovered, but there's more." David leaned closer to Alicia's ear. "If you're backed into a corner on Billy, I suggest you look closer at Ray."

Her eyebrows shot up. "What do you mean?"

"Ray may be siphoning off some of The Devine Music's money. He subcontracted quite a bit of work through a secondary management firm, and they've racked up a lot of fees."

"It could be legit. Ray said he was having financial problems due to Jerri's concert tour being canceled."

"Ray owns that other management company." David punched numbers on his phone and put it to his ear as he headed out the door.

Alicia's mouth dropped open, but she couldn't move or speak as she watched him go.

Carlton came up behind Alicia. "I'd heard he looked like Kevin, but the resemblance is uncanny. Are you okay?"

"Yes, I'm good." Alicia turned to face Carlton. "I kind of like that about him."

Carlton frowned. "Not too much, I hope."

Alicia shrugged and went to sit next to Ray as Carlton strolled down the hall. Her temples pulsated as her blood pressure rose, thinking of Diana's carelessness and neglect of her duties. Ray sat, holding his head in his hands. *He couldn't be the killer, could he? Why would he pin the crime on Jerri? He loved his brother and he loves Jerri.* The pain and anguish Ray appeared to be suffering by worrying about Jerri's condition didn't make it seem possible that he would murder his brother and place the blame on her.

Carlton returned to say he was leaving. "Hang in there, Ray. I'm sure Jerri's going to be fine. Call me with any updates, okay?" Carlton signaled to Alicia with his eyes he needed a word with her in private. "Tell the press Jerri's suffering from exhaustion, will you?"

With a nod, Alicia shook his hand, and he departed. She reached for her cell phone to call Diana when Bryan came rushing into the waiting area.

"Where is she? Can I see her? Is she going to be okay?" Dressed in denim with a bad case of bed head, Bryan was visibly distressed.

Ray jumped up, confronting Bryan. "What are you doing here?"

Bryan's concern was palpable. "It's all over the news that Jerri got rushed to the hospital. What happened? Is she all right?"

Alicia stepped between the two men, relaying the doctor's prognosis to Bryan. "The doctor believes she'll be fine, but Ray is right,

Bryan. You shouldn't be here. I'll call you and update you on her condition when I know more."

Brian smirked. "Oh yeah, like you called me to let me know she was in here?"

Before Alicia could respond, the doctor returned to the waiting room and announced, "Good news. Ms. Devine is awake. She's asking to see Ray."

"Thank God," Ray said, following the doctor toward the treatment room.

"Tell her I'm here," Bryan called out. Ray turned back and gave him a glare that said he would do no such thing.

The doctor returned shortly and asked Alicia, "Where's the guy from the district attorney's office? I've got the results of the blood tests."

"He's outside making a phone call."

"Please inform him that no other drugs were found in Ms. Devine's system. I strongly recommend she remain here rather than moving her to another hospital right now."

"Thank you, doctor. I'll let him know," Alicia replied before turning her attention back to Bryan. "You really should leave now. I promise I will call you later and let you know how Jerri is doing."

Anguish oozed through Bryan's voice. "You don't understand how much I love her, and she loves me. Jerri needs me right now. None of this would have happened if you hadn't ordered her to stay away from me. I make her happy. I keep her sane."

Alicia guided Bryan to a seat in the corner of the waiting room. She acknowledged the pain churning in his sea-blue eyes by squeezing his hand. "I understand how you feel, and I know it's difficult, but if you truly love Jerri, you'll do what's best for her right now. We can't have nurses and other hospital staff watch you fawning over her. It will start another scandal like the newspaper photo did. We just clarified your relationship with the media. Please don't muddy the waters now." Bryan broke their eye contact and looked down at his own wringing hands. Alicia continued to plead with him. "Jerri will be home in a day or so. I'll arrange for you to see her in private." She gave his hand another squeeze.

Bryan glanced at her. "You promise?"

"I promise."

Reluctantly, Bryan rose, slightly hunched over, and slowly departed.

Swiftly dialing Diana's number, Alicia arranged a meeting at the office.

As she headed toward the exit, David returned. "You leaving?"

"Yes, Jerri's awake, and Ray's with her now. The blood tests were negative for any substances beyond alcohol, and the doctor said she should stay here. I've got to get into the office and do some follow-up on a tip I received." Her gaze caught David's eyes scanning the room. "If you're looking for Carlton, he's gone."

David looked into her eyes. "Are we meeting on Saturday? I've made plans for us. Monteverde at nine."

Smiling, Alicia replied, "I'll see you at the gala," and left him standing there.

Outside, she faced the reporters with a reassuring announcement. "You all will be happy to know Ms. Devine will be fine. She's been under tremendous stress and collapsed due to neglecting her health and sheer exhaustion. That's all for now. Thank you."

Ignoring the clamor of questions, Alicia strode to her jeep and drove home. After a quick shower, she changed into a black Jones New York pantsuit and headed to the office, stopping at her favorite deli for a grilled chicken Caesar salad on the way.

Diana was seated in Alicia's office reading a newspaper when she arrived, clad in her navy Dickies, a white thermal shirt, and a red down vest. "Hey, girl. How's Jerri doing?"

"Thankfully, she'll live." Alicia settled down behind her desk. "The doctor said they'll release her tomorrow morning if all goes well. Meanwhile, we've got a trial date set, so we need to develop a comprehensive strategy to cover our bases. Starting with Ray." Alicia gave Diana a stern look with a firm tone. "No more kid gloves with Ray. I know you like him, but he's a suspect now. Did you talk to him after I left last night?"

"Yes. Ray denied having a relationship with Ella. Said they messed around on occasion, but it was never anything serious. Why are you saying he's a suspect?"

"On top of Ella's revelation, it's possible that Ray may be pilfering money from The Devine Music."

Diana's face twisted up. "Where did you hear that?"

"From David at the hospital this morning. We need to do a deeper dive into The Devine Music's financials and Ray's personal finances today. Did you ever find Teddy Vaughn?"

"Tracked him down last night in Biloxi, Mississippi." Diana sighed. "Teddy's been dead for about ten years. My girl, Parker, talked to his mother on the phone. We verified with the Biloxi police that Teddy was found beaten to death behind a juke joint not far from her home. No one was ever arrested for the crime. It's a cold case."

"That's not good. Jake and Ray probably killed him and Ray lied about it. Did Parker find anything suspicious in the fan mail?"

"Nope. There were a few crazy emails, of course, calling Jerri a demon and other unseemly things, but no one made a direct threat toward Jerri or Jake."

Alicia opened her salad and offered some to Diana, who declined. "I already ate. I'll have Parker start pulling together Ray's financials and check in with you later," Diana said as she left Alicia's office looking somber.

As Alicia savored her meal, she jotted down the loose ends she intended to tie up. The weekend was already booked with the gala tomorrow, and she refused to miss two Sundays in a row with her sister Faith, which meant the interviews with Billy, Walter, Matt the drummer, and the security guys would have to be scheduled for Monday. Determined to crack Billy during a mock court session, Alicia planned to grill each of them as if they were on the witness stand, giving testimony. By Monday, with Jerri resting at home, Ray shouldn't have any excuses for not bringing them to her office. Alicia made a mental note to grill Ray, too. She guessed there was no news on Lena Martin's whereabouts since Diana didn't mention her, but Alicia still intended to get Lena subpoenaed.

Once her stomach was satisfied, Alicia leaned back in her chair, and thoughts of David floated to the top of her mind. *How presumptuous was he? To make plans for us at Monteverde? I never agreed to meet with him after the gala.* Envisioning his face, the warm, deep brown eyes and inviting smile, warmth flowed up through her body as she relived the feel of his hands and his lips. The desire to wow him at the gala surged. *What should I wear? Presumption be damned.* Charlotte E. Ray's eyes pierced her from the picture frame on her desk, and sanity rushed back in. "I know," she said to Charlotte, "I can't."

Interrupting her reverie, Diana knocked and entered with a pile of papers. "Here, you start with Ray's finances, and I'll review The Devine Music's." She plopped half of the stack on Alicia's desk and sat in the chair across from her. They both got down to work.

After an hour of pouring over documents, Alicia was blurry-eyed. "Find anything interesting yet?"

"Many of the expenses incurred by The Devine Music over the last year were from professional fee charges from the Covington Management Corporation. But there's no description of what those fees were for. What about you?" Diana responded.

Alicia said, "Ray has been receiving income from Covington. This must be what David was alluding to. We need to verify Ray owns Covington."

Diana rubbed her eyes and yawned. "The only other item of note was a large cash disbursement to Jason Meeks about five years ago. Three million dollars. That's a lot more than the routine withdrawals of a few thousand dollars that we know he was gambling away. We will need to get details on his finances to determine what Jake did with that money. I'll get Parker on it. This weekend, I'll be going around to veterinarians showing Billy's picture."

Chapter 23

Saturday morning dawned with rain drumming against Alicia's windowsill, rousing her from slumber. With a heavy sigh, she pushed herself upright. Feeling the weight of exhaustion clinging to her limbs, she collapsed back down onto the mattress. Mercifully, no work was on the agenda, just preparations for the upcoming gala, granting her the luxury of lingering in bed a while longer. Her earliest appointment was at ten for a manicure and pedicure, followed by a hair styling session at one. As she lay there, her mind drifted to David, envisioning an evening in his company. After allowing herself an hour of reverie, she rose from the bed, determined to refocus her thoughts, and made fresh coffee to accompany her prayer time.

Recharged with the scripture, she went to her special closet in the guest room that housed her elegant gowns and cocktail dresses. Hanging in clear plastic wrapping was the golden Calvin Klein halter dress she'd impulsively purchased during a recent shopping trip with her sister. Peeling away the plastic wrap, she ran her hand over the soft, satin bodice. The skirt flared from the waistband with an intricate star pattern that hit her right below the knee.

Faith had oohed and aahed when Alicia emerged from the fitting room of Nordstrom's. "That dress looks amazing on you. What a showstopper!"

Alicia felt like a supermodel wearing it and knew she had to have it, but until now, there'd been no occasion to show it off. Her instincts said tonight was the night for that stunning dress paired with a white satin wrap. Next, she chose the perfect gold Jimmy Cho lace-up high-heeled sandals and a gold and white Coach evening bag to complete her outfit. *David will fall out of his chair when he sees me tonight. How will I tell him there will be no date at Monteverde?*

In the kitchen she prepared a simple breakfast of yogurt and fruit, unable to keep her mind off of the case. *Why did David even bother to check Ray's finances if he planned on prosecuting Jerri? Is he being influenced by that second tox screen after all?* The new evidence surfacing around Ray added to her confusion. *He was amused when I first told him Billy killed Jake. Was it because he knew Billy was innocent? Maybe, like DeLeo, I've rushed to judgment on who the killer is.* To clear her mind, she grabbed a legal pad and wrote some questions to ask during the witness interviews on Monday.

The rain ceased by the time Alicia left the house for her nail appointment. She relaxed and enjoyed all the pampering at the salon she received from Mei, her nail technician, and later from Glenda, the hairstylist. The finger wave hairstyle Glenda gave her elevated her classic look, and once her makeup was done, she'd be the cat's meow. It was already three o'clock when she returned home, and the car service was due to pick her up at five. A message on her answering machine from Carlton, saying Jerri had been released from the hospital provided much needed good news amidst the chaos of the Devine case. After a light salad to stave off hunger, she readied herself for her debut as the new and improved AK Stone.

The black Lincoln town car pulled up promptly at her townhouse at five, and Alicia strutted out to the car looking and feeling fabulous. Upon arriving at the country club, her driver navigated through the line of cars creeping along the circular driveway, dropping guests at the grand entrance of the sprawling gray brick building. With assistance from the doorman, she stepped out of the vehicle and entered the large ballroom to find the gala already in full swing.

Elegant glass chandeliers cast a soft glow overhead, illuminating round cocktail tables around the room's perimeter. Guests mingled amongst the tables draped in white cloths with brilliant bouquets of colorful flowers atop them. Light classical music piped softly into the air.

As Alicia searched for a familiar face, a waiter offered her a flute of champagne from his tray, and she accepted. Spotting Carlton dressed in a black tuxedo, conversing with two gentlemen toward the back of the room, she made her way over.

Carlton abruptly stopped speaking when Alicia approached. "My dear, don't you look stunning this evening. Gentlemen, please meet one of our prominent attorneys, AK Stone."

The tall, slender white man with salt and pepper hair extended his hand first. "Judge Roger Perry. So pleased to meet you. Carlton has been singing your praises."

"Yes, he has." The shorter dark-skinned man who was balding and had a pooch of a belly, grabbed Alicia's hand, and stroked it. "What he didn't say was how captivating you are. It's a pleasure to meet you. I'm Judge Tyler Jackson." Judge Jackson's eyes roved over Alicia's entire body and settled on her bosom as if she'd been stripped naked under his gaze.

"The pleasure is all mine, your Honors." Alicia politely slid her hand from his grip and sipped her champagne while glancing around the room, looking for an out from Judge Jackson's ogling eyes.

"Carlton says you're handling Jerri Devine's defense." Judge Jackson's eyes slowly rose to meet Alicia's, and he winked. "That's quite a responsibility he's placed on your shoulders. I have an extensive criminal law background. Perhaps I can give you a few pointers."

Carlton chuckled. "Oh, that won't be necessary. She already has me acting as her co-counsel. Besides, this isn't her first rodeo, you know."

"You've made certain both of us are aware of it," Judge Perry said. "Good luck with the case, Ms. Stone."

"Thank you. Will you gentlemen excuse me? I see an old college friend who just arrived." Alicia quickly shook both judges' hands. "It was so nice meeting you both. Enjoy the evening."

"You as well, my dear," Judge Jackson said. "Perhaps you'll save me a dance later."

Not on your life. Alicia turned and walked into the crowd. Snagging a mini crab cake from a passing waiter, she popped it into her mouth and washed it down with the remainder of her champagne. Open glass doors at the back of the ballroom provided access to an outdoor terrace. Alicia stepped out to get some fresh air and found David standing a few feet away, staring pensively over an expansive green lawn. Her face flushed as a smile blossomed on her lips. *He looks positively scrumptious in his black tuxedo and red bowtie.* His face lit up as he turned and caught her gaze, immediately stepping in her direction.

"David, there you are." Janice DeLeo cut through the moment, approaching him from the other end of the terrace. David turned away to greet his boss, wearing a sleek black sheath dress with pearls around her neck and black Louboutin heels. DeLeo spoke too low for Alicia to catch her words as she looped her arm into David's and led him back into the ballroom.

Suddenly self-conscious, Alicia's eyes darted around the terrace to see if anyone else noticed what had just happened. *DeLeo wants to show off her latest acquisition and star of her latest big case. She'll probably keep David occupied all evening. It's all for the best. We shouldn't be seen ogling one another at this event anyway.*

"Boo hoo. Rendezvous spoiled." With an evil giggle, Valerie Upton emerged from the shadows of the terrace waving a half-filled champagne flute. Regally dressed in an apple-red, form-fitting Dior gown, Valerie's face bore a wicked grin. Alicia's body stiffened as she approached and whispered into Alicia's ear. "You shouldn't be so obviously smitten my dear. It has people talking."

Stepping away, Alicia replied, "The only person talking is you, because you have a vivid imagination, Valerie. Nothing is going on between me and David King."

Valerie smirked. "But you wish there was, don't you? A chance to relive your fairy tale romance with Kevin." A cackle of laughter fell from her painted-red lips.

"I'm not going to have this discussion with you," Alicia replied, striding into the ballroom through the glass doors. Flushed with heat, she mingled with the crowd, attempting to lose herself.

A light tap on her shoulder startled her. "Hi, Alicia."

Turning, Alica came face to face with Margaret Brice, another attorney from her firm. Margaret and Alicia had worked together under Valerie Upton in the matrimonial law division. Margaret became a mentor and friend to Alicia as she tried to get up to speed in the new area of the practice. Short, squat, and chocolate-toned, Margaret's flowery, flowy red and white sundress paired with a red bolero jacket, covered all the curves of her large figure. Long black curls fell around her round face.

Alicia hugged Margaret. "How are you? I haven't seen you around the office much lately. Everything okay with you?"

"Yes," Margaret laughed. "I know you're busy working on your big case. And I know you don't want to run into Valerie's bitchy ass if you don't have to, but I'm doing fine. You know, staying busy. Val's got me working on two cases right now but thank goodness only one of them is messy. We sure do miss you down in divorce court."

"I miss you too," Alicia said, "but definitely not Valerie. At least you've still got James on your side." She was referring to James Robinson, another divorce attorney and elder statesman of Burke and Powers at the age of eighty. Always dressed in a tweed jacket and a bow tie, with a kind word for everyone, James refused to retire. He didn't appear in court anymore, but he was still one hell of an advisor and researcher.

"Yes," Margaret said. "Thank God for James." She wiggled her empty flute glass around in the air. "I could use another one of these. How 'bout you?"

Alicia acquiesced and followed Margaret further into the ballroom. It only took a moment for a waiter to pass by with a champagne tray. As they each grabbed a glass, a loud gaggle of laughter pierced through the crowd's chatter. It was Janice DeLeo laughing loudly as David entertained her and her husband, alongside two other couples, with a story. Gesturing wildly with his hands and smiling as he spoke he had his audience captivated and at the story's conclusion, the group roared with laughter once again. Unexpectedly, David looked Alicia's way. Gripped her with his eyes.

"How is it, going up against David King?" Margaret asked as she sipped her drink. "I can't get over how much he looks like Kevin. Is that weird for you?"

Tearing her eyes away from David's, Alicia focused on Margaret. "It was at first, but I've gotten used to it. I don't see him often anyway."

"Well, that will change once you go to trial. You don't think his looks will distract or disarm you in court?"

"Nope. I won't let it. Jerri Devine is innocent, and I'm going to get her off."

Margaret tipped her glass to clink against Alicia's. "You get 'em, girl."

David broke away from the group and strolled toward Alicia as a tall, light-skinned man came up behind Margaret and lightly touched her arm.

Margaret turned and squealed with delight. "Thomas, how good to see you."

Thomas bent to kiss Margaret on the cheek. "Hi, beautiful. How are you doing?"

As Margaret introduced Thomas to Alicia, David joined their group. "How's everyone doing this evening? David King." Extending his hand to Thomas and Margaret, he greeted them with a warm smile before turning his attention to Alicia. "Counselor, you're looking lovely this evening."

Alicia's skin burned under David's gaze. "Thank you. I see you've been busy entertaining the troops. Whatever that story was, I must hear it. I didn't know DeLeo had such a ferocious laugh." Margaret and Thomas drifted away, engrossed in their own conversation.

"Neither did I." David chuckled, grabbing a glass of champagne from a passing tray. "Care to get a little air outside?" Alicia nodded and followed him out onto the terrace. Standing on opposite sides of a round topiary bush next to the low stone pillar fence surrounding the terrace, they gazed at each other while sipping their champagne.

"Mm, Ms. Stone, you look like a golden goddess," David said in a low, husky tone. "Please tell me you're going to meet me later."

Alicia was busy drinking him in as he attempted to sound pitiful. His tux was barely holding in his biceps as he lifted the flute to his mouth. His lips were wet with champagne, and she wanted to drain them dry with her own. "I would like to but…"

"There he is. David King, my man." The booming voice interrupted the moment, redirecting their attention to a tall, thin, chestnut-

194

colored man in a black tuxedo waving his arm as he strode in their direction. He had a young lady on his other arm, dressed in a silk fuchsia pink mini dress with off-the-shoulder sleeves. David turned and waved back at the man. "Judge Harrington." He quickly turned back to Alicia and said, "Excuse me," then hustled to greet the judge.

Alicia guessed the woman on the elder Judge Harrington's arm was his daughter because she appeared too young to be his wife, though some men skewed that way. Once they were only a few feet away, she recognized her from the newspaper photo, and David confirmed her suspicion when he said, "Hello, Elizabeth," as he bent to kiss her on the cheek. Alicia turned to walk back into the ballroom because she didn't want to catch more of the conversation. Seeing the way Elizabeth was dressed, accompanying her father to a boring gala, Alicia deduced she must want David back.

As a waiter walked by with a tray of grilled lamb chops, Alicia snatched a small plate from it. Moving through the crowd, she found an empty table against the wall and set down her glass and plate. Tears stung her eyes as she bit into the lamb chop, heat rising from her feet to her hair. Her heart pounded in her chest. *Why am I so angry about Elizabeth showing up? I have no claim to David.* After all, she was about to tell him she would not meet him later before they were abruptly interrupted. She viciously attacked the lamb chop, cleaning the meat from the bone, and downed the remainder of her champagne. *I guess he'll be taking her to Monteverde's tonight.* While dabbing her mouth clean with a napkin, Carlton with his wife on his arm, approached her table, and she plastered on her fake smile.

Chapter 24

As David spun around, his eyes shot wide open. Elizabeth, standing next to her father caught him off guard. *What in the world is she doing here? She always hated coming to functions like this.* He firmly shook hands with the judge and greeted Elizabeth with a soft peck on the cheek.

"David, wonderful to see you." Judge Harrington beamed with delight. "I couldn't miss this opportunity to celebrate your new career in Westchester. I've been hearing nothing but great things about the work you're doing up here. You've already got Jerri Devine on the ropes. So proud of you, my man."

"Yes, me too," Elizabeth grinned. "You look fantastic. Must be all this fresh air."

"Yeah, must be," David replied. "You look great, too. Guess being in love agrees with you."

"Hmm, not so much," Elizabeth said. "But we'll talk about that later."

"Yes, later," Judge Harrington said. "Let's get some champagne to toast this young man." He lifted his hand to beckon a waiter, and they each took a fluted glass from the tray. "To Mr. Assistant District Attorney David King. Long may he reign." They all lifted their glasses to clink and sipped their wine.

David cleared his throat. "I must say, sir, I'm surprised to see you here. This is sort of far out of your territory, isn't it?"

"Nonsense. I keep my finger on the pulse of all the happenings in the tri-state area. And I haven't spoken to you in some time." The judge glanced at his daughter. "When I heard the ABA was having a gala tonight, I said this is the perfect time to catch up with you."

"And I agreed with him." Elizabeth smiled, batting her eyelashes. "I always knew you would do great things, David."

David had to admit Elizabeth looked smashing. The dress bodice dipped just enough to show ample cleavage, and the way her long locks of curly black hair flowed down and bounced around her breasts was incredibly sexy. But he knew the hair and the boobs were fake, as well as the eyelashes she kept batting at him and the glittering white teeth in her mouth.

"Thank you. But I must ask, what brings you out this evening, Elizabeth? I know you don't like attending these kinds of events. Is Stephen out of town on business?" David put a particular emphasis on his name.

"No, Stephen and I are no longer a couple. I thought you might like to know." She continued to smile and bat her eyelashes as she gazed at him.

Judge Harrington placed his hand on David's shoulder. "You were always like a son to me. I think this breakup between Elizabeth and Stephen is the perfect opportunity for you two to reconnect. I never understood why you ended the engagement."

"Because Elizabeth said she was in love with someone else, sir. I think you know that." David tried not to get agitated with his mentor, but he couldn't believe the man was feigning ignorance.

Judge Harrington smiled. "Well, now, she sees the error of her ways. Don't you, dear?"

Elizabeth stroked David's arm and drew nearer. "I do. I don't know what that was with Stephen, but it wasn't love. Not like the real love we shared."

The judge added, "You know, I always wanted you to be a part of our family."

David put his hand over Elizabeth's and gently slid it away from his arm. "I am so flattered the two of you drove all this way to congratulate me, but I'm sorry. I'm going to have to decline your offer. You see, I am starting a new life here. As a matter of fact, I just purchased a condo in White Plains, and I am swamped with work, so I won't have time for fun and games with you. Judge, it's been great seeing you. Now if you'll excuse me." Abruptly, David turned away to return to the terrace's low stone pillar fence, praying Alicia was still there.

How dare Elizabeth come here thinking all she has to do is bat her eyes and smile to get me back. Did she really think it would be so easy? Once outside, David took a deep breath and began stroking his mustache. *The nerve of her. And Judge Harrington. How could he go along with her cockamamie plan?* Bending to grip the fence with both hands, David took another deep breath, to stop his blood pressure from rising further. Alicia was nowhere in sight, and he turned to view the crowd mingling in the ballroom. He didn't want to go back in there, but he had to find Alicia. Checking his watch, it was still early. Silently, he sent up a prayer that she had not left the gala and strolled inside through the open glass doors.

After a moment, David spotted Alicia amidst a cluster of people, her laughter mingling with the group's chatter as she enjoyed her champagne. A tall, rotund, dark-skinned man animatedly held court, captivating his listeners with a tale. David edged close enough to listen in, aiming to get her attention so they could discuss this evening's plan. He stared, admiring her beauty while waiting to catch her eye until finally, she acknowledged him with a nod. She wriggled herself away from the group to join David's side.

Locking eyes with her, David spoke with intensity. "Counselor, may I have a word with you outside?"

Alicia walked out to the terrace with David following closely behind, admiring her backside sway. Once they reached the fence, Alicia spun around to face him.

"Is the engagement back on?" She smirked as she sipped her champagne.

"No, absolutely not."

"But that was Elizabeth, wasn't it?"

"It was. It was very nice of her and her father to come here to congratulate me, but that's all it was. I'm sorry we got interrupted earlier. I just didn't want things to get awkward."

"Well, we must keep up appearances, mustn't we?"

"Not once we leave here." He stepped close enough to her to smell her sweet scent as he gazed into her eyes. "You are going to meet me later, aren't you? I can't tell you or show you how amazing you look tonight or what it's doing to me. You did wear this for me, didn't you?"

Alicia blushed as she giggled. "Not exactly. But I'm glad you appreciate my efforts. It took all day to get this glamourous."

"I bet undoing it won't take long." The prospect of getting alone and naked with her made him warm in his tuxedo and his manhood stiff.

Her eyebrow arched. "Is that what you had in mind?"

"After a sumptuous meal specially prepared for the two of us in our private suite, yes. That's exactly what I have in mind. How else will we get to know each other better?"

She eyed him warily while draining her champagne flute and handed him the empty glass. "Sounds tantalizing. I'll be there." Tightening her grasp on her wrap, she waltzed back into the ballroom.

David's eyes followed her back into the room. He wanted to shout YES and jump for joy, but he kept composed and searched for somewhere to place the empty flute. As a waiter passed by, he put the empty glass on the tray in exchange for a full one. He toasted himself in the air and strolled back into the ballroom. No sooner did his foot get in the door did he run into DeLeo.

"There you are," she said. "I've got someone else I want to introduce you to."

David followed her to a group of men, but he tuned out after the first introduction to Senator Gray. All he could think of was Alicia and the evening ahead. He couldn't stop smiling. Elated, he pretended to care what anyone was saying.

The room fell silent as flatware clinked against glass, commanding attention. A stout white man in a black tuxedo with a full head of white hair stood on a rise behind a small podium on the right-hand wall.

"Good evening, ladies and gentlemen. My name is Richard Gardner, and I am the president of the Westchester branch of the American Bar Association. I want to thank you all for attending our gala this evening. I hope you all are enjoying yourselves. I would like to take a moment to acknowledge some of our distinguished guests and allow some of our judges who are running for reelection this year to say a few words."

David groaned inside as the speeches started. Amidst the crowd, he sought a glimpse of Alicia. Instead, he spotted Judge Harrington and Elizabeth heading for the exit. Relief washed over him. They would not be accosting him again tonight. Continuing to gaze around, his eyes connected with Alicia's. He winked and chuckled softly to himself as she shook her head and looked away. *She looks so cute, pretending to care what this blowfish judge is saying.*

Glancing at his watch, it was almost seven-thirty. Once all the speeches were done, the crowd would dissipate, and he and Alicia could escape. He assumed she'd hired a car for the evening and wouldn't have any problem getting there since she said she lived in the area. Unable to inspect the room in person, he questioned whether it would be as elegant as it appeared in the pictures on the website. At least the food they served at the inn was excellent. It had been a bold move for him to plan their rendezvous without first getting her permission, but he was fairly certain she experienced the heat of his kiss. Soon, he would bestow more on her. His body tingled with anticipation, wanting to hold her, kiss her, and so much more. People around him broke out into laughter, and he guessed the little old lady speaking now had made a joke. He couldn't focus on anything being said. It all sounded like gibberish in his ears. Shifting his weight from one foot to the other, he clapped lightly when appropriate, and smiled, waiting for the gala to end, his mind solely on how he would pleasure Alicia tonight.

Finally, Richard Gardner retook the podium and gave his closing remarks. David said his goodnights to Janice DeLeo and her husband and made his way to the door. He wanted to arrive at Monteverde's before Alicia so he would be there to greet her. While Alicia was engrossed in conversation, he made a beeline for the valet to retrieve his car and depart before the exodus of guests flooded the exit.

As he drove up the parkway to Monteverde's, David couldn't shake off the audacity of Elizabeth's actions. The memory of that fateful night was seared into his mind. She'd come home late, smelling of cognac and an unknown musky cologne. He was working in the study as she stumbled through the front door. When he approached the doorway, she fell into his arms and said, "I think I'm going to be sick." He carried her to the powder room, placed her beside the toilet, and held her long tresses behind her neck as she wretched into the bowl. Elizabeth coughed and gagged and wretched some more. David wet a washcloth with cold water and wiped her face once it seemed she was done. He lifted her off the floor, carried her to their bedroom, and laid her gently on the bed.

She sat up as he removed her shoes, shouting, "I can't do this anymore." David dropped her stilettos and reached under her emerald green dress to remove her pantyhose. Elizabeth hit him repeatedly on the arms, yelling, "Stop. Stop. I want you to listen to me."

"Elizabeth, you're drunk. You need to sleep it off." David finished removing her pantyhose and stood by the side of the bed.

"No, I can't do this anymore." Sniffling, she whimpered. "Do you want to know why I'm drunk? Do you?"

"Not really, but I guess you're going to tell me anyway."

"Because I didn't want to come home to you."

David smirked as he leaned down over her. "And where did you want to go? To another party?"

"No. I wanted to stay in bed with Stephen."

David's head jerked up, and he stood frozen. "What?"

"I don't love you anymore. I'm in love with Stephen, and I wanted to stay in his bed." Elizabeth fell back flat on the mattress. "I'm sorry," fell softly from her lips as she closed her eyes, drooling on the bedspread.

"Who the hell is Stephen? What the hell are you talking about?" David leaned over and patted her on the cheek. "Elizabeth, what are you talking about?" But she wouldn't answer him. Shaking her head, she turned her face away with her eyes closed. Furious and bewildered, he retreated to the study.

The GPS told him to make the next left turn, and David slowed and slid into the left lane. As he approached the traffic light, Beyoncé's voice blared from the radio, "Got me looking so crazy right now," and he turned the volume up.

"No more crazy for me," he declared and joined in singing along with Beyoncé, "Uh oh, uh oh, uh oh, oh, no, no."

It was a little before nine when he pulled into the inn's parking lot, anticipation humming in his veins. When the black town car pulled into the lot, he stepped out, ready to greet Alicia. With a peck on her cheek, he gently took her hand and led her to the entrance, his pulse quickening at her presence. "Thank you for meeting me here."

"From what you said earlier, it looks like the pleasure will be all mine." She giggled as she glimpsed up at him.

Once inside, David checked in with the concierge to secure the keys to their suite. Taking Alicia by the hand, he said, "Right this way." He guided Alicia up one flight of the carpeted stairway to Suite Two, his excitement heightened.

Entering the suite, they were greeted by a cozy sitting area with two plush beige loveseats accented with small square green and gold pillows, each set across from one another. A glass coffee table adorned with a bouquet of fall-colored mums sat in the center. Beyond the sitting area, the drawn-back brocade green curtains exposed a wall of windows. Positioned directly in front of the windows, a round, white-clothed table set for two, allowing the diners to enjoy the glorious view of the Hudson River and a lit Bear Mountain Bridge. A fireplace was on the right-hand wall, filled with logs waiting to be lit.

David was impressed with the room, and from the expression on Alicia's face, she was too. "This is pretty spectacular, isn't it?"

"It's amazing." Alicia handed David her wrap and headed towards the windows.

"Dinner will be arriving shortly. I hope you're hungry." David laid the wrap on one of the loveseats and stepped behind her to take in the view. Gently rubbing her arms with his hands, smelling her sweet fragrance, his heart was pounding, and he hoped she couldn't hear it.

"I'm starved. I don't know why I thought the gala would be more of a sit-down dinner." Alicia turned around to face him, and he wanted to kiss her but didn't want to be too aggressive or eager. "I would have never worn these shoes if I knew I'd be standing in them all night. Do you mind if I take them off?" The way she was looking at him was driving him insane. It was innocently authentic. Nothing about this woman was fake.

"No, of course not." David stepped aside allowing Alicia to make her way to one of the loveseats. As she sat down to remove her sandals, her gaze snapped to the king-size walnut four-poster bed, covered in a luxurious green and gold comforter and pillows. David observed her frozen stance, curious about her thoughts. He removed his tuxedo jacket and joined her on the loveseat. "Need some help with that?"

Alicia turned to face him, and they were a breath away from each other. David leaned in to kiss her, but she quickly turned back to her sandaled foot, working on undoing the strap. "No, I've got it."

Removing his bowtie, David kept an eye on Alicia's hands, noticing a slight tremble as she fumbled around with the sandal straps. Once the straps released, she pulled the sandals off and placed the pair to the side of the loveseat.

"Better?" he asked as she turned to face him.

"Yes, much. I see you're getting comfortable."

"I hope you don't mind. My tuxedo was feeling a bit snug. I think I've put on a little weight since last I wore it."

"I thought it looked great on you."

"Thank you. And you look amazing. Did I already tell you that?"

"You did." Alicia blushed, attempting to turn away, but David wouldn't let her. Unable to wait a moment longer, he held her chin between his fingers to lightly kiss her lips.

A knock interrupted the moment and David stopped to stare at the door. *Really? Now?* Turning to Alicia, he said, "That must be dinner," and went to answer the door.

The waiter rolled in the serving trolley and nimbly prepared the plates and poured the water. A bottle of champagne remained in the ice bucket on the trolley alongside a water pitcher. David tipped the man and he departed. He pulled out a chair for Alicia and sat across from her. She lifted one cloche to find oysters Rockefeller, oozing with cheese and spinach. Another plate held grilled filet mignon surrounded with new potatoes, and another had breadcrumb-crusted fish. They each had a garden salad plate and warm knots of bread in a basket.

"This looks delicious," Alicia said, spreading her napkin on her lap. "What kind of fish is this?"

"Chilean Sea Bass. I hope you like it."

"Oh, that's one of my favorites. How did you know?"

"I told you great minds think alike. Please, help yourself. Ladies first."

"You are a man of your word, Mr. King," Alicia said as she scooped a few oysters on her plate. She took the smaller of the two filets and of the fish along with a few potatoes. "This is indeed a sumptuous meal." She smiled and bowed her head to say grace. "Lord, bless this food we're about to receive and bless the hands that prepared it. In Jesus' name."

"Amen," David murmured, filling his plate with the remainder of the meat, potatoes, fish, and several oysters. With appetites whetted, they both dug in, savoring each bite. "I was starving, too. They really didn't have much food at the gala."

"Nothing like this," Alicia said. "This is great. Thank you for arranging this. You outdid yourself here, counselor."

"I would have never known about this place if it hadn't been for you, so thank you. But remember, we're not supposed to be attorneys tonight. No more calling me counselor. Okay?"

Alicia nodded. "Agreed."

They ate silently for a while, and then Alicia put her fork down. "Are you going to tell me what happened with Elizabeth?"

"I thought I already told you."

"Come on, David. You don't expect me to believe she came all the way from Brooklyn, dressed like that, just to congratulate you."

Her stare told him that she wouldn't let this go. "Okay," he sighed, putting his fork down. "She wanted to let me know she is available now. And I let her know I wasn't interested."

"Why would she do that? I thought you said the breakup was mutual."

"I might have told you a more simplified version instead of what actually happened. The truth is Elizabeth cheated on me with another man." Alicia's eyes widened and her mouth opened at the revelation. "That's the real reason we broke up, and there is no way I'm ever going to forgive her for it."

"Oh, David. I'm sorry. I had no idea."

"I know. How could you know? Anyway, it's all behind me now." He picked up his fork and resumed eating his food, but Alicia remained still.

"So, am I the rebound chick?" she asked skeptically.

He stopped mid-chew, incredulous, then swallowed. "What do you mean?"

"I mean, you were deeply in love with her, and she broke your heart, but if she hadn't, you'd still be with her. But because your pride won't let you be with her, well, here I am."

David dropped his fork. "No, that is not it at all. I was not deeply in love with Elizabeth. I thought she was what I wanted, you know. She's beautiful, educated, and comes from a prestigious family. Her father was my mentor and friend, and I wanted to please him too. I was with her because it made sense at the time, but I never felt passionate about her." Taking her hand, he rubbed it gently with his thumb. "Not the way I feel about you. Her cheating was just the topper because, honestly, I didn't want to be married to Elizabeth. That part of the story I told you was true. After living with her and seeing what the rest of my life would be like, I was relieved to move out of our house." He stood, stepped over to her side, and pulled her out of her chair, his eyes ablaze with intensity. "Now you. I wanted you from the moment I saw you in the parking lot." He kissed her softly at first, but as she responded, the kiss deepened. Pausing to take a breath, he composed himself because if he didn't, they wouldn't make it to the bed. Holding her face between his hands, he pressed his forehead against hers. "I hope the fact that I look like your husband isn't the only reason you're here."

Alicia pulled his chin up with her finger to gently kiss him on the lips. "It isn't."

Chapter 25

The large wooden poster bed sent a shiver down Alicia's spine. She froze.

This just got real.

In the town car's back seat on the way to the inn, she'd spent most of the ride convincing herself this would be a casual evening between friends. Seeing Elizabeth and David together triggered unexpected pangs of jealousy and to cover her hurt feelings, she flippantly agreed to meet him. But when David opened the car door and reached out his hand to help her, the intense gaze in his eyes said that tonight would be much more than friendly.

Walking hand in hand, electric tingles surged through her as they ascended the stairs. Upon entering the room, the view was breathtaking. Immediately drawn to the window, she forgot why she was there for a moment, but David quickly reminded her. Heat radiated from his body to hers as he stood behind her, his breath tantalizing her neck. Getting feverish, her skin burned where he rubbed her arms. She wanted to be with him in her heart, but there was still the question of Elizabeth. And the Devine case.

Intent on breaking the mood he was trying to set, she whined about her stomach and feet. But catching sight of the bed while removing her sandals, set off a stick of emotional dynamite. BOOM. *This just got real.*

Thankfully, the food arrived when it did. Otherwise, she wasn't sure they would have taken the time to eat, let alone talk about Elizabeth. Initially, the knock on the door irritated her. He was just beginning the kissing, and she didn't want him to stop. Fortunately, food brought her back to her senses and gave her time to straighten her head. When David confessed that Elizabeth had cheated on him, she felt awful for pressing the matter, and she believed him when he said he didn't love her. And when he'd asked about Kevin, she gave him an honest answer. She wasn't there to be with Kevin. Kevin was dead. She was there to be loved by a living, breathing David King. Nothing held her back now that they'd gotten Elizabeth out of the way. Tonight was all about them, not Kevin or Elizabeth.

Once they started kissing again, they completely forgot about dinner. David's kisses were intoxicating, rendering her on the verge of passing out. He gently took her hand and led her over to the bed. Alicia's heart pounded with anticipation. Sitting on the side of the bed, he pulled her close between his legs. "My golden goddess," he whispered into her bosom as he began kissing the top portion of her breasts exposed over the bodice of her dress. Her nipples hardened, and she wanted to moan, but tightened her lips around her teeth to keep silent. It was unfathomable why his lips were not getting scorched, because she was on fire. Upon standing, he filled the space between them and covered her mouth with his own. Their tongues clashed and flitted around each other until his mouth captured her tongue completely and lightly sucked upon it. From there, he sucked on her bottom lip and kissed her neck, then her earlobe. Ablaze, she closed her eyes, losing track of where all the beautiful sensations were coming from. His manhood hardened as he pressed against her, and when she reached up to rub his firm buttocks, he stiffened even more.

Slowly, David eased himself away. "As much as I love this dress," he said in a low husky voice, "do you mind if I help you out of it?"

Alicia turned, saying, "Please do."

Kisses fluttered down her bare back before the undoing of the button behind her neck, reigniting the fire in her core. She held the halter to her chest as he slowly dragged the zipper down her back. Stepping out of the dress, the cool air assaulted her as she stood naked save her lavender lacy undies. Shivering, she covered her bare breasts with her arms.

"Amazing," David whispered as he took the dress from her hand and laid it on a loveseat. "So freaking sexy." Their eyes locked as he unbuttoned his shirt and admired her gorgeous body.

Sitting on the side of the bed, Alicia crooked her finger at him. "Come over here and let me help you out of that shirt. And those pants." David quickly kicked off his shoes and padded over to her side. While she was messing with buttons, his mouth was on hers and back to her neck until she was breathless. "How am I supposed to get these buttons undone when you keep doing that?"

"I don't know, woman," he said between kisses on her neck and the top of her breasts, "figure it out." Finally, with the last button undone, her hand glided over his silky-smooth muscular chest. Lost in the sensations of his mouth and his hands, caressing her skin, she slid her hand down his taut stomach. As she fumbled with loosening his belt, David abruptly stood up.

"You are taking too long," he said, removing his belt and pants. Through his black boxer briefs, his erection stood out.

She took in the length of it. "Yeah, I guess I am." They both laughed as he leaped around her and jumped on to the middle of the bed.

Pulling her on top of himself he kissed her again. "You are so beautiful," he moaned as he suckled one nipple and the other.

Alicia threw her head back, bursts of electricity coursing throughout her body as he teased her breasts with his mouth, her core burning with the fire he was stoking. She was wet and pulsating between her legs as he slid his hand down into her lace panty. Slipping a finger into her moist opening, she softly moaned. After teasing her clit with his fingers until she let out a series of gasps, he sat up.

"Enough of this," he said huskily, removing the lace panty, tossing it aside, and slipping out his briefs and socks. Gazing intensely in her eyes, he continued, "Now we can get down to real business."

Light kisses floated from her breasts down her belly until he slid between her legs and used his tongue to discover her pleasure spot. Alicia moaned, "Oh, David," when he found it, teasing it until she grabbed his head with both hands and called for the lord. Slowly, he crept up and kissed her passionately, with a sweet taste lingering on his lips.

"Are you ready for more?" he whispered.

"Yes, please don't stop now." She massaged the length of his hard penis, and he moaned. He was ready, too. Bending down to find his pants, he pulled out a condom. He handed it to her, and she slid the sheath on his thick, stiff rod. Easing his way atop, he gently penetrated her, and she was aching to receive. As they created a rhythmic flow, she encouraged him into powerful strokes, pulling him deeper with her hands firmly on his buttocks. The pleasure mounted as they rocked against each other, breathing hard, skin slick with sweat. The pressure continued building deep within her. After a few minutes, she exploded with ecstasy, calling 'yes, David, yes,' and he came right behind her, moaning, "Oh yeah, you've got it, baby. Alicia, baby, you got it."

They lay holding each other, breathing hard, sweaty, and worn out. As Alicia's heartbeat slowed, David left her arms and entered the adjoining bathroom. A broad grin filled his face as he returned, handing Alicia a warm wet cloth and cleansing himself with his own.

"Woman, you are amazing. I hope you're as pleased as I am." Alicia nodded as a little yawn slipped out. He chuckled, "Don't even think about trying to go to sleep now. How about some champagne?"

"I'll take water." Her throat was like the Sahara. Amused by David parading around naked, she noticed the ugly scar on his thigh. Guessing it was his gunshot wound, she did not want to ask about it now. By the time he opened the champagne, poured himself a glass, and poured her a glass of water, she could barely keep her eyes open. After a few sips from the glass he handed her, she laid back and closed her eyes, losing all sense of time. Later, David's hands massaged her back and his hard member pressed against her butt cheek. Rolling over, her hand stroked his face, and her mouth welcomed his kiss, exploding with happiness inside. They made love again until they were both fully drained. She fell asleep again, spooned against David's body, and didn't rise until the birds were chirping.

At dawn, Alicia's sensibility returned with a tinge of guilt. David's gentle snoring made her smile, and, for one brief moment, she couldn't bring herself to be mad at either of them. The evening had been thoroughly enjoyable, but now it was Sunday morning. Faith was expecting her for brunch, as she'd promised.

Moving as stealthily as possible, she found her undergarments on the floor, retrieved her gown from the loveseat, and dressed. She tiptoed into the bathroom and checked her face in the mirror. All considered, not too messy, and she finger-combed through her wavy hair and pushed it behind her ears. Finding a little bottle of mouthwash on the sink, she rinsed her mouth, then wiped her face with a wet washcloth to remove the mascara smudged around her eyes.

Her intention to leave was halted by the realization that she didn't have her Jeep and needed David to drive her home. As she emerged from the bathroom, he was feeling around the empty side of the bed with his hands. He sat up, rubbing his eyes. "Damn, you're already dressed?"

"Sorry, but I've got a brunch date with my sister this morning." She picked up his boxers from the floor and handed them to him. "Would you mind getting up to drive me home? It's not far from here, and afterward, you can come back and get some more rest if you like."

"Yeah, sure," he said as he stretched. "I didn't know you had plans. Just give me a minute to freshen up." He passed her to enter the bathroom and shut the door. Alicia got a glass of room-temperature water and sat on the loveseat to put on her sandals. When he came out, he quickly put on his pants and shirt. Gently grabbing her arms to pull her off the loveseat, he kissed her softly, and as she responded, the kiss deepened. "Good morning Ms. Stone."

Alicia pulled away, not wanting to look into his eyes. She was vulnerable, and if they kept kissing that way, there would be no brunch with Faith.

"What's wrong?" David asked. "You're not worrying about getting caught with me in the light of day, are you?"

She answered with a sheepish grin. "Yeah, kind of. I never intended to spend the night with you."

"I hope you're glad you did. I know I am." Grinning, he said, "I thought we'd spend some more time together today, but if you've made plans with your sister, I guess we should be on our way."

David slipped into his tux jacket as Alicia took up her wrap. They walked hand in hand down the stairs and out to his car. "Are you going to give me your address for the GPS?"

"You don't need it. It's only a few turns to my place." Alicia guided him through the streets and they began to ride up the steep incline of Hudson Avenue. "Since it's a new day, counselor, I have a question about the case. How did you know Ray was stealing money from the Devine Music?"

"I don't agree with DeLeo's decision to gloss over the drugging incident. I don't think Jerri Devine drugged Jake, and I certainly don't believe she drugged your investigator. Since you were already working the Billy angle, I decided to look deeper into Ray's affairs. There is no chance DeLeo will drop the murder charge against Jerri unless she has the actual killer in hand."

Alicia turned to face him. "Do you agree with me now that Jerri is innocent?"

With a side glance, David admitted, "Just between us, yes, I do."

Reaching over, she squeezed his hand, smiling. *Hallelujah, he's on my side.* She directed him into the Briar Hill Townhomes, and he pulled into her driveway next to her Jeep. "Would you like to come in? I could make some coffee."

David leaned in, cupping her face in his hands, and kissed her passionately. "When am I going to see you again?"

Alicia melted into a puddle, meeting his intense gaze with one of her own. "I had a wonderful night with you and look forward to doing it again. We'll arrange something soon. I promise." Returning his fervent kiss, she exited the car and headed into the house.

She hurried to the kitchen window and peeped through the blinds to watch David's Benz back out of the driveway and head down the road. Her body was still pulsating with the sensations of his kisses and his touch. Shedding her clothes, she stepped into the shower, singing with joy. "I'm in love, finally. I've found someone for me." She couldn't hit all the notes as Patti LaBelle did in her song rendition, but she didn't care. Everything felt good all over and she couldn't contain her excitement that she and David had consummated their relationship. The hard part was going to be keeping it a secret. She was grateful to be meeting with Faith today since she was the one person she could talk to about her newfound love without worrying about judgment.

Arriving at Faith's apartment in Ossining around ten am, Alicia sported a casual ensemble of jeans, a vibrant red cowl neck sweater, and sneakers. As she stepped inside, Faith greeted her with a warm hug. "Hey sis, come on in."

"I'll just be a minute," Faith said as she disappeared into the bathroom. Her little one-bedroom apartment was a mess, with school papers spread over the small oak dining room table and assorted clothes scattered around the plush taupe sofa and recliner chair. In the kitchen, a pile of dirty dishes were brimming out of the sink.

Faith returned in a moment, smiling. "I'm glad to see you. I missed our brunch last week." She could pass for Halle Berry's sister with her short pixie haircut. "I know you're busy with your big case, so I wasn't sure if you'd make it today." She wore jeans and a Howard University sweatshirt Alicia had given her years ago. Tying her sneakers, she asked, "How are you holding up?"

Alicia smiled brightly. "I'm doing great."

"Great? Really?" Faith raised an eyebrow. "Are you talking about the case you didn't want to take or something else?"

"Come on, I'll fill you in on what's been happening in the car." On the way to the diner, Alicia recounted how she met David and all the drama surrounding Jerri Devine.

Once seated in a booth by the window in the diner, Faith said, "I can't believe you've fallen in love with a Kevin look-alike. What are the odds of even meeting someone like that?"

"Believe me, it caught me totally by surprise. I thought I was done with love after Kevin passed away. But now I know I had just shut myself down to the possibility. I stuffed down all my feelings because I didn't want to wallow in the pain of losing him. I was afraid to put myself out there because I assumed that even if I found someone else, love would be snatched away again."

"Everyone grieves in different ways. But you're not feeling that way anymore?"

"Not after last night." A broad grin filled Alicia's face.

"I'm happy for you. Honestly, I didn't think you'd ever give any man a chance. David must be very special to have won your heart." The waitress came over, taking their order for western omelets, home fries, and coffee. When she left, Faith continued. "It's too bad you have to keep this a secret. Do you really think Carlton would disapprove of you finding happiness, even if it is with a prosecutor?"

"I think Carlton would disapprove of anyone unless, of course, it was him."

"And I'm surprised at Diana discouraging you. She's usually your biggest cheerleader."

"I know, but I understand where she's coming from under the circumstances. I feel as if I behaved irresponsibly and guilty for being unprofessional. After all, I told her to keep her hands off Ray. But I don't regret it at all, especially now that it's possible he's the villain in Jerri's story."

"I'm glad you didn't let Carlton or Diana stand in the way, and you need to stop beating yourself up and feeling guilty. You're a grown woman, and you're entitled to have a personal life. Once the case is over, you all can come out of the closet and fully enjoy one another."

Alicia could only hope Faith was right. She thought about Jerri and whether it was time to make a disclosure about her relationship with David. "Enough about me. Tell me, what's been going on in your world?" She listened intently as her sister updated her on all the action at school and with her students.

Later that afternoon, upon returning home, a message from David awaited on her answering machine. "Hey, beautiful. I hope you enjoyed your brunch with your sister. Please call me. I can't stop thinking about you and last night. Call me back." Memories of their night together sprung to the forefront of her mind, but she hesitated to return his call. *Tomorrow, I have to go to the office and pretend nothing has happened. Take some time and let the fire die down.*

Retrieving her notes on the legal pad from the day before, Alicia contemplated her next steps while trying to figure out what to say when she questioned Billy. The phone rang, and she froze, letting it go to the answering machine.

"Hi, it's me again. I thought you would be home by now, but anyway, please call me. I just want to hear your voice, okay?" David's voice made her melt inside, and she wanted to talk to him, yet resisted the urge. Instead, she called Ray to check on Jerri and tell him to gather his people for interviews tomorrow.

Chapter 26

When Alicia woke to rain pattering against the window, irritation prickled through her. She longed for her morning walk, the ritual that kept her calm. Contemplating a gym session briefly, she instead opted to dive straight into her prayer routine. While waiting for the coffee to brew, she bowed her head, seeking divine guidance for the day ahead. *Lord, I need You today to guide me through these witness interviews.* She didn't expect any problems with the band members or the security team, but Billy was a wildcard.

The questions she'd prepared for him were on the legal pad on the kitchen table. With a final scan of her notes, she grabbed her oversized mug, filled it with steaming coffee, and settled onto the sofa, Bible in hand.

After an indulgent, steamy shower, she emerged feeling refreshed, ready to tackle the task of getting Billy to reveal his secrets. She slipped into a deep red Calvin Klein pantsuit, pairing it with comfortable black pumps, knowing she would be on her feet for hours. The goal for today was not to push for a full confession, but it was time to test some threads of her theory.

On her way into Burke and Powell, her cell phone rang.

"Hey girl, I'm going to be late getting to the office. Please go ahead and start the witness interviews without me," Diana said. "I talked to about ten veterinarians about Billy this weekend and I got a call back this morning. A vet in Ossining says his father used to work for the Devines. This could be the break we've been looking for. I'm headed there now and I'll call you if I get good news."

Goosebumps popped up on Alicia's arms. *Billy is going down today.*

Rather than use her own office, Alicia elected to use the same small interview room Diana had used for the last round of band interviews. It was better equipped for more precise recordings of what each person said, and there were fewer distractions for the interviewee since the walls were bare.

As she sat at the small wooden desk, reviewing her notes, Carlton stepped in and closed the door. "I wanted to have a chat with you before you started your mock court," he said. There were lines in Carlton's normally smooth, composed face.

"You look worried," Alicia said. "Did something happen with Jerri after she was released from the hospital?"

"No," Carlton replied. "I am worried, but not about Jerri. I'm worried about you."

"Me?"

"More specifically, you and David King."

Alicia looked down as she placed her notes on the desktop. "Oh."

Carlton came closer to give her an intense gaze. "For a few days, I've heard complaints from Valerie. Until the gala, I was able to ignore her accusation that you were getting personally involved with a prosecutor. But seeing you two together, I must say, it does appear there is some chemistry happening and I do not want to see you get hurt. You do realize that David King may look like Kevin, but he is not your friend."

"Carlton, I admit there is an attraction happening between me and David. But did it ever occur to you that I am using that attraction to my advantage? To disarm the ADA from doing his best in the courtroom?"

A skeptical look crossed Carlton's face as Alicia continued. "You don't have to worry about me and David. I am handling Jerri's case in the most dignified and professional manner possible. I believe in her innocence and would never do anything to jeopardize this case. Yes, I am attracted to

David, but I have promised to put my personal feelings on hold until Jerri is vindicated."

"Ok," Carlton said as he went towards the door. "You know I have confidence in your skills as an attorney, but I worry about you guarding your heart. You're still vulnerable."

"I appreciate the concern, but I'm putting you on notice. Once this case is over, I may be exploring a personal relationship with David. He's truly impressed me."

"I hope he's worthy of your trust," Carlton replied, shaking his head as he left the office.

Billy showed up a little before nine am with Walter and Matt in tow. She offered Billy and Matt bagels and coffee in the firm's breakroom and then did the first run-through with Walter. He recounted his version of the day at the rehearsal studio in pretty much the same fashion that he originally had, and afterward, Matt did the same. Finally, it was Billy's turn.

"Just a suggestion," Alicia said, "on the day you testify in the actual trial, you might want to try to look interested in the attorney's questions rather than annoyed."

"I'll keep that in mind, but since this isn't real, let's get on with it." Billy shifted his weight in the steel folding chair with a scowl. Alicia was grateful he wasn't wearing his musty army jacket but a clean white shirt and khaki pants. Sweat marks formed on his armpits, and his face slightly flushed.

Standing before him, Alicia began the mock interrogation. "Mr. Whitmore, please tell the court your current occupation."

"I'm the business manager for Bryan James, a musical artist and songwriter."

"And what was your relationship with Jake Devine?"

"We were business partners during a collaboration between his wife, Jerri, and Bryan. Together, we produced an album or a CD, whatever you want to call it, *Ms. Devine Rocks!* My client wrote the music, and together, they performed the songs." Billy met Alicia's gaze directly. "Do we have to rehearse all this stuff? I know you're going to ask me about receiving the phone call from Jake, and you already know how I'm going to answer that question. I've been a witness in court before. Can't we just skip to the part you really want to know?"

"What do you mean?"

"You know, the part about me killing Jake. I know you think I did it, but I didn't."

Alicia tried not to let her shock from his calm frankness show on her face and forge ahead. Leaning back against the desk, her shoulders relaxed.

"Okay, if that's how you want to proceed, we'll get to the pertinent points. Isn't it true you arranged for Nate and Connie James to fake an emergency to get Bryan to leave town quickly?"

"Yes. When I became aware Jake had found out about Bryan and Jerri's affair, and he was threatening to kill Bryan, I called Nate and asked him to come up with something, anything, serious enough to convince Bryan to come home. Nate and Connie came up with the heart thing on their own."

"And how did you become aware Jake threatened to kill Bryan?"

"I heard him yelling at the rehearsal studio, and later, Ray called and told me. He said I shouldn't worry about Jake and to keep his bogus death threats to myself. He would take care of everything. But as a precaution, Ray thought it was a good idea for me to get Bryan out of town."

Alicia's eyebrows shot up. "What?"

"Yes, Ray said he would work on calming Jake down and renegotiating our agreement, and Bryan and Jerri would no longer work together."

Alicia slammed down her legal pad on the desk. "When did Ray call you?"

"I guess it was after his 'discussion' with Jake." Billy used two fingers of each hand to form quotation marks in the air when he said the word, discussion. "Right after I dropped Walter off, I got the call from Ray, and then I called Nate."

"And Ray called you, I assume, on your prepaid cell phone? The same one you say Jake called you on?" She started pacing around in front of Billy.

"Yes, he did. Since you brought up Jake's call, I want you to know I only gave the number to that phone to two people. Bryan and Ray. I guess Ray gave it to Jake 'cause I was shocked as hell when he called me that night."

"Are you certain it was Jake who you were talking to?"

"Like I told you before, the call woke me up out of a dead sleep. He said this is Jake, and it sounded like him, so yeah, it was Jake."

Doubt seized Alicia. Shaken by Billy's testimony, she couldn't go on with the interview. She stopped pacing and stood in front of Billy, with her hand on her forehead, shaking her head in disbelief.

He squinted at her. "What's the matter? Is this not part of your plan to prove I'm the killer?"

Alicia could hardly speak. "We're done here," finally fell softly from her lips. Putting out her hand to Billy, she looked him in the eye. "I'm sorry." Billy shook her hand and left the room.

Sitting behind the small desk, Alicia snapped off the recorder and attempted to gather herself. *People always tell me that Faith and I sound the same on the phone. Was the same thing true of Jake and Ray?* Billy's testimony rang true in her ears. Ray had said the exact same thing to her…he calmed Jake down and got him to agree to renegotiate Billy and Bryan's contract. Billy wasn't lying, and anger boiled up realizing that Ray had duped her once again. She left the small room, retrieved her coat and tote from her office, and headed for the Jeep.

Within twenty minutes, she was pulling up in front of Ray's three story red brick row house on Edgecombe Avenue. Sugar Hill had been the haven for wealthy African Americans during the 1920s, named for the sweet life other black folks assumed they were living. Now the Harlem neighborhood was transforming, illuminated by a plethora of white people mixed in the groups of people walking the streets. She took a few deep breaths before getting out of the car and going to ring the doorbell.

Chris answered the door. "Hey, Ms. Stone. I thought we were coming to see you at your office this afternoon."

"Change in plans," Alicia said, stepping inside. The foyer radiated elegance with its black-and-white tiled floor and a grand brass chandelier. Partially closed ornate wooden pocket doors were to the left, and an entryway to a dark room was to the right. A wooden staircase stood directly across from the front door, and beside it, the tiles continued down a narrow hallway toward the back of the house. "Is Ray here?"

"No, he said he'd be back to pick us up around noon. You want to see Jerri?"

Alicia nodded, and Chris led her up the wooden staircase to the second floor. He knocked on the door to the right of the stairs and called out, "Jerri, your lawyer's here."

Jerri opened the door wide, wearing her floral silk robe. "Alicia, what a surprise. Come in." Jerri picked up some clothing scattered on a brown leather sofa in the room. "Please excuse the mess, but I wasn't expecting company. I thought we were going to see you in your office this afternoon. Have a seat." Walking back into an adjoining room, she tossed the clothes in and closed the door. "How do you like my new digs?"

Alicia looked around the large sitting room. The maroon curtains on a bay window with mini wooden blinds were partially pulled back, facing the street. A black entertainment center filled the left-hand wall with a big television, stereo, and an extensive record album collection. Two tall brass halogen lamps lit the room, and directly in front of the sofa was a low, oval wooden coffee table.

As Alicia sat on the couch, she said, "It's nice."

Jerri picked up a glass full of a light brown liquid from the coffee table, holding it high for Alicia to see. "Don't worry, it's apple cider. After that stint in the hospital, I'm pacing myself. Can I get you anything?"

"No, thanks. You look good. How are you doing?" It was true. Jerri's skin and eyes appeared brighter than before. She was as lovely as ever without wearing any makeup, her hair pulled up into a red scrunchy.

Jerri sat on the other end of the sofa. "I'm feeling better. Thank God for Ray. If he hadn't found me when he did, who knows if I'd even be alive."

"Yes, thank God for Ray," Alicia said. "Do you know where he is? I need to talk to him."

"He said he had some business to take care of, but he'll be back soon. Since you're here, why don't we go over those questions you have for me? Save me another trip to your office."

Alicia retrieved her legal pad and pen from her tote, flipping to the page marked 'Jerri.' "I wanted to ask you about the cabin. Did you go there often? Do you have a key?"

"Occasionally, I went there, but I don't have a key," Jerri replied. "When Jake first bought that place, I thought he was crazy. But he was doing a lot of weird things back then."

"What do you mean? When did he buy it?"

"It was in back bout five years ago. We hadn't made any music in a while cause Jake couldn't write a thing, and we were getting restless. Jake kept saying he needed to be inspired, so we started traveling around to start checking things off his bucket list, you know, the things you want to do before you die. Even though we had traveled the world doing tours, we never got to enjoy the cities where we performed. It was always about work, but not this time. We gambled in Las Vegas and Monte Carlo. Toured London, Madrid, and Paris. We went to Hawaii, saw black sand for the first time, and rode every ride at Disneyland in California. I was surprised by some things on his list, but nothing seemed to stir his spirit until we went to the Kentucky Derby in May. Even though he liked to bet on the ponies, Jake had never been to a racetrack before and fell in love with the horses. We met up with some big wigs down there, racehorse owners and breeders, and they conned him into buying a horse. They told him he could make lots of money using him as a stud. That's how Apollo came into our lives."

"Jake had a horse?"

"Yup, and the horse needed a place to stay, so he bought the cabin in Katonah. There used to be a stable on the grounds there. Anyway, Ray was furious when Jake told him about his breeding plan. It was the only time I saw the two of them have a serious argument, and Ray didn't speak to Jake for weeks. Ray wanted to focus on investing in real estate, not horses. He said Jake didn't have a clue about breeding horses, which was true, and it was a big waste of money. But Jake didn't let that stop him. He hired a guy to take care of the horse and started spending more time with

Apollo than with me. Ray and I couldn't stand that smelly beast. He was scary to me. For months, I had to go up to the cabin if I wanted to see Jake, which was okay, cause it was a nice place, and I did enjoy the swimming pool. Luckily, his Kentucky contacts did come through with some folks who paid for Apollo's sperm. When Ray realized Jake was actually making money, they made up and started working together again."

A sinking feeling spread throughout Alicia's body, but she acted upbeat. "Really?"

"Ray was the one who talked Jake into joining the real estate group that got us the penthouse, so they kinda did both. You know, the breeding and real estate investing." Jerri sighed heavily. "Lord, do I miss the penthouse." She finished her glass of juice and placed the empty glass on the table.

"You said the cabin used to have a stable. What happened to it and Apollo?"

"It was tragic, really. During a bad storm, lightning hit a big old tree near the stable, split it right in two, and started a fire. Half of it fell on the stable while Apollo was inside. I don't know how he did it, but Apollo got loose and survived the fire, but he was never the same after that. He got real wild and wouldn't let anything get near him. Not people or other horses. The vet said Apollo was traumatized." Jerri shook her head. "I didn't know a horse could get traumatized, did you?" Alicia shook her head no. "The whole situation devastated Jake. Apollo was running around loose in the fields, and the only way to catch him was to drug him. Jake got one of those guns that shoot darts to put the horse to sleep from the vet. It was the only way to milk him for his seed, but that didn't work out too good. No breeders wanted to do artificial insemination. I think those guys get off on watching the horses have sex, you know. Anyway, Apollo eventually hurt himself running through those fields. His foot got caught in a gofer hole, and he broke his leg. He had to be put down."

A sourness filled Alicia's stomach, and her throat was dry. "Do you have more cider? I think I'd like some now, please."

"Sure." Jerri picked up her glass and went back to the other room. In a moment, she returned with her glass filled and a second glass, which she handed to Alicia as she sat down.

"I have a frig in my bedroom. I love it because I don't have to run downstairs to the kitchen every time I want something." Jerri sipped the juice and eyed Alicia gulping hers down. "I have to say Ray is doing everything he can to make me comfortable here."

"Thank God for Ray," Alicia repeated as she put the empty glass down, nervously glancing at her watch. It was almost noon. "Have you spoken to Bryan lately?"

Jerri looked wary. "No, you told me not to."

"He came to see you at the hospital. I promised him I would arrange for you two to get together once you got home. Would you like to see him?"

"Of course, I would."

"Why don't you call him and see if he's free?" Alicia asked.

"Right now?"

"Yes. I will take you both to my office, and you can visit there. Would that be okay?"

Jerri's face lit up as she jumped off the sofa. "That would be great. I'm going to call him right now." She almost ran to the bedroom and shut the door.

Alicia went to the window to peek through the blinds. *Please, Lord, don't let Ray show up until after I leave with Jerri.* Strings of terror stretched from her heart to her limbs, breeding fear for her and Jerri's safety. *Please, Lord, let Bryan be home.*

Jerri flung the door open. "He said yes. I'm going to get dressed," and swiftly closed the door again.

Alicia paced around the room, hoping Jerri would hurry. The front door slammed closed and voices echoed in the foyer below. Then the front door slammed again. Peeking through the blinds, she observed Chris walking down the block. Getting out her cell phone, heart racing, she dialed David. Mercifully, he answered after two rings. He started to speak, but Alicia cut him off in a low, hasty tone.

"I'm at Ray's house. Please hurry. He's the one." David was still talking when she pressed 'END.' Heavy footsteps were coming up the stairs, and she whispered another silent prayer.

Chapter 27

The first thing David did when he woke up Monday morning was check his cell phone for messages. Nothing. *I can't believe this woman won't call me. I know she heard my messages. Is she being paranoid, or has she changed her mind about us?* He stared at the phone momentarily and then stopped that line of thinking, remembering Alicia's cautious nature.

Shrugging off his concerns, he leaped out of bed and hit the gym, determined to focus on something other than Alicia. But she persisted in his mind, lingering like an unresolved melody. Even as he dressed and made his way to the office, his mind wandered back to her, pondering their next encounter.

Seated at his desk, he dialed her office, anticipation tingling in his veins. Yet, no answer. Frustration bubbled within him like a simmering pot ready to boil over. *Where is she? Did she just fall off the face of the earth?* Taking a bite of his glazed donut, he hammered away at his keyboard to boot it up, and the ALT key popped up and fell over. With a deep breath, he gently pushed the button back into place, guessing it wouldn't halt the computer's startup. The computer beeped and made a grinding sound until it stopped, and the main screen came up. *You need to calm down. She'll call. It's only been a day.* But his mind wouldn't rest, and as hard as he tried to focus on something else, he couldn't. The prosecution strategy required his attention. DeLeo expected to receive it today. He stared at the screen for a long while until DeLeo's presence loomed in his doorway.

"Good morning David. I need a word. Can you come to my office, please?" Not waiting for an answer, DeLeo strode down the hall. Without a word, David quickly rounded his desk to follow her.

Once inside her office, he closed the door slowly. "Good morning. I am putting the finishing touches on the prosecution strategy. You'll have it this afternoon."

DeLeo brushed the lapels of her forest green suit as she strolled to her seat. Folding her hands atop her massive mahogany desk, her lips pursed. "Very good, but I wasn't concerned about that. There's something else I need to talk to you about. Have a seat." She gestured toward a winged back chair at the corner of her desk.

With a straight back, David sat, giving her his undivided attention.

Relaxing her shoulders as a small smile crossed her face, DeLeo said, "Did you enjoy the gala? Several of my colleagues were very impressed with you."

Leaning back, David replied, "I did enjoy the gala and I appreciate all the introductions to Westchester's legal elite. I wanted to make a good impression. Sounds like mission accomplished." He gave her a weak grin.

"However, there was something I didn't expect." The smile drained from DeLeo's face and her red lips formed a straight, tight line. "I saw you with Ms. Stone on the terrace. Your body language said you weren't discussing the case." DeLeo arose from her chair and sauntered around the desk. Once behind David's chair, she asked, "You're not succumbing to her charms, are you, David? If the rumor mill around here has done its job, I know you're aware of your resemblance to Ms. Stone's late husband. I expected your appearance to have a detrimental effect, perhaps even reduce her effectiveness in the courtroom."

Pulsing with apprehension, David attempted to shift around in his chair to make eye contact with DeLeo, but she kept pacing around without looking at him. "Yes, I have heard about and seen for myself the resemblance. However, I assure you, I am not falling for Ms. Stone. Yes, she is indeed a beautiful woman, but I am a prosecutor before anything else. Ms. Stone will not be charming her way into winning this case."

DeLeo stepped beside David's chair and brought her face close to his, searching his eyes. "That's good. I'm glad to hear it. I'd hate to have make a change in the Chief Prosecutor of this case."

"That most certainly will not be necessary," David said adamantly. "I'm going after Ms. Stone with everything I've got. We will get a conviction."

With a determined stride, David returned to his office and picked up his notes for the prosecution strategy report. Once he got going, he became engrossed, and time seemed to fly by. A rumble from his stomach told him it must be lunchtime. Rubbing his eyes, he went to see what Eddie was up to. Today, he would buy him lunch as a gesture of goodwill. After David cleared the air and let Eddie know that his spying activities were exposed, he chose to keep more to himself.

Eddie, engrossed in his tasks, was diligently typing on his computer when David showed up at his open door.

"Hey, how's it going?" David asked.

Eddie spun around in his chair to face him. "Good. I've got our man on high alert. As soon as we get the approval from the judge, he'll deliver the subpoenas to our hostile witnesses. Great idea to put Bryan James on the stand as our star witness against Jerri. There's no way that good old American country boy is going to commit perjury on the witness stand when you question him about his affair with Jerri. Right now, I'm studying case law, searching for reasons we can use to counter the admissibility of evidence related to the drugging. I agree with you that it's best to be prepared for this move by the defense, even though DeLeo wants to ignore it. It's a tough nut to crack, but I'm going to get something soon."

As David prepared to broach the topic of lunch, his cell phone rang in his pant pocket, and he instinctively answered it. "Hey, I've been trying…. What? What are you saying?" Holding the phone at arm's length, he glared at it. "She just hung up on me."

Eddie's curiosity piqued. "Who was that?"

David furrowed his brow, still staring at the phone. "A friend," he mumbled. Lifting his head, he gazed intensely at Eddie. "I think she's in trouble. Excuse me."

Jogging back to his office, he grabbed his suit jacket and car keys. He scrambled around his desk, searching for Ray's dossier. When he found it, he hastily jotted Ray's home address on a scrap of paper, shoved it in his pocket, and headed for the parking garage. Once in his car, he retrieved a small metal case from under the passenger seat and nimbly opened it. The Beretta glistened in the dark gray felt casing. David took the gun out and opened the glove compartment for his ammunition box. He swiftly loaded the gun and stowed it in the glove compartment alongside the ammo box. After placing the case back under the seat, he started the car and sped off to Harlem.

****** ******

Ray knocked twice on Jerri's suite door before swinging it open. He sported the same look he had the first day Alicia met him. "Hey, I heard you were here. Where's Jerri?"

Alicia held the phone against her ear, raised her other palm towards Ray, and turned to face the window. "Yes, that's right. I'm conducting the interviews here, and I won't return to the office until later. Okay, Carlton.

I'll see you then." She turned to face Ray. "How are you? I finished early with the other guys and decided to come here to interview you and Jerri. I hope that's all right." Alicia trusted her voice sounded normal because her heart was racing.

"Sure, it's fine. I just sent Chris out to get a couple of sandwiches from the corner store."

"Jerri's getting dressed. Is there somewhere else we could go talk? Give her a little privacy?" Alicia asked.

Ray smiled, holding the door open wider. "Come on down to the kitchen. We can talk there."

Turning her back to him, Alicia moved to the sofa. Sensing Ray's eyes crawling all over her, she quickly bent to gather her notes and put them in her tote, along with her cell phone. She forced a smile, draping her coat over her arm before facing Ray. "All set. You lead the way."

Ray chuckled. "Oh no, lady in red. After you."

Alicia held her breath as she passed him into the hallway and down the stairs. The thud of his footsteps behind her thumped in her head, and her heart pounded like a drum. *What am I going to say? I have to calm down. He doesn't know that I know.* Reaching the foyer, she spun around as Ray descended the last steps, his demeanor relaxed, a smile playing on his lips as his hand glided down the handrail. She maintained her smile as beads of sweat popped up along her hairline.

"Which way to the kitchen?" Alicia asked.

Ray stepped to the left of the foyer and reached his arm around the wall into the darkened room. It sprang to light, and he raised his left arm to point out the direction. "Right this way."

Taking shallow breaths, Alicia entered the cozy family room. A grand fireplace with a marble surround and opulent wooden mantle dominated the space, and a plush gray sectional sofa faced it. The room opened to the kitchen. A large white island complete with sink and bar stool seating for four served as the divider of the space. Pulling out a stool to sit on, she regarded the stainless-steel appliances against the back of the kitchen wall surrounded by white cabinets. Alicia laid her coat on the seat beside her and placed her tote on the floor.

Ray strolled behind the island to the refrigerator. "Can I get you something to drink? I have some iced tea here."

"Yes, tea would be perfect. Thanks."

Ray took out a large bottle of Arizona Lemon Iced Tea, then glided down to the other end of the galley kitchen and retrieved drinking glasses from one of the white cabinets. "You already talked to Jerri? Asked her all of your questions?" He filled the glasses with tea and handed her one.

"Not all of them, but we covered a lot." She took a long sip of cold tea. Her heart slowed to a normal pace as she regained her composure. "I was going to take her out to lunch, since you no longer need to drive to White Plains. Do you mind?"

"Heck no. Jerri needs to get out of the house. Where are you planning on taking her? Maybe I'll join you."

"No offense, but we need to have, you know, a little girl talk."

"You didn't do that already?" Ray laughed. "It's okay. You ladies, go on and enjoy yourselves." He kept his eyes trained on her as he sipped his tea and put his glass down. "It's probably going to be awhile before Jerri finishes getting dressed. She's a real slow poke. You want to get started with me? I know you've got a lot of questions for me."

Alicia reached down and took out her legal pad and pen from the tote. "Sure, why not? Cause you're right, I do have a lot of questions for you." She flipped through the pages of the pad and stopped on the one she'd marked with his name.

"Do you remember what Jake was wearing when you went to see him at the cabin that night? I wanted to have a look at the shirt he was wearing."

"Hmm. I think Jake was wearing a wife beater with gray sweatpants," Ray replied. "I don't know if the police took it, but it's probably in the hamper in the bedroom."

"Where were you when you talked to him? In the media room?"

"Yeah, it was his favorite room in the house." Ray bent down as she wrote on the pad, and Alicia heard metal clinking but couldn't see what he was doing.

"Did you ever ask the DA when I'd be able to get Jake's body?" Ray asked. "I want to lay him to rest." He stood up and laid his hands flat on the countertop.

Alicia glanced up from her legal pad. "I'm sorry, Ray, I didn't. I'm going to write myself a note right now, and I'll get back to you."

As she wrote, Jerri's heels clicked down the stairs. "I'm ready. I can't wait to see Bryan. It's been too long." Jerri rounded the corner, decked out in her black catsuit and purple cape, wearing her wide-brim hat and holding her sunglasses in her hand. "Hello, Ray."

With agitation flickering in his eyes, Ray barked at Jerri, "You are not going anywhere to see Bryan." Ray glared at Alicia. "Didn't you tell her to stay away from him?"

Jerri sighed. "It was her idea. Wasn't it Alicia?"

Alicia's eyes widened as they darted back and forth between Jerri and Ray. He looked down, shaking his head, arms tensing as he leaned on the counter. He quickly squatted, popped up holding the dart gun, and fired at Jerri. Alicia gasped as Jerri dropped her sunglasses and placed her other hand on her chest, gripping the small dart with orange feathers between her fingers. Jerri's eyes widened as she stared at Ray. "What did you do?"

"You are not going anywhere." Dropping the dart gun on the floor, Ray swiftly came around the island to swoop Jerri into his arms. He sat her down on the sofa, pulled the dart from her chest, and looked down at her face. "You'll be all right." Jerri slowly slumped over and passed out.

Ray turned his piercing gaze to Alicia, frozen in her seat. Her heart was beating so fast she imagined it might leap out of her chest. "Billy called me and told me what happened this morning. That's why you came here, isn't it? Because you don't think he killed Jake anymore."

"If I had any doubts about who did, I don't anymore." Alicia's voice trembled. "How could you do that to Jerri?" *What are you going to do to me?* Sweat trickled down one side of her face as she silently prayed David would get there soon.

With two long strides, Ray towered over Alicia. "She'll live, which is more than I can say for you. That dart was supposed to be for you." He snatched her by the arm, and she struggled against him as he yanked her from the stool and dragged her out of the room down the narrow hall. "Damn stupid police," he grumbled, tugging on her arm. "I gave them all the evidence they needed."

He opened a steel door under the staircase, and another set of stairs went down into the dark. He forced her down the steps, and when they got to the bottom, he pulled a chain, and a sole light bulb illuminated the space. Glancing around the gray basement littered with junk, terror flooded her body as she kept whispering, 'Jesus, help me,' over and over.

"Carlton said you were rusty, but you're a clever bitch. Now I'll have to leave the country sooner than I planned. Once I decide how to get rid of you." Ray pulled her back into his chest tightly with one arm and covered her mouth with his other hand when the doorbell rang.

****** ******

David's Benz rolled to a stop when he spotted Alicia's Jeep parked down the block from Ray's doorway. He parked nearby and removed his gun from the glove compartment. Walking to the front door with a purposeful stride, David slid the weapon inside his belt above the small of his back and covered it with his suit jacket. His senses heightened, he listened at the door for any sign of activity. The silence was ominous. He pressed the doorbell, waited a beat, then banged on the door with his fist. Anxiety clawed at him. *This isn't good. I know they're in there.*

Approaching the first-floor window, David strained to peer through the drawn blinds, but darkness shrouded the interior. A flicker of light emanating from a long, low basement window drew his attention. Dropping to the concrete ground, he crawled to press his face against the window. Ray held Alicia in a bear hug with his hand clamped over her mouth.

Ignited with rage, David shattered the glass with the butt of his gun. Shards of glass grazed his skin as he pushed his upper torso through the window. "Let her go, Ray, or I'll shoot. Believe me, I'm a perfect shot." A wooden door stood behind Ray that David deduced led to the backyard. He did not want Ray to make a run for it, taking Alicia as his hostage.

Ray turned toward David with his gun pointed directly at him. Pulling on Alicia's arm, he tried to bolt in the opposite direction, towards the wooden basement door. Alicia resisted and mustered enough strength to deliver a solid kick to his shin with her heel. With a yelp, Ray released her. David's breath hitched as she ran up the stairs, and then he fired. Slowly, he withdrew from the broken window and stood on the concrete slab. The gun was still in his right hand, hanging at his side.

Alicia burst out the front door and ran to him. Bewildered, she gazed at him as he folded her into his arms. "You shot him?"

"Only grazed his leg, so he can't run. He'll be okay." David gazed deep into her eyes. "Are you all right?"

"Yes, thanks to you." Alicia put her hand on a bloodstain on his shirt. "Are you okay?"

"It's just a nick from the windowpane." Leaning down, David covered her mouth with his own, and they held on tightly to each another for a brief moment. Releasing her, he used his free hand to pull his cell phone out of his pant pocket and call 911.

It didn't take long before the block filled with NYPD cars and two ambulances. They immediately rushed Jerri to the hospital with Alicia by her side in one ambulance, and David rode in the other ambulance, sitting beside the gurney where Ray lay handcuffed.

"Do you want to make a statement before I charge you with murder?"

"Jake got everything he deserved. He was a selfish bastard who never appreciated a single thing I did for him." Rocking his head from side to side, Ray's words spilled forth, filled with bitterness. "Jake was going to run our business into the ground if I didn't stop him. Wasting away our money like water on racehorses and gambling."

He glanced at David. "Our father used to say, 'Ray got the body, but Jason, he got the brains.' Ha! That dummy actually believed I wasn't smart like him." Straining at the cuffs around his wrists, Ray growled. "I could've had Jerri if I wanted to, you know. She lusted after me first, but I already had my pick of the girls, so I let Jake have her. Puny shrimp wasn't getting any action anywhere. I was the best player on the football and basketball team in high school. It takes brains and a body to be a great athlete. Girls were always hanging on me, but there was just something about that little redhead." Ray finally relaxed and laid back. "Jerri turned out to be a little ungrateful bitch too. I knew Jake wasn't satisfying her, you know, but when I offered to give her the loving she deserved, she slapped me in the face." Ray looked up at David with wide, watery eyes. "Can you believe she took up with that white boy?" Rocking his head back and forth, he closed his eyes.

Epilogue

Tiny snowflakes danced lightly against a darkening sky as David and Alicia cruised from Monteverde to her townhouse.

"That was quite the wedding, wasn't it?" Alicia excitedly clasped David's right hand while he expertly maneuvered the steering wheel with his other.

"Yes, it was. Jerri looked amazing in her wedding dress. I would have married her if I wasn't already in love with you." David stole a glance at Alicia with a mischievous grin. "I think I could take Bryan out. Do you?"

"Oh, Bryan's no match for you, Mr. Bond. He's just a nice country boy." She smiled, nestled snugly in the Benz's heated seat. "I'm glad they took our suggestion and had their wedding at Monteverde. The two of them singing their vows to one another was so touching. I've never seen anything like that before, have you?"

"No, I have not, but I did enjoy it. They harmonized beautifully together at the end."

"They both looked so happy. Now they have a new record deal with Clive Davis and Arista Records, and *Ms. Devine Rocks* is moving up the pop charts. I bet the pictures of them standing in front of that Hudson River view will be magnificent. And once again, the chef outdid himself with the food. Did you taste the stuffed crab? It was delicious." She rubbed her full stomach.

"Yes, everything was wonderful, except the cake." David wrinkled his nose at her. "There was way too much icing on the cake."

"You didn't need to eat too much of it, anyway," Alicia giggled. "Your tux is getting snugger."

"Oh, hush." David pulled into her driveway, parked next to the Jeep, and they went inside. "Want to light a fire?"

He shook the snowflakes from his overcoat before removing it and then helped Alicia remove her coat. Again, he admired her beauty in her tight, light gray cashmere sweater dress.

"What a great idea. While you do that, I will get out of this dress and these shoes."

As she was in her bedroom changing, David removed his jacket and bow tie, placed a log on the fireplace rack, and lit it. Going to the refrigerator, he took out a bottle of champagne, popped the cork, and poured two glasses. Alicia, wearing a light blue flowered silk robe, joined him in the kitchen and he handed her a glass. They clinked their glasses together in a toast to Jerri and Bryan. Then they snuggled up on the sofa in front of the crackling fire.

"I still can't believe Ray killed his brother and wanted Jerri to take the fall for it because she rejected him," Alicia said. "How can a person walk around smiling and pretending they love you while harboring so much hatred in their heart?"

"I don't know. There are a lot of terrible people out there." David gave her a peck on her cheek. "I'm just glad I still have a job. I don't believe DeLeo bought my story of receiving an anonymous tip to explain why I was at Ray's house in time to save you and Jerri. Thankfully, the press she loves so much made me out to be a big hero. As angry as she was, DeLeo would have looked foolish firing her newest star, knowing I delivered the real killer right into her hands." Silently, they both stared into the fire for a moment. "Our jobs would be much easier if killers looked like killers, but they don't. Speaking of killers, what's going on with your new case?"

"It's a clear case of mistaken identity," Alicia replied. "That little old lady thinks all black people look alike. I already have proof my client was nowhere near the crime scene when it happened."

"What kind of proof?" David asked.

"Security cam footage from a casino in Atlantic City. He was there playing blackjack. It's ironclad." She glanced at David from the crook of his arm with a grin. "Though I was kind of enjoying the idea of taking Eddie on in court."

"Well, Eddie will be relieved he's not going up against you. He's been shaking in his dusty shoes all week." They both laughed and toasted again before quietly sipping their champagne. Their bodies relaxed against one another in a warm embrace. The fire crackled, intermittently breaking the peaceful silence.

"I'm grateful you agreed not to take any new cases I'm prosecuting. I don't want anything to come between us ever again," David confessed, his fingers gently threading through Alicia's hair.

"Me neither," Alicia murmured, lifting her head to meet his gaze. "That's why I did it." David leaned in for a passionate kiss and she eagerly accepted.

"I love you," He whispered as their lips parted.

Eyes glistening, she replied, "I love you, too."

Did you enjoy reading this book?

Dear Readers,

I hope you enjoyed Alicia and David's story. If you did, I would appreciate it very much if you wrote an honest review. It does not need to be long or complicated. Just a simple statement that you liked the book and what you found interesting about it – or for that matter, why you did not like about the book.

Anywhere you post the review will help spread the word about this book and I thank you for it.

I would truly appreciate an Amazon review.

Please help me fulfill my dream. A review goes a long way to help sell books.

Thanks! I truly appreciate your support.

And please go to my website, www.lorilynwhite.com to sign up for my newsletter and stay up to date on the news related to book signings, new book releases, and additional content.

Lorilyn White

OTHER BOOKS BY LORILYN WHITE:

She Wouldn't Wait

No Big Easy Love

Available now on Amazon!

ABOUT THE AUTHOR

Lorilyn White is a retired corporate finance manager and teacher who lives in Virginia Beach, VA. Originally from New York, Lorilyn relocated after retiring. She began writing poetry and short stories at an early age for school publications and pleasure and now fully indulges in her passion. Lorilyn is also an avid reader and loves to travel.

You can connect with her by visiting her website, www.lorilynwhite.com,

or via email at lorilynwhite@gmail.com.